MAXIMUM GUILT

For Kesha, Jacob and Terrence

DEDICATION

I would like to dedicate this book to three special people who have helped sculpt my life in more ways than one. My younger sister Kesha, my younger brother's Jacob and Terrence. Being the oldest sibling comes with a lot of responsibility. Some pleasant, other's not so pleasant. Sometimes it feels like the weight of the world rests on your shoulders. Did you go to class? Have you talked to the boss? Did you talk to the teacher? Have you finished your homework? Here's some money have fun. Don't be out too late. Don't hang with those guys. He's not good for you – neither is she. The list goes on and on. I've done a lot of teaching but as I sit back and reflect I believe I've learned more from them than they may have from me. Each of them has qualities that I do not possess, that I envy and try to mimic as I evolve each day. It is often said that God will never give you more than you can handle. Well I don't believe that – not even a little bit. You see God gives each of us WAY more than we can handle *on our own*. But he never intended us to go it alone. We have brothers, sisters, teachers, parents, aunts, uncles, cousins, friends, classmates, co-workers and even strangers we can lean on to help us fight the daily battles of life. And more importantly that he intended us to lean on. Make sure you are leaning on the people God has placed in your life and being a pillar to those around you who may depend on you.

MAXIMUM GUILT

Prologue

John Blake thrashed in pain as he stared at his hand on the floor and blood painted the walls of the room a deep mahogany. As he lay in agony, tied up in the motel bed, he knew he'd been drugged. His head rang and the room spun. His arm throbbed where his hand had once been. Many thoughts raced through his mind. What would his wife think? His children? What kind of legacy would he be leaving behind? What a fucking mess he had gotten himself into. And somehow, deep down, he knew this would be his last night, his last hoorah. He felt sick in the deepest pit of his stomach.

The lights in the room were dimmed. A large duffel bag sat on the table in the corner. A cell phone sat on it too, classical piano humming from its' speaker. Everything else appeared to be normal for a hotel room. What the fuck was this he wondered.

"You bitch!" he yelled as the woman ripped the tape off his mouth. But he knew the words fell on deaf ears.

"Aww, John, do we have to call names? You told me you wanted a bad girl, didn't you? Hey, I'm talking to you! Look at me!" she said, yanking his head around. "Listen, I have a job to finish here. Let's just get through this, can we? I need to bandage that nub of yours so you don't bleed out on me before I'm finished."

"Fuck you!" he said, spitting on the floor beside her feet.

"You sure wanted to, now didn't you? Maybe, just maybe, if you had elected to stay home with that beautiful wife of yours . . . what's her name? Patricia? You wouldn't be staring at your hand here on the floor. Hey! Wake up! Don't you go passing out on me. I want you to feel this—all of it. Isn't that what you told me fifteen minutes ago? Fucking prick."

"Why are you doing this to me?"

"Are you kidding me, John? Why were you trying to do me? That's the real question, or at least it should be. You don't deserve that family you have, the job, the life . . . any of it. I mean, instead of being at home tonight, you're out trying to fuck women who aren't your wife."

"Who made you the morals police? You're a fucking stripper," he said, looking at her in disgust.

"Now, now, John. Name calling again? I'm a whole lot more than that, don't you think? Hold that thought."

She reached over, grabbed the tennis ball from the table, and shoved it back into his mouth. Then she duct taped it in place. Next, she picked up the hacksaw and went to work on his left hand. He squirmed, kicked, and seized in pain, tears rolling down his face until the job was done. But his agony didn't make her stop; she actually enjoyed it more when he showed her how much it hurt. Before tonight, she hadn't realized how much she would enjoy such gruesome entertainment, but it gave her a high. Goosebumps ran down her arm. With the hand gone, she took out a lighter and burned the wound to stop the bleeding. The smell of warm blood and burning flesh turned her stomach a little, but it had to be done. Hopefully she'd get used to the smell over time.

"John! Hey, John, can you hear me?"

He struggled to open his eyes as she slapped his face. His body twitched uncontrollably.

"Okay, now that I've got your attention . . . I know this is going to be hard, but I want you to try. You're a big boy. I've got faith in you. 2003 bachelor party for your brother. You called an escort service to hire dancers. Hey! Wake the fuck up!" She rapped on his face again.

He slowly raised his head and opened his eyes again.

"It was for my brother Carl. Yes, I remember." He barely sputtered out the words.

"We told you no sex. You remember that? You don't have to answer. You remember taking a girl to a room for a private dance? Told her you'd give her $1,000?"

"Maybe. I mean, I don't know. I was probably hammered out of my mind."

"Oh yeah, you were. All of you were, as a matter of fact. You remember drugging that girl and raping her?"

"What?"

"Oh, don't act so innocent, like that's beneath you or something. I'm sure I wasn't the first girl you raped, you piece of shit, but you won't be raping anyone else!"

She went over to her purse and came back with a pair of gardening snips. She slowly opened and closed them a few times to gratify herself.

"Now, John, what do you think I'm going to do with these?" she said with a huge grin on her face.

John started to yell, but she shoved the ball back into his mouth again and taped it shut. She reached down and grabbed his limp penis. She put the metal blades of the tool against it, but then she had an idea. She wanted to toy with him a little. She began jerking him off. At first nothing happened, but she kept tugging.

"John, you aren't playing nicely. Come on! Can't this little thing get hard for me? Aren't you attracted to me, John? *Goddamn you're hot, baby. I wanna fuck your brains out!* What happened to all that?"

Just then, she felt his penis stiffen a little. She looked at his face and could see pain and disgust as she pulled and pulled.

"Ahhh! There we go. Get it nice and big for me, baby," she taunted.

As John's erection grew, she stopped tugging, grabbed the snips, and cut off his penis—all the way to his testicles. She watched as he flailed in pain.

"You won't need that anymore."

She waited a few minutes to let him mull everything over.

"Okay. Okay. Maybe I remember, but what the fuck did you think I was paying you $1,000 for, huh? A goddamn lap dance?"

"John, I don't know what you were paying for, but I told you no sex—more than once, if memory serves. Well, that is before my memories stopped that night."

"Do you want money? Is that what this is about?"

"You're pathetic. After all this, you really think I want your fucking money? No, John, I want you to meet your maker tonight. That's what this is about. That's really all I want. You know what it's like to be raped, John? Do you? You even called your brother in to get a little. I'll see him in a few weeks, by the way. This is about karma. This is about revenge. This is about justice."

John's eyes closed, he started to fade but the quick slaps on his face woke him up again.

"Listen, let's be rational here. I mean, I can give you enough money to change your life."

"Can you give me enough money to buy back that night you took from me, John? Do you have enough money to erase my memories? Do you have that much money? Of course you don't."

She tapped her fingers on her forehead and waited a minute for him to respond.

"Nothing to say, huh?"

"You know I can't take back that night. And if what you said really happened, I am truly sorry."

"Ohhh listen at you! *I am truly sorry.* No, I don't believe you. I believe *you are truly sorry* that I am about to blow your fucking brains out."

She walked over to her purse, pulled out a pistol, and slowly put the silencer in place. She returned to him and pressed the gun to his forehead.

"By the way, the name's Brittany; that is who I am. Brittany Foy. Not bitch, hoe, stripper, slut, or any of the other names you pieces of shit refer to us as. And it damn sure isn't Candy Cane. Stupidest stripper name ever, I fucking swear. It's fucking Brittany. Just Brittany. But I would like to thank you, because there is a silver lining here, and I don't want it to go unnoticed. Thank you for helping me understand what I was placed on this earth for. I'm ready to fulfill my calling—helping rid the world of douche bags like you. So thank you, John. I truly mean that."

Then she fired two shots into John's head. She watched with pleasure as the rise and fall of his body slowly stopped. Brittany stepped back and looked at John's lifeless body. She thought she'd feel remorse or sadness after her first solo kill but she didn't. It made her feel empowered. Like she had taken something back that belonged to her. She sat down next to her victim and gently stroked his hair. She took a paintbrush from her purse and walked to the wall behind the bed. She used the splattered blood on the wall to write MORE TO COME "BF" AKA WIDOWMAKER! Then she carefully removed the two pairs of gloves she was wearing and put the inner pair in a plastic bag. She tucked the bag, her gun, and the silencer back into her purse, grabbed her sunglasses, and left.

Chapter 1

I glanced around the room, looking for a hidden camera. This had to be some sort of sick reality show I had somehow become the star of. This couldn't be real, I thought—but it was. After finally getting my wife, Miranda, back, I immediately lose another loved one to the same fate? How could this be? I was happy and heartbroken again all at the same time. I felt drained and empty. I fought back the urge to puke. I looked around the room again, but she was gone. It was no dream; my Karen was gone.

A nurse walked up to me and placed her hand on my shoulder. "Detective Porter, what's wrong? Is everything okay? You're pale as a ghost."

I didn't feel like explaining to her that Stacy's little note wasn't some cute love letter. Instead, it was confirmation that she was as sinister as . . . Hilary had been trying to warn me all along. The room was spinning. My head pounded. Why was everything moving so goddamn fast?

I slammed my fist on the counter. "No! Everything is not okay. Take Miranda back; get her checked from head to toe," I demanded. And then it was lights-out.

"David? David! C'mon! Wake up, kid," Wilcrest shouted as he slapped my face. I opened my eyes to find the captain hovering over me.

My head throbbed as I struggled to figure out where I was and what was going on.

"David, look at me. Come on. There you go. No, no . . . don't sit up. Just open your eyes."

I had fainted. First time I'd ever done that. I guessed the nurse had been right when she said I looked pale as a ghost. I struggled to my feet, despite the warnings from everyone to stay put. It felt as if I'd just spun around in circles for five minutes or had been playing beer pong for three hours straight.

"I'm okay," I said. "I just . . . I just . . . I don't know. I just fainted, I guess." And we all shared a brief chuckle at my expense. Even Miranda was smiling. Man, it was good to see her smile. I stood for a second longer trying to shake off the cobwebs. I leaned against the wall to regain my balance. Everyone stared at me like I was some kind of freak. *Come on, Porter, get it together.*

"David, you should go back with Miranda," Wilcrest said. "We'll get started at the house. Go! That's an order, son," he said when I hesitated to move. "I have every cop and then some looking for Karen and Stacy. We'll find them."

I knew Wilcrest had guys on it, but I also trusted my instincts more. I didn't want to leave Karen's fate in someone else's hands. I also knew I wasn't one hundred percent, even though I was faking it well.

"Yes, David, please come back with me. I don't think I can be without you right now," Miranda said, her voice weak. She held her arms across her chest, and I noticed how they were trembling.

The cop in me wanted to begin questioning Officer De Luca to find out the details about her brief captivity and the basement her and Miranda had been held in. The father in me wanted to set the streets ablaze and hunt Stacy down like a bloodhound. I knew the hot trail Stacy surely must have left behind would become cold rather quickly. I was hoping to capitalize on any mistakes she might have made in her haste, as leaving like this was probably spur of the moment. I trusted Wilcrest, and I knew without a doubt that the boys would give this the highest priority. Maybe they would track her down as I sat this one out. Stacy was no different than any other criminal. Sooner or later she'd make a mistake.

Wilcrest was right—Miranda needed me as a husband right now and not a cop. It would be a balancing act from this point on, because I knew I needed to spend ample time tracking down Stacy before it was too late. I believed she was capable of not only hurting Karen but killing her if she got in the way. I couldn't begin to imagine how confused Karen must be right now. I'm sure she wondered why she and Stacy had run off all of a sudden.

They led Miranda and me down a hall toward a testing room. I imagined they would run a million tests to see just how bad off she was physically. Doctors and nurses approached and asked question after question, making notes and probing Miranda. *God, I hope this will be over soon.* "This is where we'll perform most of our tests, Miranda," a nurse said. "You okay here?"

"Yes, I am fine," Miranda replied, looking over at me.

I couldn't tell how many pounds she'd lost, but I did know it was significant. I knew she was fighting hard to hold back a slew of pent-up emotions from her time in captivity. It must have been eating her up inside. Miranda prided herself on looking her best, even at home.

"I'm so blessed to have you back in my life, Miranda. You look beautiful," I said, trying my best to comfort her.

I sat beside Miranda and held her hand as the doctors ran test after test. My mind, however, was traveling at warp speed. My oldest daughter Hilary felt uneasy about Stacy from the moment she appeared at Miranda's funeral. Even I thought her "outofnowhereness" seemed a bit strange, but no one could have imagined this. How could I have been so blind? So stupid? It all made sense now—her eagerness to become a part of our lives, move in . . . the pregnancy. The pregnancy! What did that mean for me now? And now I would have to explain it all to Miranda, including the college fiasco I thought I'd left behind. I wondered how Miranda would react to everything. All of this on top of Karen's disappearance and the healing process Miranda would have to endure as a result of her own abduction. I had never taken advantage of the psychiatric counseling we had available, but now seemed as good a time as any. For all of us. I held Miranda's hand as tight as I could and just stared at her. It seemed unreal that she was here again, here with me.

We spent over two hours in the examination room. They'd given Miranda multiple IV bags of fluids and had even mentioned a possible blood transfusion. Finally, the door opened and the head doctor entered.

"David, we've given Miranda a thorough once-over. Other than the expected dehydration and malnourishment, everything seems to be okay. I'll have you bring her back in two weeks, and we'll take a look at that finger she lost and see what, if anything, we can do from a cosmetic standpoint. We can keep her here for a few nights or you can take her home, but you'll need to make sure she gets plenty of rest and continues to hydrate. She's also going to need some counseling. Most abduction victims find it speeds up their recovery. Here's my cell phone number. I usually don't give it out, but I figured what the hell. Everything you guys have gone through with Karen and Miranda would be hell for anyone. Call anytime. I mean anytime, David."

I took the business card with Dr. Peter's information and stuffed it into my wallet. I reached out to shake his hand and thank him for everything he'd done for my family.

"Take me home please," Miranda whispered to me as a stray tear trickled down her cheek. She wouldn't look at me. I knew she didn't want me to see her like this.

I hated what I had allowed to happen. She looked so weak, so fragile. I walked beside her as the nurse wheeled her out to my truck. Hilary trailed close behind us.

The walk to my truck seemed to drag on forever. I hit the button on my key fob to unlock the door, and then I reached down to help Miranda in.

"You ready to do this?" I asked.

"More than you know."

After I got Miranda buckled in, I walked behind my truck, tears streaming down my face. I stopped for a moment and rested my hands on the tailgate. Right now, for everything that was right, a million other things were broken. Shattered. Everything needed fixing.

Chapter 2

I drove home faster than usual—way too fast, actually, according to the speedometer. Too many thoughts racing through my head, I guess. My mind was so jacked I didn't even notice red lights versus green. I was really *just* driving.

"Dad, what are you going to do about Karen?"

"I'm working on it, Hil. I have some ideas. I'm going to get her home, you can bet on that. The whole station is looking for her."

"David, I need you to know I don't blame you for any of this. You couldn't have known I was alive, and though it hurt a little, deep down I knew you needed to move on."

I was more than a little shocked that, amidst all that was happening right now and everything she'd been through, Miranda was trying to sort through it all so quickly. I imagine she'd processed a lot while being held captive, given she didn't have many options.

"Well, I blame him! If he hadn't raped Stacy back in college, maybe she wouldn't have come back looking for revenge! Maybe Rodney would still be alive. I mean, is it true? What I read? How could you, Dad?"

I knew I needed to address the elephant in the room—well, in the truck—but I didn't want to do it like this.

"Hilary, what are you talking about? Your dad never raped anyone. David, what is she talking about?"

"Just try to rest, Miranda. We'll talk about all that later. Hilary, it's a long story and it's complicated. There are parts of what you may have read that are true, but I didn't rape anyone. I was young and stupid, and I made some poor choices, yes; but I never raped anyone. That part is not true."

I tried to use my training to defuse the situation, but with Hilary I knew it would be of no use.

"I'd really like some fast food," Miranda said. "How about Jack in the Box?"

"I can do that!"

We went through the drive-through and ordered one of almost everything. I guess its true how much we really take for granted— like eating fast food. As we continued toward home, I watched in amazement as Miranda ate like a fourteen-year-old football player.

"I'm sorry. It's been a long time," Miranda said through a mouthful of fries.

I didn't know whether I should laugh or cry, so I just smiled and nodded.

"Dad knew Stacy back in college. She didn't just happen on us. She planned this whole thing out. She's been watching us and planning revenge on Dad for what he did to her in college."

"Hilary, enough. Your mother needs to rest. And I didn't know her as Stacy in college; actually, I didn't *know* her at all. Right now I need to use all the brain power and energy I have left to track down Stacy and your sister before . . ."

"Before what? Say it, Dad. Before she's dead?"

I could see that Hilary put the blame for all of this squarely on my shoulders. Maybe she was right. She was clearly angry, hurt, and confused. I needed to give her my side of the story. Maybe that would help. Maybe it wouldn't. But I had to tell her and tell her fast. I tapped my hands nervously on the steering wheel as I drove.

"Hilary, it's really, really important that I explain to you and your mother what brought all of this about . . . and I will. I'm just not sure right now is the best time. My—our—first priority should be on finding your sister and bringing her home. And being there in whatever way your mother needs us."

"David, I feel like there is a big something that both of you know about that I don't. What is Hilary talking about?"

Just as Miranda finished speaking, we pulled up to the house. I knew I needed to get it off my chest, and it was clear neither of them was willing to drop it.

I gestured toward the house. "C'mon. Let's go inside first," I said as I turned the engine off.

I walked around to Miranda's side and helped her out. Arm in arm, we trudged toward the house. Miranda was so weak she could barely stand. I opened the door to lead Miranda in. She was so weak from muscle atrophy that I was all but carrying her. She broke down in tears when she looked around, home again at last. I held her tight—tighter than I had ever held her before.

I got Miranda settled on the couch and sat beside her. This was a big moment for us. I felt sick to my stomach. I wanted to throw up.

I stood up and paced a few steps. "Listen, both of you," I said as they sat, eyes and ears glued to me. "I don't know why I was so nervous but I was. Like I was a rookie cop back in court for my first firearm discharge case.

"Miranda, Stacy used to attend Wayne State back when I was playing football there. I didn't recognize her or know any of that before. Rodney stumbled across some old files on her laptop, or so I'm told. That's how he found out who she really was—Lisa Crease."

Miranda had a confused look on her face. "So what, she's an old girlfriend from college or something? How does that explain all of this?"

There was no beating around the bush on this one. Time to lay it all out on the table.

"Well . . . not a girlfriend, exactly. It's going to sound gross and terrible, but it's the truth. So here goes. We had a rule on the football team that all incoming freshmen had to have sex with a random girl at a party. Some stupid macho thing, I know. Anyway, you go up to some girl you don't know and make it happen that night. To prove, you know, who the biggest stud was. Finding the hottest girl you could, of course. If you didn't, you'd face some pretty harsh hazing. I'm not the most outgoing guy in the world, and I felt weird about the whole thing. Well, the guys didn't know it, but I had spoken with Lisa before the party, and we had sort of a deal. We agreed to have sex at the party, and I agreed to pretend to be her boyfriend for . . . I don't know . . . a few weeks afterward. So she'd look cool or whatever. So here we were at the party. Everyone was drinking and being stupid. I went up to Lisa, made it look like we'd just met as we had planned. She was hammered to the point where I didn't even know if we were going to be able to do anything or if she'd blow the plan all to hell. I thought maybe we'd just disappear and pretend we'd messed around. She'd been drinking, for sure, but seemed messed up enough that I figured drugs were involved, too. We went to the back room, and she sobered up some. One thing lead to another . . . you get the idea."

I paused to catch my breath. The only sound I heard was the blood pounding in my head.

"Then about twenty minutes in, the door flies open. The guys start going on and on about how she used to be a stripper or prostitute or something. They're yelling and screaming and acting belligerent. At this point, she could barely hold her eyes open, but we had talked some and I knew she was coherent. In fact, she was better off than I'd previously suspected. They start talking about wanting some of the stripper, too, and how I had definitely gotten the hottest girl. I told them no, it wasn't right. And it certainly wasn't the plan. Try reasoning with ten to fifteen drunken football players. I'd been drinking, too, so I probably didn't seem like the best person to listen to. An upperclassman pushed me out of the way, and that's when the shit hit the fan. Everything got crazy. They took turns with her. All of them. At one point, one of them could tell I was clearly bothered and asked if I knew her or something. I wasn't supposed to, according to the plan, so I said no. I tried to make it seem like I didn't care one way or the other. No vested interest. In other words, don't stop on my account. And I *didn't* know her, but like I said, I knew it wasn't right. She didn't fight them, and I couldn't really tell if she wanted them to stop or not or if she was too messed up to even know what was happening. Everything was moving really fast. There was yelling, laughter . . . It was wild and out of control. At least that's what I tried to make myself believe.

"I left before it was over. Looking back, she probably thought I set the whole thing up, but that wasn't my plan at all. I looked for her around campus the next few days, to talk to her, but I never found her. A few days later, she filed rape charges against me and the team. We had a lawyer who volunteered to defend us, some big shot alumni ex-player. His first words to us were, 'No one speak to her—ever.' So I stopped looking for her. Then he told us not to worry; with her checkered past it would never even make it to court. And it didn't. In a few weeks it all blew over.

"So . . . I did not rape Lisa, nor did I set up the team to do so. The whole thing was a bad deal that spiraled out of control a lot faster than a bunch of drunken kids could handle. And now, hindsight being 20/20, I should have reported every single one of my teammates. I should have told the cops exactly what happened. It would have meant me losing my scholarship, probably, and being ostracized from the team, but it would have been the right thing to do. It's easy to say now, but I'm not an eighteen-year-old college freshman who's just trying to fit in anymore either. It's hard to admit, but I was a coward—at least at that moment. None of us ever saw her or heard from her again. I figured she just left school and went back home, wherever home was for her. I felt terrible for what happened to her, but I didn't plan it nor did I realize the intentions of the upperclassmen. They were basically using us to get some free playtime, as they called it; it had been *their* plan all along.

"So there you have it. I'm not a rapist or any of the other awful things she thinks I am. I didn't set her up to be gang raped!"

I looked from Hilary to Miranda, who looked pale and woozy. I knew this was a major revelation and had to be a huge disappointment, given how long we'd been married. You always think you know someone and then . . . *bam!* I wasn't a rapist, but I'd allowed it to happen, and I sure as hell hadn't stopped it. This was a pretty big *bam*.

"Dad, I can't believe you would do such a thing! What a creep! All you jocks are just assholes!" Hilary yelled as she jumped from the couch and headed for the staircase.

"Listen, like I said, to me it was nothing more than two college kids having sex at a party. I never planned for any of that to happen. And I already admitted I acted cowardly when I realized what the others were doing." I yelled back, heading for the staircase to cut Hilary off.

She tried to push me aside. "You didn't stop it either. You're just as guilty!"

I tried to reason with her. "I wasn't a grown man, husband, father, or officer. I was a stupid eighteen-year-old drunken kid. It's not a good excuse, but it's the truth."

"Both of you. Please." My wife had found her voice. "Hilary, you've heard and said enough. All you need to know is, while your dad isn't perfect, he certainly isn't a rapist. And although he should have reported his teammates, you can clearly see how a person in his position wouldn't have. I probably wouldn't have and neither would you. I don't blame your father for what his teammates did. You shouldn't either. And in the midst of it all, I do not believe Lisa would have believed your story, David. If it had been me, I sure wouldn't have. From her perspective, you look like a monster who set her up to be gang raped. You look like an asshole jock and a terrible person."

I leaned against the banister and buried my face in my hands. I was embarrassed and humiliated, just as I'd been so long ago.

Miranda came over and wrapped her arms around me. "This doesn't change how much I love you. It doesn't change who I think you are—who I know you are. I wish you would have somehow found a way to tell me about all this. I do wish that. But my time away from all of you makes me appreciate every second we have together—even now. I want to spend every minute I have left loving you and enjoying our life."

I couldn't believe my ears. After knowing I was basically responsible for how she'd spent her last year, all the pain and torment she'd been through, she was still the same kind, forgiving, loving person. What an amazing woman—a truly amazing woman.

I hugged Miranda again and gave her the warmest kiss I could muster up. I hated letting her down and seeing a look of disappoint in her eyes.

"I'm sorry I never told you about all of this. I never in a million years thought Stacy and Lisa were the same person. It was all so long ago. I suppose I was afraid . . . . afraid of what you'd think of me and my cowardice." We hugged again. Then I reached down and gently kissed her lips.

"Well, Dad, you're on a roll. Anymore skeletons you want to unload while you're at it?"

"Hilary, that's enough," Miranda said. "We've all been through so much. And it's not over, not by a long shot. All we have is family, and right now one of us is missing. I need your dad to suck it up now and find my baby!"

That was exactly what I intended to do. Time to track down Lisa "Stacy" Crease and find my Karen.

Chapter 3

Miranda lay down on the couch to take a nap. I was glad she decided to crash there. I was hopeful that Stacy had left something that could help me track her down behind. I went upstairs to my room to see what I could find. I scoured the room for her laptop, but she must have managed to grab it. There were clothes and other things I needed to rid the room of before I would feel comfortable bringing Miranda back into the fold, so to speak. I didn't want her to hurt any more than she already had. She'd definitely been through more than enough.

Miranda's return was bittersweet. Having her back was an answered prayer, but in return, I'd lost my little princess. I heard my cell phone ringing on the table.

I reached down to answer. "Hello?"

"David, it's me, Wilcrest."

"Hey, Cap. What's up? Tell me you found Karen and its over."

"I don't even know where to start, David. I got some boys over at Stacy's . . . you know, Lisa's place trying to get a bead on where she's run off to. So far we've come up empty-handed. I mean, we've found a lot of things here but nothing that indicates where she may have run off to."

"I have some things to clean up here while Miranda is resting. I'll be another hour or so here then I'll be over to help."

"I got even more bad news for you, David. One of the officers called in a possible homicide. I haven't been out to check on it yet. If I had to guess, Stacy left a going-away present for us. The vic is almost an exact match to Karen. Height, size, weight—"

"I got it," I said, cutting him off. "Goddamn it, I got it!"

Was Stacy just reminding me who she was and what she was capable of? Or maybe it was Karen. I felt directly responsible for her kidnapping in more ways than one. In bringing Stacy into our lives and our home, I'd allowed her to be in this position. With all the murder cases I'd worked, all the years of experience, there should've been no way that could happen. But I'd allowed her beauty and sexuality to cloud my judgement. I was overlooking things that a detective with half my experience would have noticed. Sometimes we overlook the most obvious things. Stacy pushed all my buttons; she played me. They say love is blind, but I guess lust is, too.

"I gotta run, Cap. I'll see you soon."

"Wait, David. One more thing. There's a new case that's probably going to need your attention—as soon as we find Karen, of course."

Like I really needed one more thing right now, especially another case to solve.

"Whatcha got?"

"Well, John Blake—*the* John Blake—turned up dead last night. Both hands sawed off along with . . . that. Yes, *that*. Someone calling herself the Widowmaker. Smeared some of his blood on the wall, threatening there'd be more to come. Quite a bloody mess she left behind. Doesn't feel like a random murder scene."

"Everyone knows Blake loved strippers and strip clubs. He try to stiff somebody? Maybe a pimp or bodyguard take him out and use some Widowmaker moniker as a cover up? Where'd they find the body?"

"Motel. Manager called it in. Of course the room was paid for by Blake in cash."

"We download security videos?"

"Already did. Got nothing. We see a girl walking in but can't tell anything else about her. The footage is too grainy."

"Blake at a strip club last night?"

"We asked around, but all the nightclubs said no sign of Blake all week."

"Doesn't mean he wasn't there. Doesn't mean he didn't meet her at one before, either. That's probably where the connection was initially made. Send some boys over to his favorite clubs. See what they can turn up. Gotta be a girl who Blake spent a good amount of time with somewhere. Heartbreakers is one minute away from my house. I'll take that one. Call me later."

It wasn't uncommon for me to be juggling multiple cases at once; actually, it had sort of become expected of me. First things first: I had to finish up here and get to Stacy's asap. I needed to get started on tracking down everything I could about Lisa Crease—who she was before college and what she had turned into after. I needed to know everything about her.

Hilary begrudgingly joined me in getting rid of Stacy's things and helped me clean up the telltale signs of their scuffle.

"Hilary, I'm really sorry you got caught up in this." I pulled her close to me and we shared a hug. I needed to do that more often.

She wiped a tear from her face. "Me, too, Dad. I'm going to my room if we're finished."

The cleanup complete, I went downstairs to check on Miranda. She was still sound asleep. I just stared at her for a moment.

It all made sense to me now. The child killings, the mysterious woman at Karen's school, the blonde at the beach while we were on vacation, the woman who dragged De Luca from the accident—all Stacy. I went back upstairs and settled in front of the computer. It was time to start searching. I pulled up one of our police department databases to see what I could find.

My initial searches came up empty. Somehow, Stacy had managed to make Lisa Crease disappear. Almost. Finally, I came across something. Crease was a native of New Orleans. I wondered if she'd gone back there. She'd grown up there and might know the area well. And they're notorious for their bayous, swamps, and all sorts of unmarked streets. Lots of good places to hide.

I'd also uncovered more about her past. Crease had been

molested by her uncle when she was five. A newspaper clipping with a hit on Crease showed he'd died in a house fire twenty years ago. I had a sneaking suspicion that fire was no accident. It also made what I'd been a part of back at Tech that much worse. It was painstakingly obvious to me now that her accusations against the team and me weren't just a ploy for her fifteen minutes of fame. The girl had been hurt that way before, at least once, and was out for blood. She'd apparently decided she would no longer be the victim, and right now I was her prize. God, how long had she been planning this thing out?

I'd made a good friend in the military that happened to be from New Orleans and was now a detective on the force there.

I pulled out my phone and thumbed for his number.

"Paul Lafitte? David Porter here."

"Hey, my friend! Long time. How the hell are you, David?" I could hear the surprise in his voice.

"Long time indeed. I wish this call was to catch up on old times, but it's not so I'll get right to the point. My youngest daughter, Karen, is in trouble. She's been kidnapped, Paul."

"David . . . man. I . . . when did this happen?"

"It's a long story; I'll fill you in later. I know who did it. Girl named Lisa Crease. Goes by Stacy Demornay now. There's a bit of history there, too. I'll have to fill you in later on that as well. Look, I know Crease is from New Orleans, so I'm thinking maybe that's where she'll run to hide. Easy to get lost in those bayous."

Lafitte had already logged into his laptop and was waiting for it to load. "I'll pull up everything I can on her, see if I can find an LKA, too. Maybe she'll go back there. It's a longshot, but crazier things have happened. Hey, I got her file up right here. Hang on a second. Yeah, I remember when her uncle's house burned down. You know, some of the boys didn't think that was an accident, but we didn't find a darn thing to suggest otherwise."

"I believe their hunch was right. In fact, I might even have dug up what would be an excellent motive. Listen, keep your eyes open and put out a soft search for Crease. If she's back or headed that direction, I don't want to spook her. Lord knows what she'll do to Karen if she thinks I'm close. I'll be in New Orleans in a few days, Paul. Thank you, my friend."

I disconnected and kept my fingers crossed that something would turn up and fast. It felt good to talk to my old friend. I'd become so busy—obsessed, almost—with my job that I hadn't done a good job of staying connected with my friends. Given the nature of my work and how quickly it could all be over, I promised myself I would do better.

Chapter 4

I walked over to the couch and tucked Miranda in then I headed for Heartbreakers to get started on the Widowmaker case while I waited on Lafitte to call me back.

It was only a short drive, but Sports Radio 610 was broadcasting the Texans game, and I found myself listening for a minute. I hated the way my football career had ended and still dearly missed playing.

I found a spot close to the entrance and parked my truck. Oddly enough, a giant J. J. Watt billboard lined the side of an eighteen wheeler parked nearby. *More football memories. Go figure.* As I headed for the front door, two guys came out. They gave me a strange look as we approached each other. I didn't recognize either of the men, but both of them looked like trouble. The taller man stood about six foot five and was built like he'd spent his last fifteen years at the Darrington Unit in Rosharon. I'd put enough guys like that away to recognize the prison tats, too.

As we passed each other, the one closest to me gave me a hard bump. I could tell it wasn't an accident.

"Excuse me," I said, making sure to give him a hard stare.

"You're excused, cop," the man replied. They both laughed.

I didn't have time to play games with these two in the parking lot, so I kept moving. *What the hell was that all about?*

When I got inside, there was a kid behind the counter; I didn't waste any time.

"Hey, everything okay out there? Those are two of my regulars," he said with a serious look on his face.

I wanted to laugh. This kid really thought he was some kind of tough guy.

He held out his hand for my money. "And it'll be ten dollars. You're not gonna have a problem here, now are you, sir?"

I was fed up with his bravado and his rhetoric. I really didn't have time for his games, either.

"Listen," I said, flipping out my ID. "I'm not some perv here to gawk at tits and ass. I'm here on official police business. You got it, J.R.?"

He backed up a half step. "Yes, sir. I didn't know. Sorry."

"Don't be sorry; just don't be a dick. I have a few questions I need you to answer. Number one, did you work the front desk last night?"

The kid stopped making eye contact with me and was kicking at something on the floor. Clearly I had already rattled his cage.

"Did you or did you not work the front desk last night?"

"I did," he said, still looking at the ground.

"John Blake—was he here?"

"I'm not sure I know him. Do you have a picture?"

This kid was good. Too smart for his own damn good, though.

"Listen, I've got way too much pent-up anger right now for you to be fucking with me."

He looked up slowly. The smart-ass grin had been replaced by a nervous smirk.

He folded his arms. "Listen, sir. I don't know nothing."

"Actually, I'm willing to bet you know a lot. But it seems like you'd be more comfortable talking about it at the station. Oftentimes people's memories clear up a lot better there," I said as I reached for my cuffs.

"Am I under arrest or something? What'd I do?"

"This is a murder investigation. I believe you're withholding evidence. It's called obstruction of justice."

He took a step back from the counter and began chewing at his fingernails.

"Listen, Blake was here last night. Went to the back like he usually does, probably upstairs after that. I don't know much else, I swear."

"He have a regular here he came to see? What's her name?"

"I don't know who he saw, honestly. He did have a few he liked more than others, but I don't know who was working last night."

"I need a list of all the girls Blake sat with on a regular basis—his favorites. And I also need a list of all the girls who worked last night and when they left the club."

"I'm not sure I'll be able to get that for you, sir."

"Fair enough. Get me someone who can."

He walked inside the club. I thought about staying in the lobby, but I didn't want them to conjure up a story for me. I decided to follow him.

As I stepped inside, I spied a tall, slender girl dancing topless on the front stage. Five men lined the stage, holding what I guessed to be one dollar bills in their hands. All probably fifty or older. *Pathetic,* I thought to myself. I didn't want to rattle everyone by giving them the cop vibe, so I just pretended to be an interested patron.

A minute later, the guy from the lobby was at my side. "That's the manager over there. His name is Steve."

"Thanks for your help with this."

I watched the kid go back through the double doors to the front. I figured I'd walk over to Steve and pretend to be holding a conversation about the dancer. Again, trying not to let anyone in on who I really was or why I was there.

"Steve, Detective David Porter HPD."

I'd extended my hand for a friendly shake, and Steve slowly reached out to take it.

"Calm down. This isn't a shakedown. Just trying to gather some information. I know John Blake was here last night. He's dead now. He was last seen entering a hotel room around nine p.m."

Steve folded his arms, a look of disgust on his face. "What does any of this have to do with me and my club?"

"I think you know exactly what it has to do with you, Steve." We gave each other a once-over and stared in silence.

"You think one of my girls was involved? You accusing one of my girls of murder?"

"Steve, I'll say it one more time: calm down. Again, I'm

simply trying to gather some information. I need two things from you, and I'll be out of your hair. I know you keep a log of when girls come and go each shift. It determines how much their buy-in and payouts are each day. So I need a list of the girls who came in last night—when they arrived and when they paid out. I need times."

"You're asking for an awful lot, considering this isn't a shakedown. You got a warrant?"

"Now I know why your guy at the desk was such a dick. Must have to be one to work here. I can get a warrant, Steve. As a matter of fact, I can call and get one over the phone and never have to leave. The minute I yell *police*, everyone's gonna dart the hell out of here. Just need the list—oh, and thing number two. I need to know who his regulars were."

"I can get you the list, but I'm not giving out names of girls he liked."

"So let me get this straight. A regular at your club was found murdered in cold blood. One of the last places he was seen alive was your club, and video at the motel shows him going in with a woman. If your girls are innocent, then you've got nothing to be afraid of. If you force me to make a scene, you're going to have more problems on your hands than you want to deal with."

Steve took a step into my space. "That a threat, cop?"

I stepped toward Steve and placed a firm hand on his shoulder. "Yes, that's exactly what it is, Steve. You're a lot smarter than you look. I was beginning to wonder."

He and I both knew such posturing was going to get him nowhere fast. If the place was crawling with cops, it'd put a serious dent in his business the next few weeks.

"Give me what I asked for, and I'll be out of your hair. And I'm kind of in a hurry, so could we get a move on it please?"

He placed a call on his walkie-talkie, and a bouncer-type guy with a shirt two sizes too small appeared a few minutes later with my list in hand.

"Good job, Steve. That's part one. Now look at this list, and put a star beside the girl who sat with John most often when he came in."

He took the list from me, scanned it, and handed it back.

"None of those girls are his regulars. Well . . ."

"Well what? Don't make this harder than it needs to be."

"Seems like he was starting too really like one of them. Barbie."

I looked over the list. Barbie Foy.

"Looks like she left around eight thirty last night. That common?"

"Girls come and go all the time but no, not common."

"You see the two of them together last night? You have any more information on Barbie? Driver's license? Address?"

"No. Don't take much to get a job as a stripper, detective. Couple of dance moves, some nice tits is usually more than enough. We pay them in cash each night. I don't ask any more about them than I need to know."

Sadly, I believed what Steve was telling me. Didn't help my investigation, though.

"What about surveillance cameras in and out?"

"We respect people's privacy, so we don't record the doors or any of the common areas."

"Got a real name on this Barbie?"

"Like I said, I know as little as I need to know. Most of the girls' stripper names start with the same letter as their real name. Maybe it's Barbara, Beth, Brittany, and Briann? Shit, I don't know; I really don't."

I stepped back for a minute and took a long, hard look at Steve, trying to determine if he was being honest or blowing smoke up my ass.

"I think this is enough for now. If I think of any more questions, I'll be back."

"Ok man I believe the girls name is Brittany – but that's all I know I swear."

I gave him a once over, nodded in acceptance of his information and turned to leave.

I walked away feeling pretty good about the information I was able to get. Maybe I'd be able to use this intel and get a step closer to catching this girl.

Chapter 5

Everything was moving too quickly. What a fucking nightmare! Stacy had a carefully crafted plan for finishing off David and his family, but this wasn't it. She wanted to kill them all, one by one. She wanted him to watch them all die horrible deaths. She wanted him to bear the pain of knowing it was his fault and he couldn't do a goddamn thing about it. Now, because of his meddling daughter, those plans—plans that were years in the making—were no longer in play.

Karen and Stacy were traveling on I-10 toward Louisiana. They hadn't spoken much since leaving the hospital in a mad dash. Stacy knew sooner or later she'd have no choice but to break the silence and somehow convince Karen that everything was going to be okay.

"Karen, honey, are you hungry? We can stop and grab something."

Karen turned and beamed at Stacy. "Where's my daddy?

Why did we leave? I want my daddy."

Stacy was hoping to buy a little time to come up with a good story since all of this had gone down so quickly. Karen was only six but not too much got by her.

"Karen, honey . . . I have some bad news to tell you. You're going to have to try to be a big girl."

Stacy pulled the car off the road and turned into a gas station.

"Listen, I have to get gas, and we have to get going again pretty quickly. This is going to be really hard for you to hear. Your dad told me shortly after your mother died that he really didn't want kids anymore. He actually said he no longer wanted to . . . well . . . even be alive. He really loved your mother and missed her so much that his heart was broken. Then I got pregnant, and he was really unhappy because he didn't want another kid to take care of. I didn't think I could take care of you, Hilary, and the baby, so I had to leave Hilary behind. That's why I grabbed you and we left. I hope she'll be okay alone with him. Are you okay? I know it's a lot to handle. I'll tell you a little secret; my daddy didn't want me either. He left me and my mother when I was about your age. I turned out pretty okay, don't you think?"

Karen turned away from Stacy and stared out the window. Her eyes began to water, and a single tear rolled down her cheek.

"Daddy wouldn't say a thing like that . . . would he?" Karen said, still staring out of the window.

"I'm so sorry, Karen." Stacy moved closer to the girl and placed a comforting hand on her shoulder.

"I tried everything I could to change his mind. That's why he offered to let you stay with your grandparents. It wasn't because you were sick. He wanted to get rid of you for a little while. Why do you think I offered to move in? It was so I could help. Don't be angry at him, Karen. Losing your mother was hard on him."

"It was hard on all of us! I *am* mad at him. I can't believe my daddy doesn't want me anymore. I don't believe you!"

The two sat in silence for a minute as Stacy gathered her thoughts.

"Honey, I know it's going to take some time, but it's the truth. It's okay that you're upset. If it helps, you can even be mad at me. There's good news, too; you still have me, and I'll do everything I can to be a good mommy to you."

Stacy climbed out and filled up with gas tank. She didn't expect anything less from Karen. She'd have to keep a close eye on her, at least for a few days.

Two and a half hours later, they crossed the Louisiana border and headed into Sulphur. Stacy drove slowly, looking for the perfect motel to crash in for the night, somewhere she could get in and out of in a hurry and without being seen. She had work to do.

At the gas station in Texas, she'd glanced over the front page of the Houston Chronicle and knew part two of her plan was a go. Detectives were hot on the trail of what they believed to be a female killer. Someone had drugged and murdered a local politician who had been known to frequent strip clubs in the area.

"She did it," Stacy muttered. "Good for her! She fucking did it."

Stacy found a motel that appeared to suit her needs and quickly pulled in. She turned the car off and grabbed the keys.

"Wait here, honey. I'm gonna go inside and get us a room."

She made sure to lock Karen in as she left the car. A few minutes later she was back, motel key in hand.

"Why do we have to sleep in a motel room? I want to go home. I want to sleep in my bed."

"Well, Karen, we're headed to my Grammy's house, but we need to rest. It's been a long day. We've been driving quite a while. Aren't you tired?" Stacy said as she leaned in nose to nose with Karen.

"A little, I guess."

"There's that beautiful smile of yours. Here's some milk for you and a pack of your favorite cookies."

Stacy made sure to spike Karen's drink with enough sedative to make her sleep clear through the night. As Karen enjoyed her late-night snack, Stacy scoured the net for her next victim. She needed to leave a trail for David, let him know where she was but not let him get too close until she could lure him into her trap.

"C'mon! I know a little town like this is full of freaking perverts," Stacy said as her fingers flew across the keyboard.

And after only a few clicks, she opened the list of local sex offenders. Next she would spend a few minutes researching each of them. She wanted a sure thing. No time to foul this up.

Karen stretched and rubbed her eyes. "Stacy, I'm getting sleepy."

"Aww. Okay, sweetie. Why don't we turn the TV off and let you get some rest? Everything is going to be okay, dear," Stacy said tucking the blanket in tight around Karen. "I've got you and you've got me. Always, kiddo."

Karen smiled and drifted off to sleep.

Stacy created a profile on a hookup website and was hoping to get a quick hit. If she got lucky, one of the names would be a match for someone on the sex offender list. An hour in, she was starting to believe it might take longer than she'd planned. She'd gotten several hits, but none were on her list. And then . . . voilà! Sam Wilson.

"Well hello, Mr. Wilson. Let's see how bad of a boy you really are," Stacy mumbled, opening a chat window.

> Hi I'm Stacy wanna play tonight?
>
> Hey there cutie – what kinda trouble you lookin to get into 2night?
>
> Trouble? Are you a bad boy? You gonna spank me? I've been a really bad girl.
>
> Maybe, if that's what you'd like . . .
>
> It is. You don't have a girlfriend or anything do you? Don't wanna get you in trouble with the Mrs.
>
> Nope, it's just me, "Sam I am"
>
> Ohhh that's cute! So am I coming over to your place? It's been way too long for me, if you know what I mean.

This was going to be easier than Stacy thought. Guys were so fucking stupid and pathetic. She checked on Karen. Milk all gone. Sound asleep. She locked Karen in and headed for 732 Moore Street.

Stacy brought her own special cocktail for her victim. No sooner had she turned her car off then Sam Wilson appeared on the porch of his single-wide trailer. He was even more repulsive in person than she'd expected: unshaven, long unkempt hair, and a ratty flannel shirt that screamed 1980.

She looked around to make sure no one was watching her arrival.

"Hey, sugar, c'mon in," Sam yelled from the porch.

"Sugar?" Stacy mumbled under her breathe as she walked toward the trailer.

"Whatcha got there, hun?" he asked with a nod at the bottle she was carrying.

"Oh a little something to help us get the party started. You okay with that?"

Stacy suddenly felt tingly all over. This was really happening. She stepped inside and immediately noticed he'd tried to pick up the pigsty he called home.

Sam held the door open, and as Stacy walked through, he reached out and got in a little squeeze of her backside.

"You like that, do you?"

Sam's eyes brightened. "Sure do, Miss Stacy. Why don't you have a seat? Let me get us some glasses and we can get some of that drink goin'."

Sam took three steps over to his kitchen and tried to wipe out two cups as best he could without being too obvious.

"Okay . . . well, I brought my own glass. I know, I know. I'm weird like that."

Stacy's glass had a built-in drain, a double layer. The second layer slowly filled as the glass was tilted at least forty-five degrees, making it look like she was drinking the contents. She would pretend to sip hers and watch as Sam drank himself to sleep.

Sam guzzled his first drink, set the empty glass down, and tried to ease a little closer to Stacy on the couch.

Sam stroked the side of Stacy's face. "Easy, tiger. We can take this slow, right? I'm not in a rush. We got all night," Stacy said, sliding away from Sam. "Why don't we have another drink?"

"Okay," Sam said. Stacy could tell by the perturbed look on his face that he wanted to get this thing started right away.

"Whatcha got there, anyways?" Sam asked, trying to slip a sneaky hand onto Stacy's thigh.

"Oh, just a little mix I make." Stacy allowed Sam to keep his hand on her thigh. She didn't need him getting too riled up before the sedative kicked in.

"Well, I like it, and I like you. You're even hotter in person than your profile pic. I can't wait to . . ."

Sam set down his drink and placed both hands on Stacy's legs.

"My, my, my," Sam said, admiring Stacy's breasts as they threatened to spill from her extremely low-cut blouse.

Stacy noticed a hint of aggression starting to set in. He probably hadn't been laid in ages. She knew she needed to buy some time.

She stood up and waltzed in front of Sam. "You mind if I put on a little show? Do you have any music?"

"Why sure! I got a radio," Sam said with a twinkle in his eyes. "You some kind of stripper or something, Miss Stacy?"

"Wouldn't you like to know?" She poured him another

glass. "Drink this and turn some music on for a girl."

Sam got up and started looking around for his radio. He seemed to be having trouble with his balance.

Stacy walked over and reached out to steady him. "You lost, sweetie?" she said, laughing.

"No, I have a radio in here somewhere. I promise." Sam chuckled but quickly put a hand to his head and squeezed his eyes shut.

Stacy knew the drugs were working. She watched Sam stagger around. His words were slurred and he seemed disoriented.

"You okay, tiger?"

"Yeah, I'm okay. That drink is pretty strong. Whatcha got in there? I can usually out drink anyone. You didn't roofie me, now did ya?"

"You gonna let a little girl like me drink you under the table?"

"Hell no! Gimme another one!" Sam insisted.

She filled up his glass and watched him slam down another one. She knew it wouldn't be long now.

"I'm getting dizzy. Whaddya put in that drink, you bitch?" Sam said as he slid to the floor.

"Aww, you don't have to be so cruel, Sam. I only wanted to make sure we had a good time." She eased closer to Sam, who could barely hold his eyes open. She unbuttoned his shirt and started to rub on his chest.

She reared back and slapped him hard on the cheek.

"Sam, Sam, Sam. You messed up this time. You really messed up, you piece of shit."

And just like that he was out. Stacy had watched Sam take

something out of one of the cabinets and hide it under a towel as he searched for glasses earlier. She stepped over to the kitchen and lifted the towel: handcuffs and duct tape. If things had gone Sam's way, she would have been raped or worse, just as she'd suspected.

"You're a real bad boy, aren't you, Sam," Stacy said, kneeling over Sam's motionless body. "Just what were you planning to do with these?" She dangled the cuffs in the air above his head.

Stacy grabbed her bag and took out her medical supplies. She had work to do.

Chapter 6

I heard noise downstairs. Miranda must be stirring around. I never thought I'd be saying those words again. I decided to check on her. It all still felt surreal. Miranda was home!

As I got to the bottom of the staircase, I found her up and at 'em.

"You're supposed to be resting, dear."

"I know, but I've gotta move around some. I've kinda been stuck in one place for a long time now," she said, grinning.

I didn't think her joke was too funny, but I understood where she was coming from. At least she still had her sense of humor.

"You or the boys got any leads on my Karen?" The conversation suddenly got intense.

"Nothing solid. Stacy/Lisa is from Louisiana. I did some digging into her past. Really troubled girl. You remember my old buddy Lafitte? Well, I put a call into him. He's doing some digging, too. I've profiled enough of these sickos.

Trust me, she won't stay in the shadows for long. She can't; she needs the spotlight, craves the attention. It's a cat and mouse game, and right now I'm the mouse."

"Well, you found me. I know you'll find Karen, too." I sat down on the couch next to my wife and hugged her tight. After a few moments, I pulled away a bit and stared into her eyes.

"I love you, Miranda Porter."

"I love you too, David, so very much."

"Dad, your phone is ringing," Hillary yelled from the staircase.

"Toss it here," I said.

She did so in record time. I looked down at the phone. Lafitte.

"Hey, buddy, tell me some good news," I said, excited by the prospect of a break in the case.

"Well, Porter, not great news but not bad either. Looks like your friend killed an ol' boy in Sulphur just last night."

"What makes you think it was Crease?"

"She left a note for you. Sam Wilson's the guy's name. I'm headed to Sulphur now to see what I can find out."

"What does the note say and why Sam Wilson?"

"I'm looking into it. I know they're checking his computer now. His last contact was some hookup site last night. Guess who he was chatting with? Miss Stacy is the profile name."

"So, she's leading me in. Taunting me. But why Sam Wilson? Wrong place, wrong time?"

"We'll know more in a few hours. She cut the shit outta this guy. Real precise, too. No mess at all. Like she knew what she was doing. Did you know this girl was valedictorian and has SAT scores on record that are top two percent ever?"

"Yeah, I know. She's intelligent, disturbed, and emotionally scarred. Bad, bad combination. Hurt people hurt other people. You know that."

"We're going to do everything we can to catch this girl and get your daughter back, David."

"I know. I should be there in a few hours myself."

I ended the call. Lafitte sounded so sure of himself. But he didn't know Stacy like I did. I knew it would be anything but easy. It looked like a road trip to Louisiana was in my near future.

"Bad news?"

"Not great news, Miranda, but Karen's okay as far as we can tell. Stacy killed a guy in Sulphur. Left me a note so we know it's her."

Miranda broke down. I knew she had to be an emotional wreck inside after her own ordeal and now Karen's. I'd expected a meltdown much sooner. I hugged my wife and whispered in her ear that I would make everything right.

I went upstairs. I needed to talk to Hilary. While I was away, she'd need to take care of her mother hand and foot.

My talk with Hilary went better than expected, and she agreed to watch after her mother.

I hated leaving Miranda. I'd just gotten her back, and I was leaving her side again.

"Stop looking at me like that, David. I know you have to leave, and yes, you have to go. Please bring my baby back home. I'll be okay, and I'll be right here when the two of you get back!"

Chapter 7

Keeping Wilcrest informed as I worked on cases was something I needed to improve. I loved him dearly, like a father. He trusted me, and that gave me a lot more rope than the other detectives had. It didn't go unnoticed around the station.

Last year, Detective Salvez and I'd had it out pretty bad, and that issue alone was the root cause. Guess he'd seen and heard enough, so he made his displeasure known loudly enough for me and the entire tenth floor to hear. Then the guy even had the nerve to confront me about it after Wilcrest basically told him to grow a pair and get lost.

In the end, Wilcrest did end up being forced to talk it out with the chief, but it was a brief conversation. Arrest records and number of cases solved speak for themselves. Even so, in order to help him save face with the other detectives, I was trying harder to check in more frequently and provide more details on my activities as well. At times the station could be a bit middle-schoolish, but I assumed most workplaces operate in much the same fashion.

I took out my cell phone and dialed him up while I had a few moments to spare.

"Cap. I'm on the road right now. Headed for Louisiana. Sulphur. Stacy killed a guy there last night."

"Jesus Christ! Let me guess; she left you a note?"

"Yes. I have a good friend, Detective Lafitte, who lives in New Orleans. He's headed there now. He agreed to help me with the investigation. I'm going to hunt her down if it's the last thing I do. I gotta find Karen and bring her home."

"Keep me posted, and find your little girl. If you can't, no one can. Now get off the phone and solve this case. That's an order!"

"That is definitely the plan," I said before disconnecting.

Houston to Sulphur was only a two-hour drive down I-10. Gave me a chance to make a few calls. I wanted to hit the ground running when I arrived on the crime scene. I was already about eighteen hours behind her now.

I started with Detective De Luca. She hadn't been in captivity as long as Miranda, but she'd have some healing to do nonetheless.

"Hey, De Luca. It's me—David. How are you?"

"I'm okay. Pissed that I allowed myself to get 'napped, but other than that I'm okay. How's Miranda?"

"She's okay, just tired. She's at home resting."

"Where are you? Sounds like you're driving."

"I'm headed for Sulphur, Louisiana. Stacy struck again there last night."

"Okay. How long before you get here to pick me up? And

what do you mean struck again? What did the bitch do now?"

"Excuse me? Pick you up? I'm riding solo on this one."

"Yeah, pick me up. I'm going with you."

"Like hell. You need to rest. I know you're tough, but you need to recover—mentally and physically."

"Listen, that bitch . . . she can't get away with this. I'm coming with you. Come pick me up."

I knew arguing with her any longer really made no sense. She had her mind made up. If I didn't pick up her stubborn behind, she'd drive herself to Sulphur anyway.

"Call Cap. Get it cleared with medical and call me back. I'm about thirty minutes from your place, so hurry."

De Luca and I both had a personal connection to this case, and neither of us should have been on it. I knew that. I'm sure Wilcrest knew he wouldn't be able to talk either of us out of it. De Luca came to our department with the highest recommendations. I was certain she would be a valuable addition to the case.

Within minutes, she called me back with the approval from Wilcrest. If I had to guess, she'd used the same speech she'd given me. I'd known that'd be the case, and I was already heading her way.

I pulled up to De Luca's house. She was already sitting on the porch, bag packed, awaiting my arrival.

"You sure you got this cleared with Cap?" I said as I rolled down the window. The look on her face told me everything I needed to know. De Luca wore a baseball cap, T-shirt and jeans, and had her hair pulled back. No makeup.

"So, what, you trade in your pumps for tennis shoes? You

know how to walk in those things?"

"Porter, you are two seconds away from the ass-whooping I have reserved for Stacy."

We both grinned. She threw her bags into the back seat, shut the door, and we were off.

I filled her in on what I knew about Sam Wilson.

"Well, other than to check on you, the reason I called was so you could get a start on Sam Wilson. We need to find out everything we can. I'm betting something he did in his past is why he's dead. We figure that out and maybe it will tell us where Stacy's headed next. Or at least what the hell she's up to."

"So what do we have? What do we know about Stacy? She killed young girls because you have two of them. She wanted to scare you. I'm willing to bet your boy Sam is a sex offender," De Luca said as she rapped the window with her fingers.

"Maybe. That's good thinking. Call Fingers. Give him Wilson's social, and let's see what we can find out."

Sometimes I felt like I shouldn't being using Fingers as much as I did. I was torn. He had done some pretty bad things, all hacker-type shit, but he was a criminal nonetheless. Police officers all had informants, and to me that's just what he was. Others on the force may have disagreed, but I wasn't exactly broadcasting my use of him either. Besides, we had our own data analysts who were good, but Fingers was a tad better.

"See? You need me, David. I haven't heard the full story, but I know she accuses you of being part of some hazing back in college. So you going to fill me in?" De Luca asked.

"Something like that. Yeah, I'll break it down for you later. We'll see about you being right on Wilson, too. Make the call."

Bad news always spreads faster than good news. Some things never change. I didn't mind De Luca tagging along at this point. I really didn't care where the help came from. I had the same sneaking suspicion she did regarding Sam Wilson. After all, Stacy wasn't exactly killing priests.

Chapter 8

"What did you find out about our vic?" I said when Fingers called me back.

De Luca tugged at my arm, trying to get me to put the call on speakerphone.

"Hey, David. Well, your guy Sam was a sex offender. He'd done some time for a DUI, too. Multiple rape cases. A few he did some short time for; a few he pleaded out. Looks like he worked as a fisherman most his life. Graduated from high school in '91, no siblings. There's more, but I'm not really sure what you're looking for."

"Told you!" De Luca said.

De Luca had been right; our guy was indeed a sex offender.

"What? Who's that?" Fingers said.

I shook my head. "She's with me. Don't worry. Thanks Fingers. You told me exactly what I needed to hear."

"What the hell did I tell you, tough guy?" De Luca said as I disconnected from Fingers. "So she's targeting sex offenders. Probably feels like she's doing the world a favor. Hell, if I wasn't a cop, I'd probably do the same thing. Or something Catwoman-like, ya know?"

I laughed. "No, I don't know exactly. So, cop or vigilante— those were you two options, eh?"

"Better than joining my family in the mob, right?"

"Too soon to tell if she's targeting anyone, but I doubt this was random. And yeah, I guess Catwoman would be better than mobbing since we're dealing in hypotheticals."

"You going to tell me what you did to piss this girl off?"

There was a long silence between us. I didn't like sharing the story. Most people would hear it and understand why I made the choice I did. Others, including some on the force, would demonize. I wasn't sure which side of the fence De Luca would be on.

I frowned. "I wasn't always a detective. There was a time when I was a stupid eighteen-year-old kid who didn't know his head from his ass."

"Yeah, we all had lives prior to joining the force. Just spit it out already."

I told her everything—every ugly detail. After I finished, De Luca just sat there with a blank look on her face. I wasn't sure how to read her reaction.

"So basically Stacy thinks you're a monster who set her up to be gangbanged by the entire football team?"

"Pretty much. But we were both fooled. The upperclassmen used us so they could get a lay. I wish eighteen-year-old me would have had the balls to stand up to them. It's not something I'm proud of."

"Don't beat yourself up. Sounds like a pretty stupid hazing

gone wrong. Ain't the first, won't be the last. Most eighteen-year-olds in your position would have done exactly what you did—stand there and watch, even if it was cowardly."

"Well thank you, Detective Big Balls, but it doesn't really help any of us right now."

"I do have one question though: if all of this was as innocent on your part as you make it seem, why didn't you just come clean with her?"

"Two reasons. One, the school lawyered us up and told us not to talk to anyone about it. Secondly, she left school. Guess she didn't want to deal with it. I did look for her—half-assed looked, anyway."

With that out of the way, we could move on. I knew she had to ask, had to know, and I was okay with that. I was glad to get it off my chest.

Chapter 9

We knew Stacy was targeting sex offenders, but there were literally thousands in Louisiana. Same for most other states, for that matter. If I planned on catching her, I'd need more information, maybe a pattern of some sort. If she was smart I wouldn't get one.

De Luca and I weren't far from Sulphur now, only about thirty minutes out. Mentally I was already hitting fatigue, and I knew we were just getting started. The thought of her having Karen and knowing what she'd done to those other kids sent shivers down my spine. My entire career I'd done things as by-the-book as possible. At least I'd tried. There were a few times when I'd allowed my temper to get the best of me, but like a fine wine, I'd gotten better with age.

"So how do we get in front of her? What made her pick this guy out? Place like this, he couldn't have been the only perv she found," De Luca said.

"I don't know. Maybe we'll get lucky. Sadly, she might have

to do this a few more times before we find a pattern . . . if one even exists."

I saw our turn up ahead. We pulled into the trailer park and stopped as close to Sam Wilson's gravel driveway as we could get. Only a few forensic folks remained. I'd asked Lafitte to have the team leave the body until I arrived. Lookie loos lined the street, all trying to catch a peek.

I turned my truck off and we climbed out. Someone needed to take control of this crime scene. There were way too many people way too close.

"Hey!" A middle-aged woman wearing a holey T-shirt, minus a bra, approached the taped-off area.

I turned slowly to give her my full attention. I could already tell where this was going, and I didn't like it.

"Yes ma'am, can I help you?"

She twirled her hair in her hand. "You a popo, huh?"

"If by *popo* you mean a police officer, then yes, I am."

"I never trusted that guy. I told my husband he was a piece of shit. Turns out I was right."

"Is there something he did to make you feel that way, ma'am?"

"Nope. Just a woman's intuition and the way he looked at me. So was he a rapist? That's what everybody's sayin'."

"I really can't comment on that, ma'am. Did you see or hear anything last night?"

"Nope."

I reached into my pocket. "Okay, well here's my card. If you think of anything please give me a call. Sometimes people remember things when they stop thinking about it."

We definitely weren't in Kansas anymore, and these people

were not Texans. It always amazed me that traveling a few hours in any direction from Houston could yield such differences in people. I doubted leaving her my card would do any good, but you never know. I wanted to end this thing with Stacy as quickly as possible.

As I walked closer to the trailer, my old buddy Lafitte appeared in the doorway.

Paul was almost my height, maybe an inch shorter, six two or something. It looked like he weighed around the same as he had when we were in the service together. It was also clear he was still spending a lot of time in the gym. Paul and I developed a forever friendship in the military that was as solid as any I had in my life. I'd die for Paul, and I was sure he felt the same way about me.

"David! You made it."

We exchanged a man hug—you know . . . the quick, back-thumping kind. It was great to see my old friend.

"Hey man! It's good to see you! I wish it could be on better terms, but . . ."

Lafitte quickly turned his attention away from me and onto De Luca. "Who's this beautiful lady you brought with you?"

Lafitte had always been a charmer. If there was a woman around, you'd better hide her or he'd sniff her out. Somehow he'd managed to sleep with three-fourths of the brass in our platoon back in our Army days.

"This is Detective Elena De Luca. She's the newest detective on our force."

"Well now, aren't you just beautiful," Lafitte said as he checked De Luca out.

De Luca reached out for a handshake, but Lafitte raised her

fingers to his lips instead.

"Nice to meet you, Detective Lafitte. I should let you know that I don't date cops. But I am flattered."

She gave him her standard line, but I noticed the huge grin she could barely contain. Something about Paul had undoubtedly caught her attention. No big surprise there.

"I typically don't date cops either, so I guess I'll have to turn in my badge today. Give me a second; let me call my chief."

He was half joking and half serious, I'm sure. De Luca laughed.

"So, I had my guys look into the account Stacy/Lisa created yesterday. What are we going to call her, anyway? We also asked around and found the motel she was staying in. We checked the security cameras. Come take a look. I had the video emailed over to me."

The video showed Stacy and Karen arriving and entering a room. It then showed Stacy leaving alone at around eight p.m. She wouldn't chance Karen waking while she was gone, so she'd probably drugged her. Then there's footage of her returning a few hours later, undoubtedly after she'd killed Sam Wilson.

"So she kills Wilson, comes back to the room, cleans up, catches a few hours' sleep, and at 4 a.m. she's gone again?"

"Question is, where's she headed next?" De Luca said.

"Anything turn up here that could help us narrow down where she's headed, Lafitte? Any other cameras in that parking lot? Can we tell what she's driving?"

"Not really. I mean, she ain't trying to hide much."

"What about the drink? What's she using to drug people? We able to tell that from the vic?"

"We'll find that out," Lafitte said.

"I have a sick feeling we'll hear from her again, sooner rather than later."

"Hey, here's the note she left you," Lafitte said as he handed me the scrap of paper.

Be sure this gets to Detective Porter 713.555.1357
David,
You screwed me so now I'm screwing you. You may get bruised a little you won't like it.
Love Stacy

"I'm going to call the office manager at the motel. I have a few questions I'd like to ask him. Did you happen to get his number, Paul?"

Lafitte handed me the office manager's card: Binoy Ansari. *Okay, Mr. Ansari, let's see how good your memory and attention to detail is.*

I made the call and introduced myself.

"This is Binoy. Am I in some kind of trouble?"

"No, sir. I'm investigating a guest who stayed at your motel last night."

"Ahh . . . the cute chick with the kid? Somebody want to tell me why she's being investigated?"

"Binoy, listen closely. That cute chick is wanted for murder. Not one, but multiple. She's dangerous, and we need to get her off the streets before she hurts someone else. That's why I need your help."

"Wow! I had no idea. How can I possibly help?"

"Are there other cameras that could have recorded her last

night, other than the one you showed the detectives earlier today?"

"No, that's the only one."

"Is there anything you can think of that might help me, Binoy? Even the smallest detail might lead us in the right direction."

"Not really. She was in and out really fast. Looking back, it was kind of odd how quickly she pushed me to get her checked in. And she was on a call with her sister, so I didn't try to strike up a conversation."

"Wait, her sister? How do you know she was talking to her sister?"

"I heard her say 'listen little sister,' like she was giving advice or scolding her or something. But again she was in and out quickly, and I only heard one side of the conversation."

"Thanks for your time, Binoy. I'll be in touch."

I always tried to get at least one piece of intel from every witness or person I talked to when I was investigating a case. My call to Binoy had paid off. Stacy, as it appeared, had a sister. Or someone she referred to as "little sister." On top of that, they were in direct contact with each other. Maybe finding this sister would be easy enough, and she could tell us where Stacy was headed.

Chapter 10

Stacy felt really good about her work from the night before. That bastard deserved to die. Actually, torturing him would have been even better, but she didn't have time for that. And it was all over the news, just like she'd wanted. Brilliant! She'd been certain the anonymous call from a screaming woman would get cops right over.

"Where are we going, Stacy? I want my daddy."

"I told you. Karen. We're going to spend some time with my Grammy in New Orleans. She's going to love you, and you're going to love her. She's special. I need you to forget about your dad for now."

Karen stared at Stacy without saying a word.

"We're going to get another room tonight, Karen. I don't drive well at night, and I'm kinda sleepy."

"It's okay. I like sleeping in motels."

"Well, good."

Stacy had gotten off the main interstate; she didn't want a

room right off I-10. When she pulled up to the motel, she got out and locked Karen in again.

Stacy didn't care to exchange pleasantries; she wanted to get the key and be off to her room. With that mission accomplished, she plugged in her laptop and started her search for a new target.

"Stacy, can you lay with me tonight for a little bit?"

"Sure, dear. How's that milk?"

"It's great! Nice and warm, just how I like it."

"Glad to see you smile, Karen."

Within minutes the girl was out. Time to see how many potentials she had. The girl's picture she was using wasn't attractive at all, but using her own photo was no longer an option, as the cops would surely be trying to catfish her.

To her pleasure and surprise, she had a hit in less than twenty minutes, and he checked out.

"Let's see here, Jon Rogers. What did they bust you for?" she muttered. "Three counts of sexual misconduct with a minor. And you're a teacher, at that. Time to pay the piper, Mr. Rogers."

Hey there big boy . . .

Hello

You got any pics to share? I wanna see who's gonna turn me on tonight.

I might have one . . . what makes you think I'm gonna do anything to you tonight?

Open the pic I just sent of me shaving last night.

(30 second pause)

Hey you still there Jon? Don't start early over there!

Yeah wow! I'm here. I'll send a pic right away! I'll send you

my address too unless you want me to come to your house.
No, I'll come to yours . . . let you take me in your bed, tiger.
Stacy checked on Karen and headed out to meet Mr. Rogers.
Guys were so stupid and so incredibly predictable.

Chapter 11

Stacy grabbed her goodie bag and bolted out the door. According to her GPS, the drive would only take about fifteen minutes, not counting a stop for gas. She pulled into the driveway and looked around to be sure no neighbors were hanging in their yards. Stacy got her lined cup and her drink concoction and walked toward Jon's front door. She was a little annoyed because a stupid dog was barking from the backyard as she approached.

The door opened. Jon Rogers looked just like she'd assumed he would: tall, dorky, poorly dressed, and in need of a good lay.

"Wow! You're beautiful! Hard to believe you don't have a million guys chasing after you."

"Who says I don't?" Stacy said, smiling. "And besides, all I need tonight is one guy, and you're in luck, mister."

"I'm definitely liking my luck then. Whatcha got there?"

"Oh, I like to bring my own drinks. I'm kinda picky. I like

what I like, you know."

Jon sat on the couch and patted the cushion next to him. Stacy walked over and offered a drink. She didn't miss the tremble in his hand or the beads of sweat dotting his forehead.

"Drink this, baby. A little nervous, are you?"

"A little. It's just . . . the girls I usually attract don't look like you. Honestly, I've never been with a girl as pretty as you are."

"Aww. That's cute, Jon. Don't make me blush. So while we're on the topic of things we usually don't encounter, I have a confession. I've never told anyone this, so I'm kinda nervous. It's a little silly, actually. Well, I'd really, really, like to . . . you know, make out with a younger guy. Like fifteen or maybe even younger. And like, just totally turn him out. Is that weird?"

Jon almost spilled.

"Well, that's a little weird. I mean, it's illegal, right?" Jon said.

"I'm sorry; you're right. Maybe I should just leave. I don't know why, but it just seems like I can trust you."

"No, no. I'm sorry. I didn't mean to upset you or make you feel bad. Okay, maybe I've thought about having a younger girl, too, once or twice. Nothing I would ever try to make happen, of course."

As he said it, he looked down and away from Stacy as if ashamed.

"Of course," Stacy said, turning her head so Jon couldn't see the look of disgust on her face. *You piece of shit*, she thought. *You've been caught three times, and only God knows how many more you've gotten away with*. No more, though. No more.

"Already pouring us another drink?" John said as he wiped sweat from his face with the back of his hand.

"What, you some kinda girly man? Bottoms up, cowboy! You got a restroom somewhere so I could freshen up a little?"

Jon pointed Stacy in the right direction. She really just wanted a place to hang out so she didn't have to look at him while the drugs took effect. It'd almost been ten minutes; she figured it wouldn't take much longer.

"Hey, you okay in there?"

Jon's speech was long, slow, and clearly slurred. Stacy heard a hint of impatience in his voice.

"I'm fine. Just wanna make sure I look my best for you, baby."

Stacy finally came out of the restroom and tried to head for the kitchen but Jon cut her off.

"Hey, there," he said. He stood directly in front of her, way too close for comfort. Stacy could tell he was begging for a kiss.

"One second. We're almost there, big boy. We aren't in a rush, are we? I got all night."

She eased around Jon, headed for the kitchen, and poured and another glass for them both.

"You trying to get me drunk, woman?" Jon said with a smile, growing more and more confident and woozy with each passing second.

"No, baby, I just wanna make sure the edge is off so we can do everything your little heart desires."

With that last bit of encouragement, it was bottoms up!

"Why don't you come sit here beside me," Stacy said. "You wouldn't happen to have any handcuffs would you, Jon?"

"I don't think so. You are a bad girl, aren't you?"

"Let me look in my bag. I might have some. If I do, you wanna put 'em on for me?"

Stacy was trying her best to make sure Jon felt comfortable with the situation. She took out the cuffs, lifted her shirt, and placed the cuffs on her stomach as she lay back onto the couch. She gestured for Jon to come closer. She grabbed his head and forced his face onto her stomach. Jon nibbled. The more Stacy moaned, the harder Jon tried to please her.

"Stop, baby. Put these on for me."

Jon did as he was told. He couldn't seem to get his fingers to cooperate, so Stacy helped him lock the cuffs into place.

"Am I drunk?" Jon said, laughing.

"No, probably not. But you are drugged and a few minutes away from passing out. How's that?"

"What?"

"Drugged, Jon; I drugged you."

"Why in the hell would you do that?" He struggled to get the words out, fighting to keep his eyes open.

"Because, Jon, you are a bad boy—a real bad boy. Be honest with me here, Jon. Do you like girls?"

"What the fuck do you mean? Of course I like girls! I'm not some faggot."

"No, no. Not women like myself. Girls. Ya know, under the age of, say, eighteen. Little fucking girls, Jon."

"What's it to you? You a cop or something? You don't seem

like no cop."

Stacy's laughter filled the room.

"A cop? No, I'm not a cop, Jon. Far from it. But I will be serving justice tonight."

Stacy walked over to her bag and grabbed her snips and duct tape.

Jon's eyes bulged as all color left his face. It almost appeared to Stacy that he'd turned into a little boy, in a way. No bravado, no yelling, no begging—just a shaking, frightened, cornered little boy awaiting his punishment.

"Jon, I don't know what happened to you, but—and I mean this—I really do feel sorry for you. But I have a calling, a duty, and this must be done."

Chapter 12

My head pounded, and I was sure my eyes were sunk deep into my head. De Luca, Lafitte, and I had stayed up all night scanning the net trying to get a bead on Stacy. We'd scoured every hookup site we could dig up. I even had Fingers working on some stuff back home. We'd managed to find the profile she'd used to lure poor Sam Wilson. She's even been brazen enough to use her own goddamn picture. None of us had been to sleep. I didn't plan on sleeping until I found Stacy and got Karen back.

"I'm sorry, guys. This all night shit ain't my cup of tea. I'm too old for this shit. I could use a cup of coffee. How about you guys?" Lafitte said.

"You guys just soft down here," De Luca said with a smile.

"Yeah well, soft or not I need some coffee. You guys want anything?"

"Why not? Biggest cup they have, two creams, two sugars," I said.

"And you, Superwoman?"

"Get me whatever you get girly-man."

Lafitte left to make the coffee run. I wanted food, too, but first things first.

I logged into my email. Fingers had sent me everything he could find out about Stacy.

"Let's see what we got here. So, Stacy grows up in New Orleans. Spends some time living with her grandmother, uncle, and in multiple foster homes."

"Yeah, and somewhere along the way somebody took advantage of her, and I'm willing to bet it happened more than once," De Luca said.

"Nothing's in her file, but I would have to agree. We know this girl is damage goods."

De Luca pulled a chair next to mine and browsed through the files with me. We gave each other a hard time, but I was glad she'd come with me to work on this case.

"So what's the deal on this sister? We know anything about her?" she said.

"No. I'm texting Fingers now. I need him to dig deeper."

We made it all the way through Stacy's file. Not a darn thing. Nothing that seemed too useful right off the bat, anyway. Our best piece of intel was the fact that she had a sister – we didn't even have a name. Now if we could only find her. And even if we did, would she be of any use?

Lafitte kicked the door open, hands full with three coffees.

"Thanks for the hand, guys."

"Do you ever stop moaning and bitching?" De Luca said with a grin on her face.

"Just come get your coffee, pretty lady. You know, you're

lucky I'm sweet on you."

I took my coffee from Lafitte, and De Luca and I made a second pass through Stacy's file. We had to have missed something.

"David, come take a look at this," Lafitte said, motioning me over to his computer.

"Well I'll be. Didn't take her long at all, did it? Morgan City man found cut up in his own home. Jon Rogers. No witnesses. No one heard a thing."

"You were right about her heading east. Looks like she might be headed for New Orleans after all, David," Lafitte said.

"Guess we're headed to Morgan City?" De Luca said.

"No, not yet," I said.

I wanted to spend a few hours sifting through the evidence that had been uploaded from the Houston killing a few days earlier. Before things got too stale, I needed to dig as deep as I could.

"Before we pack up, let's spend some time going over the John Blake murder."

"You looking for anything specific, David? I mean, I'm sure the boys back in Houston are working on it, aren't they?" De Luca said."

"Yes, but they don't know everything we know. I'm just looking for a break here any way I can get it."

She gave me her maybe-you're-right look and said nothing else. We all sat down in front of our laptops and read through the details of the Blake murder.

"You guys notice anything out of the norm here? I'm not seeing a thing." I said, leaning back in my chair.

"Me either," Lafitte said.

"John Blake has no criminal background, so why was he targeted? Seemingly no enemies, something isn't adding up."

"Well, he was a powerful guy. Maybe he did something to someone and it was covered up?" De Luca said.

"Maybe. You could be onto something there."

"Makes sense. Guy had enough money to buy anything he wanted," Lafitte said.

I looked through the pictures again, and all at once it hit me like a ton of bricks.

"Picture forty-eight—the last pic taken. Look at it." I waited for them to catch up.

"Okay . . . now what are we looking for?" Lafitte said.

"BF. Recognize those initials?"

"No, should we?" De Luca said.

"Brittany Foy—Stacy's sister. It's a long shot, but it isn't that far-fetched. Think about it. Both of these girls bounced from home to home. They're only fourteen months apart. It's a safe bet that whoever molested Stacy did it to Brittany, too. No way he'd get one and not the other."

"Goddamn, David! You may be on to something," Lafitte said.

"I think you may be right. I'm with you too," De Luca said.

"Let's keep searching this case, at least another hour or so. Look for anything else we overlooked," I said.

I didn't want to bring anyone else in on this, at least not yet. And I certainly didn't want to let the girls know we were on to them—if indeed we were.

"We need to pull up everything we can on John Blake. We

know he was into strip clubs. We need to find out which ones he frequented the most. I'm betting Heartbreakers is going to be on the top of that list. I'll call Cap and have him get someone on it. The more we find out about Blake, the closer we get to Brittany Foy."

Chapter 13

"Carl Blake, come on! Do something fucking exciting, would you? You've got to be the most boring guy ever," Brittany mumbled.

She'd hoped to gather information fast enough to be finished with this job in two days—three days max. Her biggest obstacle seemed to be getting him alone. Her first day of following him had been pretty uneventful. He left the house at six thirty a.m. and made a thirty-five-minute commute to work. He left for lunch at eleven forty-five with a group of coworkers. Returned at two minutes to one. Left for the day at six forty-five and made it home by seven thirty. Not a shred of excitement in this guy's life.

Eight. Eight thirty. Nine. Nine thirty. Nothing. Brittany was bored and started playing a game on her phone.

Another twenty minutes went by. "Okay . . . what do we have here?" Brittany said, looking up from her phone.

She watched as Carl stepped out front to take a phone call.

Could be nothing but it could be big. She watched as he moved about and noticed how he looked over his shoulder every few seconds.

"Who are you talking to, Carl?" she whispered. She had to admit that, in another life, she could see herself with a guy like him. He was well-dressed and ruggedly handsome. After several minutes of passionate discussion, Carl raced back into the house and slammed the door.

 Less than five minutes later, Carl's car sped down the driveway. She finally had the break she needed. Where was he going in such a hurry so late at night?

She started her car but made certain her lights were off for now. She followed as he drove like a madman across town, ignoring stop signs and running red lights all the way. Twenty minutes later, they arrived at Cabo, a bar in Kemah

"Who are you meeting at a fucking bar at ten p.m. while your wife is at home with your kids, Mr. Blake?"

Much to her surprise, Carl stayed in his car. Three minutes later, out came a twenty-something blonde—tall, super skinny, very pretty. Carl got out of his car, and Brittany watched as the two had an intense make-out session against the passenger-side door. The microphone she'd placed in his car wouldn't pick up much more than a mumble unless they got in. Must be her lucky night. The two finally got into Carl's Lexus, and the pair began talking.

"I came as quickly as I could. You know this is difficult for me, and you know how hard it is for me to get away so late."

"I know; I'm sorry. You know how I get when I drink, but I needed to see you, baby. And what do you care about her anyway? You told me you were going to leave her soon."

"Yeah, well, that's easier said than done. She is the mother of my kids, and I have a lot of assets, business. There's a lot to think about before I make my move. You understand that, don't you?"

"I guess. I just want you now. I don't want to wait any longer. We've been doing this, whatever this is, for over a year now. My friends all say I'm stupid and that you'll never leave her."

"Fuck your friends. I *am* going to leave her. Sorry if that sounded mean. I don't dislike your friends, but this thing is going to take some time, okay?"

"Okay, but not too much more time, you hear me?"

"I hear you. Now bring that sexy little body over here."

What a fucking pig, this guy. No better than his piece-of-shit brother. Stacy was right.

"Okay, I gotta run. Cindy is going out of town this weekend, remember?"

"Yes. Are you going to spend some time with me?"

"Yes. I'll call you tomorrow. She flies out first thing in the morning. I have some business to take care of then we can hook up. Sound good to you?"

"Deal. I'm gonna make you forget all about that wife of yours!"

"Okay, baby. Now get back in there with your friends. I gotta run."

"Gotcha, you bastard. So tomorrow it'll just be you, huh?" Brittany muttered. She watched as the girl got out of his car and stood there as he drove off into the night.

"Hey you!" Brittany said to the woman, who looked around

the parking lot trying to figure out where the voice was coming from. "Yeah, you!"

"Me? Do I know you?" the young woman said as Brittany drove up beside her and rolled down the window.

"I'm new to the area. I'm looking for a good spot to hang out and make some friends. This place any good?"

"Yeah, it's okay. Good dancing, two floors of music, and usually a live band, too. My friends and I like it."

"Friends?" Brittany said, looking around.

"Oh they're inside waiting on me, so I gotta run. It was nice meeting you."

"Oh, okay. I thought I saw you making out with some guy a few minutes ago. That your boyfriend? Got a night out on your own, huh?"

"Yeah, something like that. What did you say your name was again?"

"I didn't. Maybe I'll see you around."

With that, Brittany left the woman standing there and sped off into the darkness.

Chapter 14

All of my intel told me John Blake's younger brother Carl was his right-hand man. If anyone knew why John was killed, it'd probably be him.

"Let's get all of this mess cleaned up and head to Morgan City before the trail goes cold. It'll take us about an hour to get there, so let's get a move on," I said.

"What about Brittany and that case?" De Luca said.

"I'll make a call on that while we drive. If anybody can give us some direction, it's going to be John's brother Carl. He handled most of his day-to-day activities. To be honest, I don't believe he's going to give me anything useful, but I need to scratch his name off my list."

We spent the next ten minutes gathering up our equipment and loading it into my truck. I planned on calling Carl Blake and putting him on speakerphone so the three of us could break down his answers after the call. We had been working pretty well together; I liked that.

"So, what exactly do you have planned for Carl?" De Luca asked.

"I don't know, exactly. I guess I'm gonna wing it. I do have an idea, but I'm willing to bet his answers dictate my questions."

I made the call, and we sat in silence waiting for him to pick up.

"Hello? Who is this?" Carl Blake answered his phone, clearly agitated.

"Carl Blake? Detective David Porter, Houston PD. Do you have a few minutes to talk?"

"Not really, Detective. I'm headed to a meeting. You got about five minutes. What is this about, anyway?"

"I'll be brief. First off, I'd like to offer my condolences to you and your family. I'm told you and your brother were close. I'm investigating his murder. Do you know anyone who wanted to hurt your brother?"

"I appreciate the concern, Detective, but let's be honest; you guys never catch the bad guys. What percentage of the murders do you really solve here in Houston?"

This guy had some nerve. Here I am trying to help find the person who killed his brother, and all I'm getting is flack.

"I'll ask the questions here, Mr. Blake. But just for the record, I actually have a pretty damn good solve rate for the cases I'm involved with. Again, do you know anyone who would want to hurt your brother?"

"No. My brother was a good man. He always looked after me, and he loved his family."

"Intel informs me that your brother used to frequent strip clubs. Seems he had an affinity for the nightlife. You know anything about that?"

"Hey, what guy doesn't like to see a little flesh from time to time? No reason to kill a guy."

"Not implying that's a reason, Mr. Blake. Just verifying my intel. Your brother a gambler? He owe somebody money?"

"No and no. We almost done here?"

"Yes, just a few more questions. Being his right-hand man, you must know how his wife felt about his need to . . . how'd you put it? See a little flesh? Other than her own, of course."

"I don't know. She isn't my wife. Is this really going to help you find my brother's killer?"

"It might. Could help me rule out or identify a motive. Your brother have you on his insurance policy? How about his business; it all turned over to you now?"

"Are you suggesting—"

"I'm not suggesting anything. I'm simply doing my job. Someone butchered your brother. If you guys were as close as I'm told you were, you'd think finding his killer would be a top priority for you. Unless, of course . . ."

"I didn't kill my brother. I don't know who did or why they'd want to. My brother's business is one hundred percent mine now, yes. I'd give it all back and then some to have my brother back. Fuck you for suggesting otherwise, Detective. So the man liked to go to Heartbreakers—so fucking what. Big fucking deal. That's not a reason to have a man killed. Sounds like you need a lap dance yourself. Have a nice day."

Blake disconnected the call, I stared at my phone for a second.

"Well, Porter, that went well," Lafitte said, laughing.

"Yeah, some go better than others," I said.

"I'm learning, Porter. Call the family, piss them off, get absolutely no leads, and then they hang up on you?" De Luca said.

"I beg to differ; I got plenty. Unless the brother and wife are having an affair, both can probably be ruled out. The wife didn't get the business, and the brother seems legitimately pissed off about his brother's murder. John did frequent strip clubs, so we validated that. We also know he doesn't owe any bookies money. So we learned quite a bit."

"And you believe everything that little jerk was spewing?" De Luca said.

"I've learned, for the most part, to remove the emotion from a suspect's questioning and dig out the root of their answers. Carl loved his brother. I'd even say he adored him. He does sound like an entitled little brat, but it doesn't make him a killer. He'd have no reason to leave behind the BF calling card. I wasn't trying to suggest Carl did it; I was trying to make him believe I was. I got him riled up, and he gave me the most important piece of evidence yet. There are about one hundred gentlemen's clubs in Houston; however, we now know the one John Blake frequented. That's where we go next. Maybe Brittany was a dancer there. Maybe Blake was one of her regulars. Maybe somebody can tell us where she lives or what she drives."

"Guess you get the last laugh, David," Lafitte said.

"I'll laugh when I have Karen at home and Stacy and Brittany behind bars."

Chapter 15

"Hey, baby, guess what?"

"What do you want, Carl? That wife of yours gone yet?"

"Actually, she is. I have to meet a few clients for dinner and then I'm free. Maybe I'll take you out to that spot you like so much—Cabo, right? I'll hang out with you and your girlfriends. We can do some dancing."

"I'd like that. I think they're going to love you once they get to know you like I do."

"I'll call you around ten after I am done. See you soon."

Brittany watched through the window as Carl got dressed. Little did he know, his time had run out. She grabbed her purse and headed for his doorstep. She pressed the doorbell and waited.

"Hello. You the new nanny?" Carl said to the woman on his porch. "My wife isn't here. Can you come back next week?"

"No, silly. You see a girl and you assume she's your nanny?"

"I didn't mean to offend you. My wife mentioned that the

new nanny might be stopping by. Can I help you with something? I'm kind of in a rush here."

"No need to rush, Carl. We got all night. Your clients and girlfriend are going to be waiting a long time."

She did one last glance back and forth to make sure no one was watching. Brittany had her Taser in hand and knew how to use it. She hit him with the taser and he dropped helplessly to the ground. After he stopped convulsing and lay limp, she injected him with a sedative. It wouldn't put him out but it would make him easily manageable. She removed two pairs of handcuffs from her bag and secured his wrists and legs. She looked around again to be sure she hadn't been seen and drug him into the house and closed the door behind her.

After about five minutes passed, Carl started to come to. Brittany could see Carl trying to process everything and figure out what happened. His eyes opened and closed slowly. A little foam had built up in the corner of his mouth.

"Who the fuck are you? And what are you doing?"

"Carl, Carl, Carl. Slow down, baby. We're gonna get to all of that, don't worry. Let's talk about some other things first. You okay with that?"

"Listen, bitch. You don't know who you're messing with."

"Oh, I'm pretty sure I know *exactly* who I'm messin' with. You think I showed up on your doorstep when your wife and kids are out of town by accident?"

"Okay, so you know who I am. That just proves how stupid you are!"

"Well, I was smart enough to land you and your pathetic brother. Let's quit playing around and cut right to the chase,

Carl."

"You killed my brother?"

He pulled and tugged at his restraints but it was no use.

"I'll make you pay for this!"

"Umm . . . I don't think so, Carl. I don't see you making it out of this one, bud. Let's play a game. Do you remember much about your bachelor party?"

"Of course I remember my own bachelor party. What about it?"

"I mean, I'm sure you remember the event, but what about the details? Did you guys have dancers?"

"What kind of lame-ass bachelor party would it have been without dancers?"

"Ahhh! Okay. Well guess what, Carl? Surprise! I was one of your dancers—the one you and your brother raped!"

Carl sat up as much as he could and Brittany could tell by the expression on his face that he couldn't believe it.

"Wait, what?"

"Rape, Carl. Forcibly entering a woman's vagina when you weren't invited."

"I understand what rape is, I just—"

"You just what? Don't remember? You and your brother and all of your guests were totally fucked up."

"So what now? This some kind of payback?"

"Justice, Carl."

Brittany walked over to her bag, reached in, and grabbed her snips and a hammer.

"Have you had anything to drink today, Carl?"

"What the fuck are you going to do with those?"

"Have you had anything to drink today, Carl? A shot? A

beer?"

"No! Why does that matter?"

"It doesn't, really, but I'm glad you haven't. I want you to feel every bit of this pain."

Brittany took his right hand and spread his fingers on the floor. She took the hammer and smashed each finger one by one as Carl squirmed and screamed in agony. She never stopped she didn't even flinch as she methodically mangled each finger on his right hand.

She grinned as he whimpered like a wounded animal. The high she'd felt when she'd killed his brother a few days before returned. She felt no remorse.

Then the doorbell rang.

"What the fuck?"

"Help! Help!" Carl began to yell.

"Shut up!" Brittany had forgotten to put the tennis ball into his mouth. She snatched it from her bag, shoved it in his mouth, and slapped a piece of duct tape across his lips.

The doorbell rang again.

She eased over to the curtains to see who it was. Some kid. Looked to be seven or eight. *He's probably selling something,* she thought. She peeked out again and noticed a car idling in the driveway. She figured she needed to get rid of him before the parents came to help. She ran to a mirror in the living room and made sure she looked presentable before heading toward the door.

"Hello. Can I help you?" Brittany said, the door slightly ajar.

"Yes, ma'am. I'm Timmy. I live a few houses down. I'm selling these cookies for school. Are Mr. and Mrs. Blake home? They usually buy some."

"Well, they're out of town, Timmy, and I'm house-sitting. Can you come back in a few days? They should be back by then."

"Yes, ma'am. My dad thought he saw Mr. Blake here about an hour ago, but I guess he didn't. Thanks anyway."

"No problem, Timmy. Bye now."

Brittany locked the door and watched through the curtains until the car backed out and headed down the street. When the taillights disappeared from view, she breathed a sigh of relief and returned to the business at hand.

"This is what I meant, Carl. I don't have all day to sit here and play with you. Be a good boy and put those hands back up here."

Brittany looked down at Carl's mangled right hand. *Serves him right, the piece of shit.*

"What's it going to be, hammer or saw?"

Carl blanched and turned his head away.

"So you're letting me pick again? Aww . . . isn't that sweet of you. I think I want a little more practice with this ole' hammer."

Carl squirmed and flailed, as much as he could but it was no use. Brittany flattened out his left hand and beat away. Pieces of finger flew and splattered the walls. Blood gushed everywhere. She made sure to give each finger the attention it deserved. The more she pummeled him, the more pleasure it gave her. Brittany never imagined such violence would bring her sexual excitement, but it had. Every swing brought her closer and closer to an orgasm.

"You will never put these hands on anyone else!"

Carl was numb, in too much pain to move. He was on the

verge of blacking out. His hands looked like they'd been run through a meat grinder. His blood freckled Brittany's face.

Brittany slapped his face. "Wake up Carl, it's not over until I say it is!"

"Okay, you win. Please stop," Carl pleaded.

"I win? This isn't a game, Carl. You're a piece of shit with no respect for women. You think we're your little sex toys, like the only reason we exist is to pleasure you."

"You're right. I'm sorry. I've been very selfish and rude to women in general. I can change."

Brittany stepped back. He actually seemed sincere.

"I'm glad you're going out with a little bit of dignity, Carl."

Brittany walked over to her bag again, grabbed her gun, and screwed the silencer into place.

"Hey! I said I'm sorry! That's not enough? What else do you fucking want from me?"

"I'm afraid it won't be enough this time. No charming your way out of this one. Let me replay the line you gave me. It's stuck in my head all these years. *Just relax baby and let it happen.*"

Without another word, Brittany stepped back, pointed her gun at Carl's head, and pulled the trigger.

She wanted to leave her BF trademark on the wall, but she remembered what her sister had told her about Detective Porter and the importance of sticking to the script. She opted to leave *Widowmaker* on the wall as her calling card instead. That should be enough to do the trick.

Chapter 16

I needed to call home and check in on Hilary and Miranda. The drive to Morgan City wasn't long, and I'd already eaten into that time by talking with Carl Blake. I still couldn't believe how much of a prick he'd been when I was trying to help him and his family.

"Hey, Sonny and Cher, keep it down a bit, will you? I need to phone home and check in on the girls."

"Funny guy, here. We prefer Bonnie and Clyde, if we have to be named," Lafitte said with a chuckle.

It was good to see those two getting along. Who knew what would spring up from their relationship.

"Hey, dad," Hilary said with more excitement that I'd anticipated.

"Good morning, honey. How are you? How's your mother?"

"I'm okay, Dad. Mom's still asleep. She mentioned going back to work, do you think it's too soon?"

"Did she? Well, she knows herself better than anyone. She's

seeing a doctor, so I'm sure the two of them will make the right choice. I'm glad to hear she's doing so well. How are you holding up?"

"I'm okay, but I'm worried. I'm afraid I might never see Karen again. I'm really scared."

My eyes began to water, and I could tell De Luca and Lafitte were zeroing in on me.

"I'm fine," I whispered to them, holding the phone away from my face.

"Hil, we're doing everything we can and then some. We're going to find her, trust me. Have I ever let you down? I don't plan on starting now. Kiss your mother for me and let her know I called."

"I love you, Dad."

"Love you, too, Hil. Bye."

The biggest fear in the world for any parent is having to bury one of their own. Despite my tough exterior, I harbored the same fear. I didn't want to find Karen's naked, decayed little body in some field. The thought terrified me.

"David, according to my map we're about five minutes away," Lafitte said.

When we arrived the place was overrun by local law enforcement. I was hoping that having Lafitte with me would continue to get me access to all the information the local guys had and, more importantly, any potential witnesses.

"That's Jim Collins. He's no doubt in charge here," Lafitte said as we passed by, looking for somewhere to park.

"That's where I need to start then," I said.

We stepped down from my truck and stretched our legs a

little. Headed my direction, to my surprise, was Jim Collins.

"Listen, I know who you are, and I know why you're here," Collins said as he extended his hand.

"Listen, Jim, I'm not here to step on your toes or get in anyone's way."

"Hell, you won't be in our way. Way I see it, this only happened here in our little town because of you. Me and my team will take any help you can give us. We're small-time here, Porter. We ain't some fancy-schmancy, big-time HPD detectives. This here is the most action we've had in quite some time. Like I said, only reason I reckon any of this here foolery is goin' down is on account of you and that maniac you're chasing."

"I'm not going to disagree with much, if any, of that, Jim. Sounds pretty spot-on to me. I'll offer any assistance I can."

Jim yelled across the way for one of his officers to come over.

"Porter, this here's Officer Blasberg. He pretty much knows everything that's happened here thus far. He'll be able to brief you and tackle anything else you might need."

"Thank you, Jim," I said, turning my attention to Blasberg.

"Before I say anything else, I just want to let you know how much of an honor it is to work with you," the officer said. "I've read all of your books. I think I'm a better cop 'cuz of 'em, too."

"Thanks. That's nice to hear. I appreciate the kind words. Now, what can you tell me about what happened here?"

We headed up the driveway. This definitely had the markings of Stacy: secluded house way off the road; quick, easy access where no one would see her come or go.

"Well, sir, craziest damn thing I've seen in my three years here. This is one psycho perp you got on your hands, sir. Vic's name is Jon Rogers. Thirty-seven years old, no wife, no girlfriend far as we can tell. Sketchy guy, too. Been arrested multiple times for having sex with underage girls. We've gone through his computer, for the most part. Visited a lotta kiddie porn sites. Got a bunch of pics saved. Looks like last night he and Miss Stacy chatted back and forth on this hookup site, and he led her right over. Any particular reason she'd choose him, sir?"

"Yes. He's a rapist, plain and simple."

We walked into the house, and what I saw next stopped me dead in my tracks. This guy sure as hell didn't end up having the night he'd hoped for. Rogers lay stark-naked on the floor—what was left of him, anyway. As I looked around the living room, I saw pieces of his body taped off everywhere. His face had been chewed to hell. *Rats, maybe*? Made sense. Nutria. River rats. Louisiana was famous for them.

"Jesus Christ, Porter," De Luca said, her face a spooky shade of green.

"You sure picked a crazy bitch to piss off, David," Lafitte said.

"Thanks for reminding me."

"Wait, am I missing something here? Do you know who did this, sir?"

"Yes, I do. All too well. She's kidnapped one of my daughters, and she's pregnant, too. And yes, it's mine."

Blasberg's jaw-dropped, his face paled.

"It's okay, son. Relax. It's a long story—one I don't have time to tell right now. What else do you know about what happened here?"

"Well . . . sorry; this is all happening really fast. The bites you see? Rats. The ME hasn't given an official cause of death, so it's hard to tell if he was alive or already dead when she let the rats free."

I walked over to the torso of Jon Rogers and knelt down beside him. Jesus Christ was right! Just when I thought she was all out of tricks. I took a pen out of my shirt pocket and poked the body.

"He was alive."

"Wait, how do you know that?" Blasberg said.

"If Porter says he was alive, he was alive, kid," De Luca said.

"Blasberg, you've done good work here. Take my card. Call me the minute the coroner completes the autopsy. You hear? And any news breaks, you be sure to let me know."

"Yes, sir. You can count on me, sir."

"Before we head out, is there anything else we need to know about this crime scene? Any notes or messages left behind?"

"No, sir. Nothing like that has been recovered."

That was strange. In the past she'd always left something behind. How many men would Stacy kill before I stopped her? Would I ever stop her? I was beginning to wonder. And where was Karen? I couldn't help by feel solely responsible once again for her abduction. God if I could just go back and change that one day, *the day I'd met Lisa Crease* all of our lives would be better for it.

Chapter 17

We left Blasberg and headed for my truck. I hoped one day soon I'd be able to get the image of Jon Rogers's limbless, rat-bitten torso out of my head. We were halfway down the drive when I saw Collins approaching.

"Blasberg give you everything you needed here? Quite the mess you've left us."

Collins was right, but I wasn't in the mood for his shit. Instead of wasting time arguing with him, I bit my tongue.

"Yes, he did."

"Before you leave, I think the three of you need to see something. Just came across my phone. Damnedest thing, too."

"What?" I said, alarm bells ringing in my head.

I snatched Collins's phone away from him and stared at the screen. Stacy had videoed the moment she released the rats on Jon Rogers's body and uploaded it to YouTube. This was her calling card, which explained why she hadn't left a note here at the scene.

I hit play on the video that already had one million views.

"Jon, one last treat to finish you off. I think my furry little friends here are going to like all this blood."

The video panned to a close-up of Stacy looking directly into the camera.

"Hi, David. Don't worry, the baby is fine and so is Karen. Jon and I were about to have some fun, but then I decided I'd be the only one having fun tonight. Tell Carl I said hello the next time you talk to him. Love you, boo."

Then the camera panned back to a barely moving Jon. Rats tore into him like starved savages.

I handed Collins his phone.

"Thanks. Get in, guys. Let's go."

I rolled the window down as we started to drive away.

"Collins, tell Blasberg I said thanks again. Tell him I said he's going to have your job one day."

I rolled the window up, and before De Luca or Lafitte could get a word in, I was already phoning Carl Blake.

"Porter, who are you calling? And where are we going?" De Luca said.

"Heading to New Orleans. Stacy's clearly headed east. Maybe she'll kill again before she gets there. Guess we'll find out soon enough. Oh, and I'm calling Carl Blake."

"Why Carl Blake? What's he got to do with this?" Lafitte said.

"No answer. Damn!" I said as I hung up the phone. "I don't think he's got anything to do with this. Hell, I'm just hoping the prick is still alive. You know our BF—aka the Widowmaker? How much you wanna bet she's paid a visit to him already? Why in the hell else would Stacy tell me to tell Carl hi in her little video?"

"Brittany kills John Blake *and* Carl Blake? What the hell did they do to her?" Lafitte said.

"I don't know. Haven't been able to put my finger on it. Maybe they went to the club one night and took her to a private room. Maybe things got out of hand, and this is her payback. We don't even know that Carl Blake is dead. It's just speculation on my part."

"Yes, we do," De Luca said, holding her phone in front of David as he drove.

There, on the front page of the digital addition of the *Houston Chronicle,* was the headline, *Local Politician Carl Blake Found Murdered in Home.*

"Well, well, well. We need to regroup," I said as I pulled off to the side of the road.

I knew neither of them would like what I was about to say.

"Hear me out on this one. Lafitte, I drug you into this thing so I could navigate Louisiana a little faster and cut through some red tape. De Luca, we know why you came, but things are different now. We can't track Brittany Foy and Stacy across two states. I need you two to head back to Houston, visit these crime scenes, and track Brittany down. I'll push east and keep pushing until I find Stacy."

"No! Absolutely not," De Luca said, crossing her arms across her chest like a pouty child.

"Listen, I'm not suggesting here; it's what we need to do. I've been through some rough shit on my own. Louisiana ain't got nothing I can't handle. There are things the two of you will see with your eyes and feel with your presence that we simply can't get from a set of pictures. Carl Blake's case is fresh; the crime scene is fresh. Start there and let's see if we can't catch Miss Foy with her pants down. She's clearly begging for attention, so let's give her some."

"Can't the boys in blue handle this?" Lafitte said.

"I don't doubt they can handle it. But I don't have three years to wait. And they don't have all the information we do."

"I guess you're right, Porter. We'll do it," Lafitte said.

De Luca was staring out of the window, none too pleased with my new strategy. I understood where she was coming from, though. Stacy had kidnapped her and held her hostage. Her interest was personal.

"Doesn't feel right," De Luca said.

"Trust me, I'd rather have the two of you here with me. It doesn't feel right to me either, but it's the best play. Lafitte, I'm taking the two of you to the nearest car rental place I can find. Get to Houston and find Brittany Foy."

Chapter 18

Funny thing how we meet people in life. You marry this person, who knows that person, who introduces you to these people. I knew it would only be a matter of time before Lafitte moved to Houston or HPD lost De Luca to New Orleans. The writing was on the wall. They both played tough, but I could feel it. And now that I'd sent them off to hunt down Brittany Foy, they'd have some one-on-one time to get to know each other a little better. Wasn't my intention. Just kind of how it all seemed to play itself out.

Hunger and fatigue had begun to overwhelm me. Both were evil necessities that dearly needed my attention. But how could I possibly sleep with this much going on and so many unanswered questions? I couldn't, and it was catching up with me fast.

I drove on as nighttime set in around me. The beady yellow eyes of gators and other swamp creatures lit up the bayous as I drove I-10 East toward New Orleans. Even at night this was beautiful country. My eyes got heavy as the loneliness set in and my tiredness grew. Just as I started to nod off, my cell phone rang.

"Porter."

"Hey, honey. It's me."

I shook the cobwebs off. "Miranda! Hey, baby, how are you? I called you earlier but you were sleeping."

"Yes, Hilary told me. I'm okay; I really am. Did she tell you I was thinking about going back to work? David, I can't just sit here every day feeling sorry for myself. I've also thought about helping Tim Miller and EquuSearch. Maybe not on Karen's case, but I want to help another parent if I can. This is terrible, David. I feel so powerless."

Tim Miller's daughter had been abducted from our area many years ago. I wasn't an officer then, but the case gained national headlines and it stuck with me. He started EquuSearch as a result of his daughter's kidnapping. They've really helped a lot of families find closure—one way or the other.

"No need to explain. I get it. I'd drive myself crazy, too, just sitting around. I think getting involved with Tim and his team is a great idea. If you're ready, I mean. It's going to make you think of Karen a lot."

"I know, but I've got to do something. Besides, I don't think I could think of her more than I already do. She's on my mind every single moment. So . . . how are you? You sound tired."

She knew me all too well.

"I am tired—exhausted, to tell the truth. I can't even tell you the last time I slept. And now we got these murders popping up in Houston, too."

"Yeah, it's been all over the news. They're trying to make a connection, but they can't."

"I have. I know who's committing those murders. As a matter of fact, I sent Lafitte and De Luca back to Houston a few hours ago to track her down."

"Her? Stacy? How?"

"No, Stacy's sister, Brittany. Keep it to yourself. No exposé, missy!"

"Of course not. I know it's ongoing. How'd you guys figure out so much already?"

"Like I said, I haven't slept in days. All my focus has been on this."

"I hope my baby girl . . . God, I can't even go there."

"I know. It makes me sick to my stomach every time I think about Stacy being alone with her. I'm doing my best to treat this case like I would any other, but in my heart . . . I'm going to find her and bring her home safe and sound!"

"I know you will, David. I believe in you. I love you."

"I'm turning off here. I've got to shut it down for a few hours and refuel this old body of mine."

"Yes, please do. Get some rest. I'll talk to you tomorrow. Don't worry about us; we're fine here."

"Good night, Miranda Porter. I love you, too."

If I drove much longer, I knew what would happen. I'm a habitual drowsy driver. I hate myself for it, but I accept the character flaw for what it is. I also remember that admitting you have a problem is step one. I'd come really close to driving off the road more than a few times. Not to mention I'd drifted into oncoming traffic more times than I cared to admit.

I pulled into a run-down Motel Six. I didn't care how the placed looked. I needed a bed and some running water, nothing more. As I walked into the lobby—if you could call it that—I noticed the place was dead. Really dead. There was a bell on the desk and a sign suggesting I ring for service. I hit it a few times and waited. A TV played across the lobby, broadcasting what appeared to be a late-night rerun of the local news.

Five minutes went by and no one came. I hit the bell a few more times, hoping someone would wake up and get me checked in. Finally an old woman flung open a door and walked toward the counter.

"You want a room?" the old woman barked in a strong Cajun dialect.

"Yes, ma'am," I said as politely as possible.

"What the hell you doin' out so late, anyways? Aint you got no wife at home?"

"Yes, ma'am, I do. But I'm traveling for work right now."

"Yeah, I bet," the woman said, glancing out toward my truck.

"Your work out in your truck waiting on you?"

It was then I realized she thought I was getting a room for myself and some company. The place was a shit hole, and the guests she got were probably here for that very reason, more often than not.

"No, ma'am. I'm actually a police officer," I said, flashing my badge.

"What the hell does that mean? You bastards are the worst ones. I get more of you than anything else. Listen, just give me your damn credit card."

I was too tired to argue. I handed her my card. I glanced over at the TV in time to see *Police hunting female serial killer* flash across the screen in big letters.

"That what you here for?"

"Well . . . yes and no. Kind of."

"Well either you are or you ain't. And where you from? You're not from here."

"No, ma'am. I'm from Houston."

"So you some big-time Houston cop, huh? You here to help us small-timers out? Show us how it's done?"

"Not at all. It's a long story, actually. And you wouldn't believe it if I told you, so I won't. You have a good night."

I took the key from her and walked back out to my truck. Grouchy old hag, she was. She seemed like a straight shooter, though, which I liked. Maybe it was the detective in me, but I preferred brutal honesty to beating around the bush.

I drove around to my room, grabbed my bags, and went inside.

Shit hole was right. The place was a dump. I guess I shouldn't have expected much for thirty-nine dollars. I sent Miranda a text telling her I was off the road and getting some sleep so she wouldn't worry.

I wanted to spend a few minutes working the case now that I was alone. I sat down on the bed and fired up my laptop. As it booted up, I struggled to keep my eyes open. Any work I tried to do now would be counterproductive. I shut my computer, plugged it in to charge, and went to sleep.

Chapter 19

I rolled over to grab my cell phone as the alarm clock sounded: five-thirty a.m. If I slept later than five-thirty, I felt guilty. Guess that was a result of my stint in the military and college athletics. The motto "We do more before 6 a.m. than most people do all day" wasn't far from the truth. Not far at all.

I grabbed my laptop. Time to see if I could get any closer to hunting Stacy down. I'd played with the idea of calling Stacy's grandmother, since I had a hunch she was heading that way. I hadn't decided whether I wanted to beat her there and wait or whether she was ahead of me. That probably depended upon whether or not she stopped for another kill along the way. I had also toyed with the idea of putting surveillance on her grandmother's home, but I didn't want to chance Stacy sniffing it out. If she suspected anything out of the ordinary and bailed on me, I might never find her or my baby girl.

I grabbed my cell phone and thumbed Lafitte's number.

"Paul, I pulled up a map to Stacy's grandmother's place. I'm thinking I'll need someone to help navigate back there. Looks like it's right in the middle of the goddamn swamp. From what I gather there's only one way in or out. You got anyone you can hook me up with?"

"Guess we skipping all the pleasantries today?"

"Sorry, Paul. Got ahead of myself, buddy. How are you and De Luca doing? Anything yet?"

"De Luca and I are doing quite well. By this time next year, she'll be Mrs. Paul Lafitte. And yes, I got somebody who can get you back there. His name is Randy Landry."

"I meant how are you doing with the case? And give me his number."

"We got in late last night. We're diving in today with a visit to the crime scene. Then we'll start chasing leads. 504.555.7685."

"I'll give him a call in a few hours. Thanks. Keep me posted."

I disconnected with Lafitte and decided to call Miss Patty Jones. It was closing in on seven a.m., and old people never slept that late anyway, or so I reasoned.

"Hello? Who's this?"

"Good morning, Miss Jones. This is Detective Porter from the Houston Police Department."

"Am I expecting your call, son? I don't have any business in Houston. I think you have the wrong number."

"No, ma'am, you don't know me, but I need to ask you a few questions about your granddaughter, Sta . . . I mean, Lisa."

The phone went silent.

I cleared my throat. "Hello? Miss Jones, are you still with me?"

"Yes, I'm here. Listen, I haven't seen or spoken to Lisa in nearly fifteen years, son. I'm not sure how much help I can be."

"I understand, but I'd like to try, if that's okay with you. I also have reason to believe she might be paying you a visit soon. It's just a hunch."

She raised her voice an octave. "I did everything I could for Lisa and her sister, Brittany. Raised 'em both like they was my own, when they'd have me. Hard seein' them up and leave. They never call or come see me. She's okay, right?"

My radar was pinging off the wall; her answers came fast and seemed a bit too perfect. "She's alive and well, ma'am. I'm sorry she doesn't contact you, Miss Jones. I need to call my grandmothers more often, too. We can be pretty selfish at times."

"Not your fault, son. So, is my Lisa in some kind of trouble?"

"I'd just like to ask her a few questions is all. No trouble yet."

"Like I said, I haven't seen her in many years. Slim chance she'll show up all of a sudden, detective."

"What can you tell me about her uncle's house burning down?"

"Not really much to say. Lisa did it. We all know that much. Can't say that I blame her. Joe messed with both of them little girls. Got what he had coming, if you ask me."

"So if everyone thinks Lisa did it, why isn't she behind bars?"

"You not very sharp for a detective. You do the math on

when that happened? Lisa and her sister were both still minors; plus, they couldn't find one shred of evidence suggesting either of them did it."

"I understand. It's very important that I talk to Lisa. If you hear from her, please call my cell." I rattled off my number.

"All them girls been through, I'm amazed it's taken 'em this long to find some trouble. If she calls or shows up should I tell her to contact you?"

That was a million-dollar question if I'd ever heard one.

"Yes ma'am. Please let her know that I need to ask her a few questions. Thank you."

I hung up. I didn't believe a word she said.

Chapter 20

I went through some files and even spent time looking over the pictures Lafitte and De Luca were uploading from Carl Blake's murder in Houston. Hunger pangs made my stomach growl as my body reminded me that I hadn't eaten anything worthwhile in several days.

I threw on some clothes and headed for the lobby. Maybe I'd find a snack machine or something to hold me over. As I approached the door, I spied the old woman who'd checked me in the night before.

"Still here, huh?" she said as I walked in.

"Only for a little bit longer. I've got a few more leads to follow up on, and I'll be out of your hair."

"Oh you ain't botherin' me none. First time a cop's done any actual police work here in a long time. You really think you gonna catch that ol' girl here in these swamps?"

"I don't know, but I'm going to try. I got a lot riding on it."

I kept moving as I spoke, trying to get to the snack machine and back to my room as quickly as possible. I wasn't really in the mood to discuss the case in the motel lobby.

"You got any coffee?" I said.

"Over there." She jerked her thumb toward and old-school coffeepot on a table in the corner.

"Ya know, captain, I may know something about that ol' girl you lookin' for."

I turned too fast and nearly spilled my coffee. I gazed at the woman, trying to read her. What could she possibly know about Stacy?

"When they showed her picture on the news as a person of interest, I recognized her right off."

"Well . . . yes, ma'am, I appreciate any information you can give me. But if her identity is all you can offer, we already know who she is."

"Well, hell! I know you know who she is! What I'm talking 'bout is something you might not know."

I walked over to the counter to listen. She reminded me of my grandmother. Maybe a few cards lighter upstairs, but all the same . . . She stood about five feet nothing and was skinny as a toothpick. Her gray hair hung in limp pigtails down both sides of her head. Her leathery face was aged way beyond her years, which I guesstimated to be seventy or so.

"You've got my full attention, Mrs. . . . ."

"It's Miss Romero," she said.

I still wasn't sure if she was pulling my leg or if she really had something concrete to share. But I'd come this far, and the coffee wasn't half bad. Might as well hear her out.

"Before I stared workin' here, I used to be a janitor at one of the high schools in New Orleans. Coupla years after her uncle's place burned down, two men turned up dead 'bout the same fashion as these new murders you got now."

"I understand. Why do you believe the cops hadn't thought about that already?"

"They probably don't know they connected, but I do. For one, they wasn't here; they was in Alabama and few months apart. Real sloppy work."

"And what makes you think Lisa was involved with those? If they were in Alabama, how would you even know about them?"

"I've said all I'm gonna say, unless you can do something for me."

I hadn't expected the shift in focus or the what-can-you-do-for-me card, but I was willing to play her game a little bit longer.

"Well, is there anything you had in mind? Anything you need? And I can only give you something if this information pans out."

"Oh, it'll pan out. I got a . . . let's just say, a really good friend doin' a nickel on a drug charge over some li'l ol' Mary Jane. Think you can get him out anytime soon?"

"That's quite the request, Miss Romero. How long has he been in?"

"A few months now. Three-time offender, too. I know that don't help none, either."

"It'll take some time for me to pull it off, and I'll need something really good from you."

"Why does this case mean so much to you anyway? You all the way from Houston chasing this girl don't make a whole lot of sense to me."

One of the things I'd learned growing up was to never judge a book by its cover. Many of my *esteemed* colleagues probably wouldn't have given this woman the time of day. But I was rolling the dice, and maybe, just maybe, she had something I could use. A lot of cops didn't like to admit it but profiling was indeed a problem within our ranks. Sure it had its uses but like everything else in life too much of anything is usually a recipe for disaster.

"I'm not making any promises. Tell me what you know."

"Okay. Well, one day I was cleaning one of the stalls. Another janitor had borrowed my cart, so it wasn't outside the restroom door. In other words, no one suspected I'd be inside. In comes Lisa, her sister Brittany, and another girl. They thought the restroom was empty, I guess, 'cuz they start talkin' 'bout the two murders in Alabama. I mean, why they did it and how after that moment it would never be discussed again. I bet you'll find those cases are still open."

I'll be damned – my heart raced I was in complete shock and disbelief. Sweat started to seep through my skin. What were the chances that some random old woman at a motel in the middle of BFE would help me with a case that I had to solve?

"I must say I am quite taken aback and impressed. How did you manage to go unnoticed? If what you're saying is true, they would have killed you had they found you there."

"I was deathly still. I couldn't believe what I was hearing. I haven't told a soul since that day—not one person on earth. I'm not really even sure why I'm telling you now. But you seem kinda desperate. Trading goods is a way of life here in the swamp, detective. So you gonna help me?"

"Why didn't you go to the authorities?"

"Didn't wanna get involved. It's not really my style. Like I said, looks like you could use some help, though," she said pointing to my inside-out shirt.

"People like you are the reason police officers solve cases. I do have a really important question that you have yet to speak on. Who was the third girl in the restroom that day?"

"You're getting' ahead of yourself, sonny. Don't you even wanna know why they killed them ol' boys in Bama?"

I was happy to be getting this information, but I didn't want to scare her off. I was willing to play her game, at least for the time being.

"Did the girls discuss that? I don't imagine they were there very long."

"Only a few minutes, and one girl did most of the talking."

"Lisa?"

"No, never heard a peep from her or her sister Brittany. Nope, the ringleader was a girl named Marci Wingup. She did all the talkin'. Really smart girl, from what I gathered. She said, 'I guess we taught those monsters a lesson.' She also said they had to learn all they could 'bout killing, 'cuz they couldn't be so careless the next time. About then, someone tugged on the door. Two of 'em hid in stalls, and one of them slowly opened the door and peeked out before disappearing."

"Miss Romero, this is fascinating information. I will work on helping your friend after I do some research on these Alabama murders."

So they had not only killed their uncle but two other rapists in Alabama a decade earlier. If the details matched up with Miss Romero's story, I'd bend over backward to get her friend out of jail. I also started to wonder if they'd pulled off other murders across the country that had never been linked together or solved.

"I'm going back to my room to work on this. Thanks for the info and the coffee. Looks like I'll be around here a bit longer than I'd planned."

"Like I said, you aint botherin' me. Fryin' some gator here in a little while. Come up 'round noon and get you a plate."

"I will, thank you."

Nothing better than a home-cooked meal. Lord knows I could use it. And Cajun food just happened to be one of my favorites.

Chapter 21

I walked back to my room, punching in Captain Wilcrest's number on my way.

"David, glad you called. It's been a few days. Things couldn't be more unsettled here. I met your detective friend Lafitte earlier. I'm actually headed to the crime scene now. I thought you'd call me sooner. I've tried you a few times now."

"Yeah, I needed Lafitte and De Luca there to work the scene. We need to catch up with her before she kills again. And I got your calls. I'm knee-deep in the middle of this thing right now, and I got a lot at stake."

"Her? Her who? And I know what you got riding on this. Chief wants an update. We have a meeting here shortly to discuss it all. He's nervous about having you on this case."

"Brittany Foy. That's her name. Stacy's little sister. I'll fill you in on everything I know for your meeting with the chief. *Wouldn't want him mad at me.*

Right now I didn't give two shits about who may be mad at me. The number one priority was getting Karen back.

"How the hell do you know that she's Stacy's sister?"

"The BF on the wall. I'm one hundred percent certain it's Brittany Foy. What I don't know is why they targeted the Blakes. They usually only go after guys who've committed some crime toward women. Neither of those guys have anything on record. Still doesn't mean they were clean, though. But I'm working on it."

"Anything else you want to tell me about what's going on here in Houston when you're a couple hundred miles away?"

"Hey, it's what you pay me for, right? And I may be onto something big. I mean *really* big—bigger than I ever could've imagined. I have some research to do, but we may have a third murderer running with these two. The three of them may actually be linked to several other murders around the country. I'm starting to think they got some goddamn group of vigilante rape victims."

"I bet you know her name, too."

"Yes, but I don't know if it's accurate. It's all speculation right now. I have a pretty good hunch about where Stacy's headed. I'm still working out the details on intercepting her or making an attempt to. My first priority is getting Karen back in my arms again."

"We'll work the cases in Houston. We can talk later tonight or first thing in the morning and exchange info."

I tossed my phone aside, grabbed my laptop, and dug in. I started with a background check on Marci Wingup. Same high school as the sisters, same age. Then something jumped right out of the laptop at me: valedictorian. I also came across a file containing an image, a picture of Marci. Marci was smart—really smart—and beautiful. Kind of girl who could probably get whatever she wanted by batting her eyelashes. And she had a clean record. Not one single blemish. Not even a goddamn speeding ticket.

I grabbed my cell phone and called Fingers.

"Hey, it's me. Porter."

"Whatcha need, Davie? I'm kind of in the middle of something here."

"The middle of something legal or illegal? Listen, I need you to research something for me. Start from twenty years ago to now, looking for murders of rapists. They would have been nasty, violent crimes—cut up, dismembered. Nothing in connection with drug cases or gang related."

"You want rapists or sex offenders?"

"All of the above. Pull some case info on each of the hits you get. I'll do the rest; I know what I'm looking for. Email me the info when you get it."

I hung up and returned to my search for info on Miss Wingup. If I got lucky, I'd find a current address; that's what I really wanted. But if she was as smart as I thought she was, she'd be using an alias. That would make her a hell of a lot harder to find.

I did an image search. After scrolling through thirty-plus pages, I finally found an old picture. I recognized Stacy—Lisa at that point in time. The other two? Brittany Foy and Marci Wingup. I'd bet my life on it. Only God knew what either of them looked like now.

My phone rang. It was Fingers.

"Give it to me," I said.

"You aren't going to believe this."

"Believe what? Tell me, goddamn it!" I said, raising my voice so high it cracked.

"I said you won't believe it, so I'll just show you. Check your email."

The phone went silent. My laptop beeped—incoming mail. I opened the file and stared at the screen in amazement.

It was starting to look like the old bat wasn't crazy after all. Her lead had checked out, and what Fingers had just emailed me was a game changer.

Chapter 22

As usual, HPD headquarters was a madhouse. The hustle and bustle of the hundreds of officers on the force was ever present. The phones never stopped ringing; it sounded more like a call center than a police station.

Captain Wilcrest strode down the hallway toward the elevators. He had a one thirty meeting with Chief Hill, and he knew promptness was of utmost concern to the chief. He'd sent guys home for being one minute late to a meeting.

As Wilcrest reached the elevator, two other detectives piled in with him.

"Heard you got a date with the chief," one of the men said.

"Yeah, just filling him in on Porter's case is all," Wilcrest said.

The detectives' faces told a different story.

"What's that look for?" Wilcrest said.

"Well, I heard he wants to pull Porter off the case. You

know he shouldn't be on it. Hits too close to home," the detective said.

The elevator stopped, and Wilcrest held the door open as he stepped out. "Yeah, and you know there was no way in hell me, Chief, or anyone else was going to stop him. Badge or no badge, he would have gone after this girl."

He hurried down the hall, dodging one cop after another. He reached the chief's office with two minutes to spare.

"Come on in; it's open."

Chief Hill was a tall, lean, clean-cut man who didn't bullshit around. Ever. He'd been chief for ten years and on the force three times as long. He was fair but short on patience. He seemed to like Wilcrest, and the two had never had a falling out before.

He moved from behind his desk and, with a vice-grip-like handshake, reached out to greet Wilcrest.

"Shut the door and have a seat," Chief Hill said.

Hill's mood was cold and direct. Wilcrest sat down on the other side of the giant mahogany desk and waited for him to start the meeting.

Hill got right to it. "Listen, Wilcrest. I know you have a special place in your heart for Porter, but what he's doing right now doesn't look good for HPD. It's just flat-out wrong and against everything I stand for."

"Chief, hear me out on this one. What you say is right. Not arguing that. I know it's not protocol, what Porter's doing, but you and I both know the best chance he's got of finding his daughter is by doing it himself."

"That may be so, but rules are rules. They aren't up for debate or interpretation."

Wilcrest knew this was an uphill battle. It almost felt like the chief's mind was already one hundred percent made up. Maybe he had someone else in his ear on it. Wilcrest couldn't be sure.

"I did talk to Porter this morning. He's close. Swears he is. For everything he is or isn't, he's never lied to me, you, or any of us. He actually sent De Luca and a detective friend of his from New Orleans back here to solve this Widowmaker case."

"Do we not have capable officers on it already?" the chief grumbled.

"We've got great guys on it, but none of them are Porter. He told me more about the case here during our five-minute call than these guys know times one hundred. And get this: the *BF* painted on the walls? Brittany Foy? She's Stacy's sister. Yes, *that* Stacy. How he figured that out I don't know, but we sure as hell hadn't."

The chief sat there and stared, peering through Wilcrest and into his soul, or so it seemed. He remained silent for a few minutes before starting again.

"That's good intel," Hill said.

"I know. I'm not asking for a super-long leash for Porter, but he's good; you know that. Hell, he might solve this Houston case from flippin' Louisiana."

"Can you control him? Keep up with him? Keep me briefed? I don't want any surprises here, and I sure as hell don't want to see HPD Detective Fill-in-the-blank in the papers. Word gets out we got guys working cases that intimately involve them, and I got questions that I don't want to answer."

"I believe so. Kinda putting my neck on the line here, but I always have and always will for him. We've all seen him grow into a fine detective—one of the best."

"God forbid anything like this happened to one of our loved ones, but would you let another detective work a case so close to home?" Hill asked.

"Honestly, sir, I probably wouldn't. I also don't have another David Porter that I could put on his own case. If I did, I'd consider it."

"What I'm hearing is Porter's got some special privileges."

"I don't see it that way. But with that said, Porter's earned some special privileges that other's haven't."

"I'll allow this to continue for now, but you better keep me up to speed every step of the way. We clear, Wilcrest?"

"Crystal," Wilcrest added.

"For what it's worth, I truly hope Porter finds his little girl. Not trying to be a hard-ass here."

As Wilcrest reached the door, he stopped and turned back to Chief Hill.

"I'll leave you with this to chew on, sir: if your daughter had been kidnapped, who would you put on the case, Porter or one of the other guys? We should afford him no less."

Hill stared at the captain but didn't say another word. Wilcrest left feeling relieved. He'd managed to buy Porter more time to solve the case, at least for the time being. He knew it probably wouldn't be the last time Hill chastised him about Porter, but his parting words to the chief still rang true. No matter how much of a conflict of interest it might be, every cop in this department would want David Porter on the case if their kid's life was at stake.

Wilcrest pulled out his phone to text David.

Chapter 23

Pasadena, California. Jacksonville, Florida. Brooklyn, New York. Denver, Colorado. All across the United States. Every murder had the same MO: rapists brutally dismembered. There was no way Stacy, Brittany, and Marci could have committed every murder. They were too many miles apart and too close in time. I couldn't believe what I was piecing together. They had formed a secret society—a society of scorned, hurt women out for justice. No . . . out for blood. My God! What a mess I had uncovered. How many women? How far back did the murders go? I had so many questions but not near as many answers.

The murders had been spread out over twenty years so as not to raise suspicion, I presumed. It had worked. I would probably be able to rule out one or two, but there were over ninety murders here. And now that I had turned up on their hit list, I had to believe someone would come to finish the job. I knew if I wanted to live without having to look over my shoulder every ten seconds, I'd have to catch every one of these women. One by one. I also knew it would be impossible to do alone.

Even more questions popped into my head. My mind was racing one hundred miles an hour. *Were they recruiting? How did they recruit? Where did they meet? How often?*

The chirping of the desk phone startled me.

"Hello?"

"It's me, Theresa Romero from the front desk."

"Yes, ma'am?"

"The food is ready. You comin' to eat?"

"I thought you'd never ask. Be right there."

When I walked into the motel lobby, the smell of Cajun paradise welcomed me. The spread laid out on the counter looked incredible.

There was a bar stool at the front counter. I sat down and Miss Romero slapped a heavily loaded plate down in front of me.

She put her hands on her hips. "You know, when I open my restaurant I'll be chargin' fourteen bucks for a plate like dis."

I shoveled a forkful into my mouth. "I believe you could easily get that and more, Miss Romero." I dug into a steaming bowl of gumbo, cornbread, jambalaya, and crispy fried shrimp.

She leaned up against the counter. "So, you gettin' my friend out or what?"

"You were right," I said, staring into her worn eyes.

"I know that. So you goin' to hold up your end of the deal?"

"I always keep my word. No promises on how long it will

126

take. I'm a long way from home where things make sense."

"Texas? How many horses you got down there?"

"I don't own a horse," I said with a chuckle.

"C'mon! All Texas boys got a horse."

"That's the common misconception. Listen, the information you gave me led to something big — huge, actually. A vast network of bad, bad news. It'd be enough to get four or five of your friends out if they needed it."

"Now that you mention it . . ."

We shared a laugh. I devoured the food and washed it down with some sweet tea. At least they got that much right. I still couldn't get over being able to buy hard liquor at the convenience store or carrying your drink with you from bar to bar, but who was I to judge?

I exchanged information with Theresa, told her I'd be in touch, and headed back to my room. I spent the next hour digging up everything I could, some of which I still needed to validate.

I took out my phone and dialed Wilcrest.

"David, didn't expect to hear from again you so soon."

I rubbed my head. "We have a huge problem."

"Who is we? We cops? We Houstonians? We Texans?"

"We the United States of America. Go find the chief, Lafitte, and De Luca. Sit them down in a conference room with a projector and call me back."

"You want me to bring anyone else in on this? Maybe the president?"

"No, not right now."

"The chief is a busy man. You sure you want to bring him in on whatever this is right now?"

"I've stumbled onto what might be the biggest case in my entire career. Get the chief, Cap."

Chapter 24

"David, this better be good," the chief said when the group was assembled and they had me back on the line.

"It's more than you can imagine," I said.

I made sure my laptop was positioned so the four of them could see me and began.

"Thank you all for joining me here on such short notice. I apologize, but this couldn't wait. My investigation into Stacy and her sister Brittany has morphed into much, much, more. We are no longer searching for just those two. I believe there is an entire network or team of women just like them who are killing rapists all over the United States. I believe they're working together."

The chief spoke up. "That's quite a claim, detective. Do you have any evidence to support this theory of yours?"

"I have uncovered at least ninety cases that all share the exact same characteristics as Stacy's recent murders and the murders of the Blakes there in Houston. I even have a witness who might have accidentally overheard the genesis of their group. A local woman here in Louisiana described that conversation to me in startling detail."

"My God!" Wilcrest said.

"I don't even know if God can help us now," I said.

"What else do you know, Porter?" De Luca said.

"It gets worse. The mastermind behind all of this is a woman named Marci Wingup. Well, that was her name. God only knows what it is now. She's not some regular girl, from the looks of it; she's a goddamn genius. Graduated valedictorian and a member of every nerd and geek squad you can imagine. President of most. So all in all, their leader is brilliant, which will make tracking her down all the more difficult."

"This sounds like some shit right out of a movie," Lafitte said.

"It's no movie, my friend. They've become emboldened. And I believe taking me on was a challenge for them, a test. I dug deeper into a few of the cases. One vic was Lonnie Jordan: white male; age twenty-nine at the time of his murder; two rape charges to his name; married and a seemingly upstanding member of his community. He was a successful businessman involved in local politics. Seems he had a knack for young interns during his campaigns. They found him cut to pieces in a hotel room off a main highway. Oh, and this was in Pasadena, California, eight years ago. Then there's Dr. Mark Wilson: Las Vegas, Nevada; age thirty-three; found murdered in his home five years ago. Three rape cases on his resume which had, for all intents and purposes, been buried. His wife was out of town on vacation, just like Carl Blake's. He too had a reputation for being a ladies' man."

"I'm not one for handing out compliments, Porter. Everyone knows that," Chief Hill said.

The group was silent. This could go one of two ways, and with this guy, that way was usually south. We all knew that.

"With that said, this is an amazing find. Captain Wilcrest and I had a brief conversation earlier regarding your involvement with this case. No one but the committee I was meeting with knows what I am about to say."

What the hell was he doing? Was I about to be fired and removed from this case? I sat up straight and perked up, making sure I looked as attentive and stern as I could.

"After researching all of your case files and taking into consideration what Captain Wilcrest has said about you, coupled with this find, I know I'm making the right decision. As of now, you are heading up a new division of HPD. We're starting a new task force. We're calling it the MCDH—Major Crimes Division Houston—and you, Porter, will be the lead detective and supervising officer. You will also serve as captain of this team. You will no longer report to Wilcrest but will report directly to me. I am also asking that Captain Wilcrest serve in a mentor capacity. He has fifteen years' experience as a commanding officer and can offer you a multitude of advice and guidance.

As I'm sure you are aware, you will need a team to take these women down. You can't go it alone. After you find your daughter and return to Houston, you'll need to pick four or five officers to work with you as detectives on your team. These can be internal or external candidates, as long as they fit your needs. I'll give you whatever you need to make this team succeed; failure is not an option. This rapist killers club will be your first official assignment. Find this Marci Wingup and arrest as many of these women as you can. You may not catch them all, but if you take down enough of their leadership maybe they'll disband. As time goes on, the Major Crimes Division will develop multiple subgroups, but for now you'll act as one team."

I heard everything Chief was telling me, but none of it really sank in. I sat in silence just trying to make sense of it all. *Captain? Major Crimes Division?*

I threw my hands up. "I don't know what to say," I finally chimed in.

No one in that room was trying to help me out much, either.

"As you have proven again today, David, there's no one on this planet better suited for this honor," Wilcrest said.

"I won't let you down, sir."

"You know anything else about this *RKC* and how they choose their targets?"

RKC. Chief had given them a name.

"I know a lot more about them. It's too early to tell if all these women are targeting men who actually raped them or not. That's what I'm leaning toward, though. If that is the case, it makes our suspect list in the low nineties. Maybe they started out that way, found they actually enjoyed it, and are now targeting any male convicted of a sex crime. These women have become judge, jury, and executioner—literally. Personally, I don't believe cutting off the head is going to kill this monster. And when they find out we're onto them, then what? Do they crank up their killing spree or lay low and go into hiding for some undisclosed amount of time?"

"Houston is one of the largest metropolitan areas in the world. When you add in the suburbs—Pearland, Katy, Alvin, Angleton, Galveston, Sugarland, The Woodlands, Pasadena, all less than an hour away—it may be the biggest. We needed a Major Crimes Division, and after studying everything you've accomplished, you're definitely the right man for the job, Detective Porter. If anyone can wrangle up the brass of this RKC wickedness, you can. And if not, God help us all."

Chapter 25

I shut down my laptop and disconnected from the call. Major Crimes Division. I'll be damned. My parents had always taught me that if I worked my hardest and did everything like my life depended on it, good things would happen for me. And this seemed pretty damn good.

While I had a second, I wanted to call Miranda and fill her in on my bittersweet news.

"Honey?" I said.

"Hey there, handsome," Miranda whispered.

"You sound sleepy. Did I wake you?"

"I was only taking a nap. I'm glad you called. I can't sleep for very long. I just keep thinking about Karen."

"I'm about to leave the motel and head for Stacy's grandmother's. I believe that's where she's taking Karen. I don't think she intends to harm her; in fact, I'm almost certain of it. I discovered Stacy is a member of a group of women who are hunting one target: rapists."

"I hope you're right. But after what she did to me, I believe she's capable of anything."

"I know, honey. I'm sorry. Talked to the chief a bit ago."

"That's odd, isn't it? What did he want?"

"He offered me a promotion."

"A promotion? Did you apply for another position in the department?"

"No. He said Houston needed a Major Crimes Division and promoted me to captain and asked me to lead it."

"Oh my God, David! That's great news! I'm so proud of you. How long before you become chief?"

We shared a laugh, the first in quite a while. I loved my wife. She supported me through thick and thin. She was my right-hand man, so to speak. We talked for a minute longer, and then I let her get back to her nap. But knowing Miranda, I'd probably ruined that for her. Her mind would be racing, filled with thoughts of me and my new position. More than anything, I'm sure she'd be thinking about Karen, becoming more and more nervous about me getting her back home safe and sound.

Chapter 26

Stacy was about twenty minutes from her Grammy's house. So far, everything was going according to plan. She wanted to get this over with and get back to her hunting. Sexual predators were everywhere, and she needed to do her part to get rid of them. Every two seconds a woman in the United States, the freest country in the world, was raped.

"Karen, honey, wake up," Stacy said, shaking Karen's arm.

"We're almost to my Grammy's house. It's going to be so much fun."

Stacy knew it would be anything but that, once her plans for Karen were carried out. It wouldn't be long now.

"Are we going to see my dad at your Grammy's?"

Stacy looked over fake smile and all.

"I believe he's coming tonight," Stacy said, lying with ease, as always. "I need to make a few calls. Can you give me a minute, dear?"

Stacy grabbed her phone and placed a call.

"I'm almost to Grammy's! Why are you calling me?" Brittany hissed. "I thought you said we wouldn't talk again until after we arrived?"

"Hey, friend. Just making sure everything is still on schedule?"

"Yes, it is. See you in ten," Brittany said before hanging up the phone.

The car turned off the main road and Stacy turned onto another dirt road. They could hardly see in front of them as clouds of dust kicked up around them. Swamp surrounded the road as far as the eye could see. About a mile in, the road split into three, and Stacy instinctively went to the far right. After another mile, the road went from shell to dirt.

"Almost there, Karen."

"Where are we?"

"Deep in the swamp, dear. New Orleans, Louisiana. You're going to love it here."

After a series of twists and turns, an old but rather large two-story house appeared in the distance.

"There it is! Can you see it?"

Karen nodded but didn't say a word. The house looked kind of spooky to her.

As she pulled up in front of the house, Stacy noticed Brittany's car parked in the driveway. *Nice ride she'd gotten her hands on*, she thought.

The house was surrounded on three sides by swampy marshland. Huge trees covered the yard, and moss hung from the treetops all the way to the ground. A light fog covered the yard, and the croak of bullfrogs rang out.

As the car door closed, a woman emerged onto the porch.

"Grammy!" Stacy called out and walked over to her for a hug.

The woman didn't respond. She stared at Karen with cold, steel-gray eyes and never seemed to blink. She wore a red flannel shirt and dirty jeans, her weathered hands fisted on her hips.

She walked right past Stacy and snatched Karen by the arm, almost dragging her into the house. Stacy said nothing as she hurried behind.

"Ouch! You're hurting my arm!" Karen squealed in dismay.

The old woman said nothing.

"I'm scared, Stacy," Karen said over her shoulder.

Stacy looked away, still silent.

Before Karen knew it, the woman had taped her hands together behind her back. Next, she wrapped tape around Karen's mouth. Karen squirmed but it was no use. The woman led Karen further into the house. She reached the basement door and kicked it open.

When Karen looked into the room, she could see candles—hundreds of them. A goat walked back and forth in the back corner. The woman pushed Karen onto the damp floor.

Brittany walked over to a radio and hit *Play*. Haitian voodoo chants filled the room. The old woman grabbed a bag of flour propped against the wall and spread it around Karen as she lay on the floor.

"Stacy!" Karen yelled through the tape as tears pour down her face.

Suddenly, the old woman began to chant along with the radio, twirling and bending as she danced her way around Karen.

Brittany beat out the rhythm on a drum.

Soon, Stacy was dancing and chanting, too. She picked up a giant knife laying on the floor and walked over and grabbed the goat with her other hand.

Karen's body trembled.

Stacy dragged the goat over next to Karen.. The old woman put one hand on the goat's back and touched Karen with the other hand. Stacy drew back the butcher knife and, with one swing, cut the goat's head off clean.

Karen screamed, but the other three remained steady, emotionless. The music grew louder and faster as blood spewed everywhere. The old woman rubbed her hands in the warm blood and then smeared it over Karen's body.

Brittany stopped playing the drum and joined in with the chanting and dancing.

Stacy knew it wouldn't be long and Karen would be changed forever.

Chapter 27

I loaded my computer equipment and clothes into my truck as quickly as I could. Stacy had a few hours head start on me, if she was indeed heading toward her grandmother's. Something about the woman's story had seemed a little rehearsed, the more I thought about it. Almost too perfectly imperfect, if that makes any sense. Like she was expecting my call and was doing her best to play along.

As I hurried along the interstate, I looked around my truck for Lafitte's swamp guide. From the maps I'd seen, her grandmother's house looked pretty isolated. As my luck would have it, it wasn't going to be easy to find. The goddamn house was right in the middle of the bayou. Whoever built it sure as hell didn't want to be easily located.

I finally found the number and punched it in.

"Hello? Who the hell is this?"

"Uh . . . this is Detective David Porter HPD and—"

"Yeah okay. What the hell do you want?"

"Hey, bud, did I catch you on the wrong side of today or something? Looking for Randy Landry."

"Listen pal . . ."

"No, *you* listen. I'm on official police business. Paul Lafitte told me you could be of service, but so far all—"

"Whoa, man. Why didn't you say you were Lafitte's friend in the beginning?"

What the hell was wrong with this guy?

"Okay, next time I'll know. So here's what I got. I need to get to an address, but the place is buried in the middle of this godforsaken swamp. It'll take me two days to find it on my own, and I've got less than two hours, I imagine. Can you help me or not?"

"Yup. Sure can. He tell you my fee, buddy?"

Fee? I should have known Paul would conveniently forget to mention that part.

"Name your price."

"Just foolin', friend. No fee."

I told Lafitte's friend I'd meet him right where the map showed the road branched off in three directions. Without a guide from there, I'd be alligator dinner for certain.

I arrived at the meeting spot and looked around. I heard a loud whooshing noise and looked up in search of what I suspected was an incoming helicopter. I saw what appeared to be an airboat off in the distance. And then, just like that, he was there.

"You Porter?" the man said, shutting off the engine.

"Yeah! Randy?"

"Yup that's me. Well, get the hell on! Let's go!"

"What in the bloody hell is this, a goddamn airboat deluxe?"

"Aww shit, this old thing? A Cajun helicopter, my friend. A must-have out here in these swamps."

"Well, I don't want these people to know I'm coming. This contraption is rather loud." *Hell, who am I kidding? It was louder than anything I'd ever heard.*

"Don't worry, we'll go a little ways in this, and then we can take my pirogue the rest of the way."

Great. Go from this oversized airboat to a POS canoe? I just nodded and along we went. Karen and I were both regular watchers of *Swamp People*, but after this I'd have a whole new appreciation. This was some rough going.

We rode for a few minutes, and before long I noticed Randy pointing ahead to a brushy area. He shut the engine off and we drifted until I saw the pirogue come into view on the banks. This idea sounded worse with each passing second.

"Alright, Captain, let's get this pirogue going."

"If you insist."

We tied the airboat off. Randy wrapped a chain around a tree and threw some locks on it.

"This won't keep anyone who really wants it from taking off with her, but this here's the thickest chain you can find. It'd take 'em a while to get through it. Reckon we'll be back before anybody could make off with her."

"Yeah, I don't plan on making myself at home here."

We pushed the tiny, canoe-like boat into the swamp and got in. This definitely was a bad idea. Two big men and a really tiny boat.

"Hey, it's worth mentioning that this thing will flip over on us if we move wrong. You can swim, right?"

"No shit. I've got couches at home that are bigger than this thing. And yes, I can swim, but I don't swim faster that alligators."

"Speaking of gators, I can smell one. A big 'un, too."

"You're kidding, right?"

"Hell no, I ain't kiddin'. And if I see it, we gon' take his ass down."

"Listen here, Troy Landry—"

"Ahhh. You watch *Swamp People*, too? No relation if you're wondering."

"Yes, but right now the only thing I want to catch is Stacy so I can get my daughter back. Can we focus?"

"So this crazy bitch got your daughter? You really gotta work on giving me all the details up front, bud."

We paddled for about ten minutes. My arms were dead; I haven't canoed since the girls and I had did it together.

We paddled for a few minutes longer, and then a house came into view.

It was a large wood cabin-type house with a wraparound porch. Smoke was spewing from the chimney. I was already looking for entries and exits from the house. There appeared to be a cellar door on the side closest to us. I found that strange, as the soil this far south typically wasn't firm enough to support such a structure. And typically the water concentration was too high. Obviously that wasn't an issue here.

"You got some supercop way you wanna do this? I'm ready for a little action."

"Yes, and first thing is, you have to stay here. I can't take a civilian with me. Could be dangerous. If she's here, she won't go down without a fight. You can bet on that."

We made landfall. I took my glock from its holster and headed for the house on foot. I was running as quickly as I could, but I had to be careful. God knows there was a little bit of everything in this place—hogs, snakes, gators—and I didn't have enough rounds to waste any.

When I got within two hundred yards of the house, I noticed three cars in the driveway. *No way the old lady needed three vehicles*. I'd been right all along; Stacy was here. I made my way closer to the house using the trees as cover. My heart was racing. If anything went wrong here, I'd probably never see my daughter alive again.

I finally got close enough to the cars to make out the plates. Two of them were from Texas. Stacy and Brittany?

All I hoped for now was a pet-free home. A barking dog would be a disaster. I did a once around the perimeter, but I didn't see a soul inside or out. They had to be here. I tiptoed onto the porch and turned the doorknob. Locked. I took a lock pick out of my vest and quickly gained access.

I slipped inside, gun in hand. I scanned the room but again saw no one. I cleared the room and made my way through the house.

I heard something, but I wasn't sure what it was or where it was coming from. It sounded like muffled music or some sort of chanting. I cleared two more rooms but still saw no one.

I moved deeper into the house. The sound was coming from below me somehow. A basement? And then it hit me. Oh God! If it was a chant, they had to be performing some godforsaken ritual! What the hell were they doing to Karen?

I kicked the door open and charged down the stairs, my gun leading the way. The room was bathed in candlelight. It took my eyes a second to adjust. And then I saw her. Karen lay motionless in the middle of the room. The floor was covered with white markings. I had no idea what any of them meant but I was certain it was nothing good. My heart dropped to my stomach and rage flooded my body.

Stacy noticed me first and made a beeline for a door in the back of the room. The music and chanting was so loud that none of them had heard me kick my way inside. Stacy's grandmother had her eyes closed and was fully into her sickening voodoo madness. The third woman—Brittany, I presumed—followed Stacy in a full-out sprint. I thought about giving chase, but the only thing on my mind was Karen.

"Freeze!" I shouted, but it was no use.

Stacy's grandmother looked up at me in shock. She turned like she was reaching for something, and I fired a warning shot near her feet.

"Don't make me shoot you, because I will. Lay down face-first, and put your hands behind your back. I'm placing you under arrest."

The old lady complied. I cuffed her and dialed 911 as I ran over to check on Karen. I was angrier than I'd ever been in my life. Karen's eyes fluttered, opened, and then closed again. Her little body was cold and limp. She was soaked in blood. Had she been cut? I searched all over her body but I didn't see any cuts right off. Some sort of tape still covered her mouth. I did my best not to hurt her as I peeled the tape off her mouth.

"My name is Detective David Porter, HPD. I'm at thirty-two fifteen LaCrouix Street. I need an ambulance and police backup immediately. Two murder suspects fled on foot."

I figured either one or both cars would be gone, so I gave the operator both makes and models along with the plate numbers which I'd memorized.

Karen's breathing was shallow, and she was totally unresponsive. It was shallow enough that I felt CPR was needed, so I began compressions.

"It's too late; she gone now. We take her to da other side," Stacy's grandmother said.

"Shut up! You shut up now!"

I couldn't be too late. I just couldn't be. I continued with the compressions, and it seemed like her breathing was slowly improving.

"Karen, it's me, dad," I pleaded with her. "Wake up, Karen! Talk to me."

This couldn't be happening. Not like this.

"I tell you already; she gone. She be free now."

"You evil bitch!" I yelled, shoving my gun in her face. "What did you do to her?"

"No matter now; you's too late," she said.

I turned back to Karen. As I knelt down beside her, she opened her eyes and let out a bloodcurdling scream.

I hugged her tight and tried to calm her. I doubted she could hear my voice over the screaming.

"Police! Freeze!" a cop yelled from the top of the basement staircase.

"I'm HPD. Here's my badge," I said, pointing inside my jacket. "I have the one you want handcuffed over here."

The ambulance arrived, and I ushered the EMTs over to Karen.

"Daddy!" Karen had opened her eyes again and finally saw me—*really* saw me.

"Karen! Hey, baby. Daddy's here."

Karen was still crying. It was a deep, hard cry and I could tell she was still trying to figure it all out. "How did you find me? I thought I'd never see you again."

"Don't worry about that right now, sweetie. Just relax and let these good people take care of you."

Chapter 28

I piled into the ambulance with Karen and held her hand as tight as I could for the duration of the trip to the hospital. I don't think I'll ever let go of her again. Stacy's grandmother was being taken in for booking. For now, the only thing I could pin on her was endangerment of a child. I was hoping to add aiding and abetting to that list, too.

The one thing I needed to do more than anything was to call Miranda. I was eager to tell her and frightened at the same time. I worried that Karen might never be able to get those horrifying images out of her young mind.

I punched in her number. The phone couldn't connect fast enough. Before Miranda could even finish saying hello, I interrupted her. "Miranda, I found her!" I wanted to get the words out before she had a chance to say anything else.

I heard a clatter as Miranda's phone dropped to the floor. Then I listened, helpless, to my wife's anguished wailing. It overwhelmed me, and I found myself crying along with her.

"Don't cry, Daddy. I'm okay now. You saved me!"

"I know, baby. I know. Daddy's just really happy."

I stayed on the line until Miranda returned to the phone.

"Is she okay, David?"

"I think she's going to be fine, yes."

"Put her on the phone. I want to hear her voice."

I hit the speaker button and laid my phone down between us.

"Hi, Mommy!"

"Oh baby!" Miranda said, choking back tears.

"Don't worry about me, Mommy. I'm okay. Daddy found me!"

"Your dad is the best. He loves you so much. We both love you so much, baby."

"I gotta go now, Mommy. I love you, too."

"Okay, sweetie. Mommy will see you real soon."

When Miranda hung up, I called De Luca. I needed their report on the Carl Blake murder. I also wanted to let everyone in Houston know the latest.

"Porter, Lafitte and I were just about to call you. We just finished up the Carl Blake crime scene investigation."

"Good. I want to hear every detail, but it'll have to wait a few hours."

"Why? Is everything okay?"

"Everything is better than okay." I felt the tears well up again as I looked into Karen's eyes.

"Porter?"

"I'm here. I found Karen. She's with me now."

"Wait, what? When?"

"Within the last hour. That's what I was calling to tell you."

"Porter, that's amazing! I guess your hunch was right all along. What about Stacy?"

"I'll do you one better. Both Stacy and Brittany are here in Louisiana. I stormed into the basement and found both of them. They escaped out a back door before I could apprehend them. I was more concerned with tending to Karen."

"You made the right move."

"I did get her grandmother. She's in custody now. I'll call you and Lafitte in a few hours for a debriefing on the Carl Blake crime scene. We're getting Karen a once-over, and then I'll get her on a plane back home."

"Wait. So, you aren't coming back to Houston with her?"

"No. Call you soon."

I could do my job and handle this case, even if it involved my little girl. I'd found her, and after I got her safely back to Houston, I would track down the other two I came for. I'd come too far, and I'd never be able to rest knowing Stacy and Brittany were still out there. They'd surely come for me if I didn't find them first.

Chapter 29

Stacy and Brittany were both traveling east on I-10, moving quickly but not so fast that they would be stopped. They needed to ditch their cars and get new ones in case Porter had given their plate numbers to the cops.

Stacy got in the right lane and exited the freeway. She saw a Walmart up ahead and figured it would be a good place to make a car exchange. Brittany followed a few car lengths behind.

Stacy drove around the parking lot in search of an easy mark. It had to be toward the outer edge of the parking lot. She came to a stop and waived Brittany to pull up beside her.

"There's one security guard making rounds. Go to the other side of the parking lot, get out, and raise your hood. Disconnect your battery. Be sure to park so he'll have his back to this side of the parking lot when he gets under your hood. I'm going to take this white Maxima to my left. Be sure to flag him down when he comes near you. After he reconnects your battery, drive around to the back of the store. That's where we'll leave your car. I'll be waiting for you back there."

"Got it."

"It'll take some time for them to realize we've ditched these cars and hopefully an hour or so before this one is reported stolen. I noticed the stickers on the back window of the Maxima—soccer mom with three kids. She also had a huge grocery list in her hand as she walked into the store, so she'll be awhile."

Brittany did as she'd been instructed, and, just like clockwork, the security guard drove over to help the damsel in distress. *Pathetic*, Stacy thought. *Go time!*

Stacy got out and jimmied the door. Within no time, she had the car hot-wired.

She drove the Maxima to the back of the store, pulled into a parking spot, and waited for Brittany.

"What the hell is she doing? Come on, Brittany, damn it."

One minute. Two minutes. Three minutes. Four. Finally, Stacy could see Brittany's car coming around the corner.

"Get in! Let's go," Stacy yelled as Brittany jumped out of her car.

In less than a minute they were back on the Interstate.

"What was that all about?" Stacy said.

"You mean, what took me so long?"

"Yes, that's exactly what I mean," Stacy said, giving her sister a hard stare.

Brittany grinned. "Well, I didn't want it to seem too obvious that I didn't really need his help. And he was kinda cute."

Stacy rolled her eyes and focused on the road. "Jiminy Cricket."

"So where to?"

"Mississippi and Florida are next. I'm quite certain those incest breeding grounds will have plenty of bad boys to choose from."

Chapter 30

Stacy and Brittany drove straight through Louisiana to Mississippi. Brittany wanted to talk about their grandmother, but she was afraid Stacy would come unglued. They both knew the odds of ever seeing her again were slim to none. And much closer to the none side. But they both knew she wouldn't talk. Not to a cop. Ever. She'd rot in jail for the rest of her life before she'd say a word.

But now that Porter had searched her out, what else would he find back at her house? Would he even go back and look? She was afraid he would.

"Grammy—"

"Don't, Brittany. Grammy knew the risks. She's a brave soldier. Don't even go there."

Brittany wanted to say more but she didn't. And Stacy was right; Grammy knew the risks. After all, this whole rapist killer movement was her idea.

"If Porter goes back to Grammy's house, he could find

everything."

"Brittany, don't you fucking think I know that already? Jesus."

"I was just saying. Don't be such a bitch, Stacy."

"Well, what were we supposed to do, hang around and get everything while he stood and watched?"

Brittany didn't respond. It was no use.

"Listen, kiddo, I'm sorry. Yes, I know if Porter goes back, he could find the vault, and he would have all of our information at his fingertips—from our leadership structure to our members. I been thinking of ways to stop him from doing that."

"How?"

"I'm thinking about having one of the girls go in and torch the place tonight. Probably the best thing we could do."

"I like that idea, Stacy. Right now he's probably at the hospital with his little girl. No way he makes it back by tonight."

"Well, I wouldn't put it past him. Either way, it's going up in flames tonight."

They drove on in silence until they reached Gulfport, Mississippi. Stacy exited the highway and stopped when she reached a wooded area on the outskirts of town.

"So what's the plan, Stacy?"

"Plan is simple. We camp out here till nightfall. Tonight we'll go into town and find some new clothes, doll ourselves up a bit, and see what kind of *fun* we can get into."

"You have someone in mind for the burn job tonight? We could send her in to get the vault and stuff before she burns it."

"Too risky. We have all the information safely stored, so there's no need for the hard copies. And yes, I do have someone in mind. We have plans for everything. I'm going to send her a text code *eight*. She'll know what needs to happen. Not to mention it's an old vault that probably weighs three hundred pounds."

Chapter 31

As I sat in the hospital waiting room, the minutes felt like hours. I was hungry and tired and worried sick that whatever voodoo bullshit Stacy and her sick grandmother had done to Karen would be permanent. *How would she ever get those images out of her head*? I wondered.

Finally, I saw a doctor heading my way.

"Detective Porter?"

I nodded. "Yes. Give me some good news, please. I could use some for a change."

"Good news is my middle name, detective. And I do have some for you. Karen is great; actually, she's better than great. I don't think she's going to have any lasting damage. She just needs to get home and get some rest. A little dehydrated, but other than that I don't see anything wrong. I'm releasing her to you here in a bit. She needs plenty of rest and lots of liquids."

I sat down and called Miranda back to give her the doctor's

report. I also let her know I wouldn't be making the trip back with Karen. I knew she wouldn't be happy about it, but she also knew none of us were safe with Stacy and her goons still out there.

I heard my name being called from a nurse at the desk. Karen's examination was complete and she was being discharged.

I hurried to my truck. I wanted desperately to get back to Stacy's grandmothers to see what I could find. I'd been called twice already by the local PD, anxious to get me to come in and give a statement. I pulled up to the back entrance of the hospital just as the doors opened.

Karen gave me a huge hug. "Daddy!"

I pinched her cheek. "Hey, sugar. You ready to go home?"

"Yes! I'm ready to see Mommy!"

"Let's get you home then."

I got Karen loaded into my truck and headed for the airport. I was told a few detectives had offered to ride back with Karen, which I appreciated.

"Daddy, why did Miss Stacy take me away? She told me you wanted to leave us behind."

"No! Don't talk like that. That couldn't be any further from the truth. Miss Stacy is sick, dear. Daddy is trying to find her so I can get her some help."

A single tear rolled down her cheek. "So you still want to be my daddy?"

I leaned over and kissed her on the forehead. "Of course. I love you, Karen."

As I'd feared, Stacy had filled Karen's head with lies. I was both angry and saddened for Karen in the same breath.

"Listen, I need to tell you something. Mommy will be waiting for you at the airport. I won't be able to go back with you. I have to find Miss Stacy before she hurts someone else or hurts herself. Do you understand?"

Karen sat in silence for a moment, staring out of the window. I hated having to put her on the plane alone, but I couldn't leave now.

Then she turned to me and smiled. "It's okay, Daddy. I understand. But I really wish you could come home instead."

I reached out my hand across the truck and held hers.

When we reached the tiny one strip airport, I parked my truck and helped Karen out. I stood there hugging her for a long time, fighting back tears—tears of joy, pain, anger, pity. I was all over the place.

"You okay, sir?" one of the detectives asked as he walked over to get Karen.

"I'm fine. Take care of my baby girl, or there'll be hell to pay," I said with a smile as I winked at Karen.

"You get some rest and get well. Take care of Mommy, and give her and Hil a kiss for me, okay?"

I bent down to give her a kiss and one last hug before I saw her off. I didn't pray as often as I should, but I said a quick one, asking God to watch over the plane carrying my baby girl.

I stood there until the plane was out of sight. Before I made it back to my truck, my phone rang.

"Porter here."

"David, it's me, Wilcrest. De Luca told me about Karen. I am so happy for you, son. I called as quickly as I could."

"Thanks, Cap. My family needed this. I don't think we would have—"

"I know, son. So you and Karen headed back soon?"

I hesitated. I knew what Wilcrest's response would be when he found out I wasn't coming back, and I really wasn't in the mood.

"I'm not coming back right now, and no, it's not up for debate. I'm going to catch her."

"David, she . . . this case isn't going anywhere. You need to come home, spend a few weeks with your family. You guys need time to heal."

"I know. And I will, just as soon as I bring Stacy and her sister in."

"I know there's no talking you off the ledge on this one, but you should listen to me on this, kid."

"I'm actually headed back to Stacy's grandmother's house now. She was obviously involved on some level. Maybe I can find some good intel there. I'm kinda banking on it, actually. De Luca and Lafitte should be on a flight back to NOLA soon."

"They're headed to the airport now. You be careful out there and get home to your girls soon. You hear me?"

"Aye, aye, Captain."

"One more thing—I'm damn proud of your promotion. It's well deserved. You and your team are going to do a lot of big things. I can feel it. I'll be here to kick your ass if you don't."

After my little chat with the captain, I was kind of second-guessing my decision to stay in Louisiana. Maybe he was right. Maybe I was pushing it too far this time. I couldn't be sure. Before I could give it more thought, my phone rang again. *Who could it possibly be this time?*

"Hello? Hello, this David Porter?"

I hadn't spoken a word and had barely gotten the phone up to my ear.

"Hello!" the voice called again, this time a little louder.

"Porter here. Who the hell is this?"

"Porter, it's Chief Davidson. I thought you were coming in. Where the hell are you?"

Damn it! This guy was persistent. I had planned on going to see him after I went back to Stacy's grandmother's, but it seemed it wasn't going to play out that way.

"I just loaded my daughter on a plane back to Houston. I was actually headed back to the scene to look for clues. My next move was to come in and file my report."

"No. I don't know how you boys do things in Houston, but that's not how it works here. Not on my watch. Come file your report immediately."

I was stomping in their territory, but how about having a little professional courtesy? I wasn't some masked vigilante running around in a bat suit.

I headed toward the NOLA police station to meet with their chief of police and give them a statement regarding what happened. Then I would head back to Stacy's grandmother's house and see what I could find. There'd probably already been a handful of cops in and out of the house. I just hoped they didn't take anything valuable or trample any of the evidence before I arrived.

I pulled into the parking lot and hurried in. I knew this had to be done, but I had more pressing things to attend to. I wasn't happy about being wrangled into doing it now.

"I'm here to see the chief. Detective David Porter HPD," I said, flashing my badge at the officer at the desk."

"Give me a few minutes, detective, and I'll run him down."

I leaned over the desk. "Thank you. I'm kind of in a rush, ma'am, if you don't mind."

"A few minutes? I don't have a few minutes," I said to myself as I took a seat. This department, at least on the surface, was a complete one-eighty from the hustle and bustle of Houston. I thumbed through a few things on my phone and waited. Finally after five and a half minutes the chief showed up.

He was taller than I'd expected probably six one or so and well built. His arms and chest bulged against his shirt. Blonde hair, blue eyes, and way too clean cut to be from here.

He stuck out his hand to greet me. "Detective Porter, the legend."

He had a firm grip. "Chief Davidson, nice to meet you. I'm afraid you've got me confused with someone else. I'm no legend, just a cop trying to do the best he can."

"Humble, too; I like that. Let's cut right to the chase, Porter. You discharged your weapon today. I have a board assembled to hear your side of what happened. And I'll need you to sign a statement, too."

A board? What happened to just writing my statement and getting the hell out of here?

"Okay. I'm here to play along. Hoping to get through this quickly so I can get back to hunting down this maniac and her twisted sister."

"Come with me. They're waiting for you in the conference room. You've traveled quite a ways, detective."

"Yes, I have. And I'm not done yet. I won't stop until I find her."

We made our way down a long hall, passing at least ten offices on our way to the conference room. When we walked in, five ranking officers were seated behind a massive, rectangular table. It almost felt like a goddamn interview or a promotion panel.

"This is Detective Porter," Chief Davidson said. "He is going to provide a statement regarding today's events. I'll turn it over to him."

"I'm not certain where you'd like me to start," I said as I took a seat.

"Why don't you start from the time you entered the house, detective?" Chief Davidson said.

I looked across the table. No friendly faces, to say the least.

"Okay. I can do that. I have a longtime friend on your force that put me in contact with Randy Landry. Randy helped me navigate the swamps. I left him behind after the house came into view. As I approached the house, I deduced from the plate numbers that both Stacy Demornay and Brittany Foy were somewhere in the house. The plates were registered in Texas."

"Is that when you pulled your weapon?" one of the officers asked.

What the hell was this? I thought. I ignored the question and kept going.

"I had spoken to the grandmother a few days earlier regarding the sisters. She told me she hadn't spoken to them in years, but it felt practiced and seemed a little stretched. Rehearsed would be a better word."

"Detective, you didn't answer the question," the officer said.

"Am I on trial here? I thought I was here to give a statement. I'm trying to do that. It'll go a lot faster if I can just tell you what happened. I didn't know this was a Q and A session."

"Detective, my team is just trying to get a feel for the events that led up to your weapon being discharged," the chief said.

"I understand, sir. Allow me to offer your team a little background information that they are clearly unaware of. Stacy Demornay is a bonafide killer. She's the real deal. She killed three children back in Houston just to get my attention. She kidnapped my wife and held her captive for a year. She also kidnapped a detective from my station. She has killed several men over the last few days, and her sister as done the same. I'm not hunting a goddamn soccer mom here. So, yes, as soon as I had reason to believe I'd located the killer I was hunting—who, mind you, also had my daughter—I drew my weapon."

"Listen, Detective Porter. I apologize if my question seemed accusatory or inflammatory. We're all on the same team here," the officer added.

"Apology accepted. Anytime I'm approaching an area where a known killer and fugitive may be hiding, I draw my weapon. That's pretty much Police 101. As I was saying, when I passed the vehicles, I drew my weapon and went around the house to make sure no one was trying to escape on foot. I went onto the porch and tried the door to see if it was unlocked."

"Detective, if you believed multiple perps were in this house, why didn't you call for backup?" another officer said.

"I didn't know how long I'd have to wait for officers to arrive, given the remote location. I also knew a child was potentially in immediate harm's way."

"Your child?"

"Yes, my child. But it wouldn't have mattered who's child it was. I jimmied the door and started clearing rooms to see if I could find anyone."

"So, do you feel you had probable cause to enter the house without a warrant, detective?"

I was about finished playing games with these armchair quarterbacks. I had real work to do out there, and Stacy and her sister were putting miles and miles between us.

"Yes."

"Care to elaborate?"

"No."

The room fell silent and stayed that way for several moments. Finally, the chief cut in.

"Detective Porter, please continue."

"Gladly. As I cleared the house, I heard music coming from one of the rooms. I couldn't pinpoint which room it was at first, but as I got closer, I realized it was coming from the basement. I ran down the hallway and kicked the door opened, but the music was so loud that no one noticed. I started down the stairs, and Stacy noticed me first. She ran for a side exit and Brittany quickly followed. Their grandmother's eyes were closed, so she never saw me. I noticed a child lying on the ground surrounded by candles, and I suspected some sort of voodoo ritual was being performed. The girl on the floor was covered in blood and a mutilated goat lay only a few feet away from her. As I neared, the grandmother spotted me and turned like she was moving for a weapon. I fired a warning shot at the ground near her. I yelled for her to lay on the floor and she complied. We done here?"

"Almost, sir. Why didn't you give chase to the other assailants?"

"Like I said, there was a child involved—a bloody one—and I wanted to attend to her medical needs. I felt like that needed my immediate attention, rather than chasing two killers through unfamiliar swampland on foot. I also had another perp in handcuffs, and I didn't want to leave her behind with the child."

"Detective, this gives me and my team everything we need. Personally, I believe everything you did here today was justified. I probably would have done things the same way. As a husband and father, I am sorry for everything your family has undergone. I can't begin to imagine. I don't believe we have any more questions," Chief Davidson said.

I got up and shook his hand then headed for my truck. By the time I got to the front door, the chief had caught up with me.

"Detective, for what it's worth, I don't believe my officers were trying to corner or entrap you. I've been working with these men and women for nearly a decade. We aren't used to the fast pace you HPD guys move at. If you hadn't noticed, things move a whole lot slower here. We've had our troubles here in NOLA in the past, but the murder rates are way down; so are the aggravated crimes. So the way one of my officers would go into a situation is probably a lot different than what you'd do in Houston."

"Got it," I said.

"Good luck finding her."

"Luck is about right. She's good—really good. I'll take any luck you or anyone else can throw my way."

Chapter 32

As I walked back to my truck, I noticed I didn't have my cell phone. I must have left it back in the conference room. Just as I turned to head back in, the chief came through the door, my cell phone in hand.

"I believe this must be yours. You just missed a call, too."

I checked my phone and returned the call as I climbed back into my truck.

"Sorry I missed your call, De Luca. You here in NOLA?"

"Hey, David. Yes, we just got off the plane. Where are you?"

"Leaving the police station. Had to give my statement. I'm about to go back to Stacy's grandmother's."

"Have they brought her in yet? Why don't you see if she's going to talk before you leave? Paul and I can start poking around at the house."

"That's a good idea. Doubt I'll get anything out of her, but it's worth a shot."

"Call me when you leave," De Luca said.

This was going to be fun. They weren't exactly welcoming me with open arms here. I went back to the officer I had spoken with upon my arrival.

I sensed a bit of an attitude.

"Let me guess; you need to see the chief again."

"If I could, please."

I leaned on the counter, hoping my wait wouldn't be too long. Just then, the chief walked around the corner.

"Detective Porter, is there something else I can do for you?" Chief Davidson said.

"Yes, I hope so. I need to ask—"

"You want to question the grandmother?"

"Yes."

"She's currently in a holding cell. I'll get her to a room for questioning. Come with me."

That went a lot smoother than I thought it would. I was nervous about leading the interrogation, because the case did involve my daughter. I needed to keep my cool here which, given the circumstances, wouldn't be easy.

I got settled in the interrogation room and waited. As I contemplated which approach I was going to use, she walked in.

I gestured toward the seat in front of her. "Have a seat. I'm Detective David Porter. I'm willing to bet you've known who I am for quite some time now. Please state your name for the record."

"You know who I am already, detective."

"Fine. Don't state your name. When I found Karen Porter, you and two other accomplices were performing some sort of ritual on her. What were you attempting to accomplish?"

"We were making her better."

"Better? How?"

"You wouldn't understand, Mr. Porter. To people like you, we are witch doctors. I won't waste your time or mine trying to explain."

"Try me," I said as calmly as I could. She said nothing, but her eyes bored into me. I was growing more impatient by the moment; this wasn't getting me very far.

"Not talking. Okay. Along with kidnapping, endangerment of a child is also on the list of crimes committed by you today," I said.

"I don't care about you or your laws."

I decided to play on her heartstrings, if she had any, to see if I could wrangle any information out of her. I doubted it would work, but what the hell.

"Do you know where your granddaughters are headed? I'm going to catch them. I'd prefer to bring them in alive. I know you care about them, so why don't you help me out here?"

"Do I look stupid to you, cop?"

"No, ma'am, quite the opposite. That's why I'm asking you to help me. We both know I'm going to catch the girls eventually. We also both know they aren't going to go quietly."

"I don't have anything else to say to you, David Porter. You are a monster pretending to be a do-gooder. I know what you did to my Lisa."

"Contrary to what you believe, my only crime was youthful ignorance."

She didn't reply. I knew this conversation was going nowhere—at least nowhere good.

"Thank you for your time," I said.

That went exactly how I'd believed it would. Time to catch up with De Luca and Lafitte to see what they had uncovered.

Chapter 33

I was able to navigate back to the crime scene without the help of my guide. It would be dark soon, and I was glad to arrive before it was a pitch-black abyss out there. It was a good thing Lafitte was there, too. No way I could have made it out of these bayous in one piece after dark.

I parked and headed for the house.

"David! You finally made it," De Luca said as I walked through the front door. "How'd the interrogation go?"

"About as good as you'd expect. Got nothing I can use. She didn't say much, but I really hadn't expected her to. You guys find anything here yet?"

"We have IT going through the computer we found, but so far nothing. Lots of books on voodoo and witchcraft. A couple books on secret societies, too."

I walked over and gave my old friend Paul a hug.

"What was that for?" Paul said.

"I love you, Paul. And I appreciate all of your help on this."

"We're brothers, man—for life."

"I know we are. I want to talk to you about joining my new unit in Houston when this is over. I want somebody I can trust. Gonna be a huge undertaking, brother. Be like old times in a lot of ways."

"I will definitely give it some thought. Honored you'd ask me, old friend. We need to brief you on the Carl Blake crime scene after we leave. Nothing earth-shattering, but we did find a few things that could help us."

"Sounds good. I still want to know why they went after the Blakes. Anyone been down to the basement yet? I'm willing to bet if there's anything noteworthy here that's where it will be."

"No, we haven't been down there," Paul said.

There was only one other NOLA detective on the scene, along with the guy from IT.

"We are going to take a trip down to the basement," I called out to the detective.

"I'm about done here," he called back to me.

"Me too, I can finish checking out this computer from the station," the IT guy said.

"Ok if you guys come up with anything let me know. Thanks for your help on this."

The three of us headed down to the basement, Lafitte and his flashlight in the lead. We reached the basement door, I opened it and pulled the chain switch turning on the lights.

We made it to the bottom of the staircase and started rummaging around. This room was filled with a lot of stuff, crates, papers just crammed full.

"Look at all this shit," De Luca said.

"Classic voodoo. I'd be willing to bet each of your family members has a goddamn doll somewhere in here, David," Lafitte said.

"I wouldn't doubt it. I'm looking for anything we can find on their little group—a list of members, leadership structure, something I can track these girls down with."

There were crates stacked everywhere. Some contained candles, drums, and other musical instruments. Others were full of paper. It'd take us hours to sift through them all, but it had to be done. We were here, and I didn't want to leave any stones unturned.

I sat down on one crate and pulled another in front of me. "Looks like we're going to be here for a while. There's got to be something useful in all of this shit."

"I don't know, David. Would you leave important files here to be found?" De Luca said.

"Good point, but they've been operating here for over a decade, and we just found it. You get complacent. They probably didn't think we'd ever find this place or tie the grandmother to any of it. If we don't find anything, we don't find anything I don't want to leave here wondering, though."

We all dug in our heels for the long haul. An hour in, none of us had come up with anything worth a shit.

"I gotta get up and stretch these old legs of mine," I said.

"Still think we're going to find something here, David?" Lafitte said.

I heard Lafitte talking, but I'd zeroed in on a vault tucked away in a corner.

"Hey, look over there. What do you guys think is in that

thing?" I said.

"Your voodoo dolls?" De Luca said.

"Very funny. Why would you need a vault for voodoo dolls?" I said.

"Guns maybe?" Lafitte said.

Lafitte and I walked over to the vault and tried to lift it. No such luck. Together, we pushed it to the middle of the room.

"Jesus Christ! What the hell is in this thing?" Lafitte said.

"Old vaults were built a lot studier than the new ones. Made out of some heavy-ass metal, that's for sure. One of you want to give me the key for this?" I said.

De Luca pulled her gun, took aim, and fired two rounds. Voilà!

"There you go, boys," she said.

Chapter 34

Stacy and Brittany were headed back into Gulfport. They'd spent the afternoon hiding out in their car in the woods.

"Stacy, let's go there," Brittany said, pointing to a Dillard's outside a mall.

"Sure. I bet they have some sexy clothes in there. Before we go in, I need to find a Starbucks. They have free Wi-Fi. We need to find our dates for tonight before we get ahead of ourselves."

"Good thinking. Did you hear back about torching Grammy's place?"

"Yes, it's being executed as we speak."

Stacy pulled into Starbucks, and the pair went inside. She plugged in her laptop, logged on to her go-to site, and started browsing. She changed her profile to read "Sis and I looking for double-trouble tonight—any takers?"

Within two minutes, Stacy had five hits. She cross-checked each with her sex offender search engines, hoping to find a match. So far, everyone had come up clean.

A few minutes later, she had three more hits.

Hey Missy. Me and my brother Claude would love to wine and dine you two sweeties tonight. . .

"I may have something here," Stacy said.

Stacy read Bubba's message to Brittany and clicked over to the sex offenders list.

Hey Missy you still there?

Hey I'm here, sorry. We got lost in your photos. You boys are handsome. We need some attention tonight if you know what I mean??? You up for it?

Stacy turned the screen so Brittany could see. "Well, look at what we have here," she said.

Both Bubba and Claude had multiple sex offender charges and a slew of DUIs.

"Real class acts, these two guys," she grumbled.

Brittany shook her head. "These guys are pieces of shit, Stacy."

"And probably very, very dangerous. We can't afford to make any mistakes tonight. We've never tried to pull this off before. A lot could go wrong."

Hell yeah we're up for it. We ain't had no sisters before. Gonna show you girls a real good time.

We can't wait. Never been to Gulfport before, you got a spot in mind? We want to do some dancing first. That ok?

Whatever you want yall call the shots. There's a place called Good Times on Graham Street.

We'll find it – ten pm ok?

See you two beauties at ten.

"Now we can go to Dillard's," Stacy said. "We got ourselves

a couple of dates."

Chapter 35

"Well, I got it open. Are you boys going to just stand there and look at it?" De Luca said.

I pointed to the shot-up vault in front of me. "Wasn't exactly what I had in mind, but I guess it'll work."

I yanked the busted lock off the vault door and opened it to find . . . more paper.

"So do we stop looking at the papers in the crates and focus on these?" De Luca asked.

"Well, somebody had these locked up for a reason. Could be a will or other legal documents in here, I guess. Birth certificates and such, good find I'll take this. Paul, why don't you give me a hand? Let's see if we can sort through these real quick."

Paul and I dug through the stack but were coming up empty-handed. My head hurt and my stomach rumbled. This wasn't manual labor, but we'd all been going strong for several days now. We'd been sorting for thirty minutes when our luck changed.

"David, I think you'll want to see this," Lafitte said, handing me a sheet of paper.

The look on his face told me it was going to be good.

I pumped my fist in the air. "Hot damn, Paul! Jackpot!"

"What is it?" De Luca said.

"A list, a roster of members. If this is in here, there's got to be more. This is a great start, but I'm sure none of these ladies are going by these legal names anymore. But at least this will give us a starting point. This is golden," I said.

I took a quick glance over the list. I didn't need to see Lisa Crease's or Brittany Foy's name, but something in me really wanted to see them on paper. As expected, Marci Wingup was listed as the head honcho, with Lisa as second-in-command. Down in the members section I located Brittany's name.

Suddenly, I stopped and looked up. "You guys smell that?" I said, turning my nose up to get another whiff.

"I don't smell anything, but I'm fighting off a cold," De Luca said.

"Smells like something's on fire," I said, concerned but not ready to panic.

"This ain't the city, David. People still burn trash out here," Lafitte said, laughing.

I chuckled. "Joke's on me, I guess. Hadn't thought about that. And you're right; we are a long way from Houston. Let's see what else we can find in this treasure trove and then get the hell outta here."

We continued to sift through more papers.

"Wait! I smell something now, too," De Luca said.

"I'll go tell the neighbors to wait until we leave to burn their trash. Geez" Lafitte laughed. "Calm down, Houstonians."

"Just go check it out, wise guy," De Luca said, enjoying the moment.

I pulled out another stack of papers as Paul headed up the stairs.

A few seconds later, I heard Paul yelling something. I couldn't make out what he was saying, so I got up and walked to the bottom of the staircase.

"Hey, did one of you guys lock this door? It won't open," Lafitte yelled over his shoulder.

"What do you mean? Just push it open," I yelled back. "Put those muscles to use."

"It's freakin' stuck, man. Like it's jammed or something."

I looked up the stairs and noticed smoke seeping in under the door.

"David, this fucking place is on fire!" Lafitte yelled.

Stacy! They were trying to burn us alive!

"David, we've got to get the hell out of here now!" De Luca said.

Lafitte took the stairs two at a time. He grabbed De Luca and started for the back door I'd pointed out to them when we came in.

"David, let's go, man. Leave all that stuff. We're gonna fucking die in here."

I hurried back to the vault and grabbed a handful of papers that I hadn't sorted through yet. Paul and De Luca had just reached the door. The smoke was starting to overtake the room and I was finding it harder and harder to breathe without wheezing.

"For God's sake, David! Come on, man!" Lafitte yelled again. I followed them, carrying an armload of papers. No way I was leaving all this behind.

Lafitte pulled and pushed on the door. "It's stuck, David. It won't fucking open!"

"This is no accident. We've been trapped in here," I said.

Paul dropped to the floor and pulled De Luca down with him, trying to stay below the smoke. I kicked the door as hard as I could but still nothing. My chest ached. The smoke made it impossible to take a full breathe. I wheezed, and inhaled a cloud of smoke that knocked me to my knees.

"We have to find another way out," I said, struggling to get the words out.

"De Luca!" Lafitte screamed.

De Luca had been overtaken by the smoke. She passed out and lay lifeless on the floor. We had to find a way out. Suddenly, the room was shrouded in darkness. I assumed that the fire had knocked out the electricity. By now, the rest of the house had to be ablaze. One of us needed to begin CPR on De Luca, or I knew she wouldn't make it.

"Paul! Paul, listen to me. I'm going to get us out of here. You've been doing CPR for over twenty years. Take care of her."

I took the flashlight and crawled to the nearest wall. I hadn't noticed any windows before, but I had to try to find one. I didn't want to die here—not like this. Paul had started CPR on De Luca; I could hear him counting the compressions. I was running my hands along the wall when I felt a sharp pain. I'd sliced my hand on something. I couldn't see what it was, but I felt blood squirting everywhere. I yelled out in pain.

"David?" Paul called out.

"I'm okay. Keep going! Don't stop!"

The fire had intensified. I could actually hear it raging above us. I was starting to think I might not be able to get us out of this one. Each breathe I took was shorter and more painful. Then I heard a loud noise at the back door. I thought I heard someone yelling, but it was probably just wishful thinking.

"David, did you hear that?"

"New Orleans Fire Department! Anyone in there?"

"Yes!" I yelled at the top of my smoke-clogged lungs. "We're trapped in here!"

"Back away from door! We're coming in," a voice yelled.

I pulled De Luca and Paul away from the door and listened as the firemen pounded their way inside. The door was solid—some sort of wood—and it was taking a tremendous amount of effort for them to get in. Finally I heard it break through. The banging stopped a gust of cold air flooded the room. I felt hands grab my shoulders and drag me out. I was still clinging to a handful of papers.

"You're okay, sir. I'm a firefighter. I'm here to help."

"What about the others?" I said.

"We already got the other two out. They're both going to be okay; all of you are. Let's get you out of here."

"Thanks. I'm sure as hell ready."

The first responders put me on a stretcher, but I was in no mood to stay there.

"Sir, we need to look you over. Please lie down and relax."

I did as instructed, but I was madder than I'd ever been. They had almost burned us alive! I was tired of being the mouse in this little game of cat and mouse Stacy and I were playing.

As I struggled to sit up again, I saw someone approaching me.

"Porter, relax. It's me. Chief Davidson. I sent a couple units over to assist you after you left. Good thing I did or you'd be toast right now—literally."

Considering the circumstances, I didn't find his pun all that funny. But he was right.

"Thanks," I said.

"This wasn't an accident. Looks like someone tried to burn the place down. They were obviously trying to get rid of something and got lucky when they found you here. There's definitely someone out there who doesn't like you, detective."

"That's an understatement."

"This have anything to do with what grandma was saying to you during the interrogation?"

"It doesn't have *anything* to do with it, chief; it has *everything* to do with it."

"You want to tell me what you could have done to her to piss her off so badly?"

"Long story."

"*CliffsNotes* version?"

"Eighteen years old, alcohol, college, hazing, football team, sex—all of that. A really bad combination."

"Sounds like it."

"De Luca and Lafitte okay?"

"Yeah, they're both fine. I'm sure you'll all be shaken up a bit. You guys take two or three days off, and you'll be recharged and ready to go."

Days off? This guy obviously didn't know me that well.

Chapter 36

Stacy and Brittany put the finishing touches on their makeup. Both of them had purchased skintight, low-cut tops, miniskirts, and six-inch heels. Stacy made sure to let everything she had hang out—and hang out a lot.

"Are you sure you know how to walk in those things, Brittany?"

Brittany laughed. "I'm sure I'll figure it out."

"Why are you frowning?" Brittany said.

"Why do you have those things wrapped up so tight? Let those girls out, sister!"

"Well, I don't want to seem too over-the-top."

"But we are, remember? We're two sex-crazed sisters in need of an intervention. We don't just want it; we *need* it. We have work to do tonight, two bad guys to rid this world of."

The pair made a few more last-minute adjustments, and then they were off. They didn't realize Gulfport would have so much going on. Every street corner had a hole-in-the-wall bar that was lit up and packed.

"There she goes," Stacy said, finally spotting their rendezvous spot.

"I'm nervous, Stacy. I mean, what if something goes wrong?"

"Nothing's going to go wrong. I know this is different and unscripted, but the only real difference is we'll get two tonight instead of one."

They found a parking spot and both took one last look in the mirror before Stacy led the way inside. They were shocked at how nice the place was—almost too nice. There had to be security cameras, probably several of them. It was a much larger audience than they'd hoped for. No turning back now.

"This isn't the shit hole I expected. Let's get these boys liquored up and out of here as fast as possible, okay?" Stacy said.

"Got it."

They sat down at the bar and scanned the joint, looking for the brothers.

"What'll it be tonight, ladies?" the bartender asked.

"Two Coronas with lime. No salt," Stacy said.

Kenny Chesney's "She Thinks my Tractor's Sexy" was playing on the jukebox, and the huge dance floor in the center of the room was packed with twirling couples. Still no sign of their dates.

"That'll be six dollars, ma'am."

Stacy handed the bartender a ten and told him to keep the change.

"Do I know you?" the bartender asked.

"No, I don't believe so. You wouldn't forget me if you did," Stacy said with a wink.

"I believe you're right about that, ma'am. You ladies have yourselves a good night."

Brittany noticed the pair first and tugged on Stacy's arm. Both had cleaned up pretty well, from what they'd seen online earlier.

"Should we walk over?" Brittany said.

"Absolutely not. Let them come to us. They're hunting right now."

It didn't take them long. "Stacy, right? Even prettier in person. I'm Bubba. Bubba West," he said reaching for Stacy's hand and laying a quick kiss on it.

"Wasting no time, I see, Mr. Bubba?" Stacy giggled.

"When a man knows what he wants, why does he need to waste time?"

"You must be Brittany. Hi. I'm Claude."

He's actually kind of handsome, Brittany thought. *Shame he'll be dead in a few hours. Might as well enjoy him now.* She introduced herself with a sexy smile.

"Quite the pair, you two. What brings you to Gulfport?" Claude said.

"Just passing through. We've got some family in Florida," Stacy said.

"Oh? What part?" Bubba asked.

Stacy hesitated for a second and Brittany stepped in.

"Jacksonville. Aunt and uncle."

"You boys are behind. This is our third drink. Have you boys even started yet?" Stacy asked.

"No, ma'am, but it won't take us long to catch up!" Bubba fired back.

"I hope not. We've been waiting all day for this," Stacy said.

Bubba ordered two shots each for himself and Claude and one round for the girls.

"Here's to a kick-ass night!" Bubba said, raising a toast.

Chapter 37

They danced to every song that was played. They even requested a few tunes of their own. The chemistry was great, and the girls knew they'd hit the jackpot with Bubba and Claude. The bar was packed now; it'd probably take a good five minutes to even get to the front door.

Stacy placed a kiss on Bubba's cheek. "Hey, baby, we're gonna go freshen up. Don't leave us."

"Leave? Hell, we ain't goin nowhere without you!" Bubba said.

Stacy grabbed Brittany by the arm, and they weaved their way in and out of the crowd as they headed for the bathroom.

They both went into a stall and locked the door.

"We've had enough fun. It's time to get the hell out of here," Stacy said.

"Why? I mean . . . I kinda like this one."

"What the hell is wrong with you? He's a rapist! Or did you

forget that?"

"Yeah, I guess you're right. He just seems different."

"Okay, so he's a charming, handsome rapist. That better?"

"I get it, Stacy."

"Good. Stay focused. Let's grab them and head back to their place."

They headed back and found Bubba and Claude right where they'd left them.

Stacy leaned in close to Bubba and nuzzled his neck. "We're ready to go. Let's go back to your place and, you know, get to know each other a little better."

Bubba perked up. "Well now, I'm sure Claude and I can make this night memorable for you."

"Oh, it will be memorable. You can take that to the bank," Stacy said.

The two couples ducked through the crowd and finally made it to the front door.

Stacy kissed Bubba lightly. "Brittany and I will follow you. How far away do you live? I kinda want to hurry, if that's okay with you."

"You don't waste any time, do you? I live about ten minutes from here. Cozy little place out in the woods. It ain't much but it's mine. Hope that's okay."

"You have neighbors that live close? If not, maybe we can play outside some. I mean, if you're up for it."

A grin crept across Bubba's face. "I'm up for whatever you throw my way, sweetheart. Claude, head for the truck. Let's get the hell outta here now!"

Stacy and Brittany headed for their car. They heard a few catcalls as they walked through the parking lot but chose to ignore them. Stacy pulled out behind Bubba's oversized, jacked-up truck, and they were on their way.

"Look, when we get to Bubba's place, you just follow my lead. No more drinking. We use our special cups from here on out. We need to have our heads in the game. You with me? I need you focused until we get these country-ass hillbillies cuffed. If they decide to get violent, we end it with this," Stacy said, pointing to her gun.

Brittany nodded. She knew Stacy was right about them being rapists, but she really liked Claude. She was conflicted about what she was about to do to him and his brother.

Ten minutes later, they turned down a dirt road and pulled to a stop in front of Bubba's house. He was right; it wasn't much to look at, but it would do.

"I like being out here alone. No neighbors to hear you scream tonight," Bubba said to Stacy as he walked her to the door.

"Maybe it's you they won't hear screaming. Ever thought about that?" Stacy said, a cunning grin on her face.

"I'd love for you to make me scream, sexy."

"Remember you said that."

Bubba unlocked the front door, and everyone piled inside.

There wasn't much to see: a tiny living room connected to an even tinier kitchen, a couch, and a table with an old-school TV.

"First round's on me," Stacy said before the door could even close. "Have a seat on the couch, boys. Mama's gonna take real good care of y'all."

The boys did as they were told and grinned at one another.

Stacy turned on some music from her iPhone.

"You think you can dance to this, Brittany?"

"Just watch," Brittany said.

Brittany had spent several months working at Heartbreakers in order to get close to John Blake before murdering him. She'd learned a thing or two and was anxious to show Claude.

Brittany moved right in front of Claude and dropped to the floor seductively. She toyed with her finger in her mouth as she rubbed Claude's leg. Claude's eyes bulged.

Stacy chuckled. It was funny to watch her baby sister being seductive. She had to admit she was doing an amazing job. Stacy sauntered over and sat on Bubba's lap to watch.

"You like what you see?" Stacy whispered in his ear.

Bubba looked like a kid in a candy store.

"Hell, yeah! You and your sister are goddesses, I swear! Where the hell'd you come from?"

"Well, if you play your cards right, maybe you can have her, too."

Chapter 38

Paul and I were sharing a motel room, and De Luca's room was next to ours. We decided to crash after we'd been released from the medical team's care. We still needed to go through the stack of papers I'd retrieved from the vault and discuss the findings from the Carl Blake murder.

I texted Miranda to tell her I was okay and that I loved her. I also wanted to see how she and Karen were doing.

"It's too early to be stirring around over there," Lafitte said.

"What do you mean? It's six a.m."

"Why don't you be a dear and go get us some breakfast from the lobby?"

What were we, an old married couple now? Lafitte rolled over and hid under his pillow. I got up, put on some clothes, and did as I'd been told. When I got back to the room, De Luca was sitting on my bed.

"I tried to wake Sleeping Beauty over there, but no luck," De Luca said.

"He's never been an early riser."

"Hey, I can hear you two," Lafitte said.

"That was kind of the point," De Luca said with a smile on her face.

"Let's see . . . I got eggs here, sausage, some bacon, and coffee," David said.

Paul rolled out of bed and rubbed the sleep from his eyes.

"So, food can get you up but not a woman?" De Luca said.

Paul stared at De Luca and smiled but said nothing.

"Wow! I've know this man for over two decades, and I've never seen him at a loss for words."

"I told you the first time I met you, Porter; you've never seen anyone like me," De Luca said.

We scarfed down our food so we could dig into the day's work and then hit the road. I wasn't sure exactly where we'd be driving to, but if my hunch was correct, it'd be somewhere east on I-10.

Chapter 39

Lafitte and De Luca debriefed me on the Carl Blake murder. The details were gruesome. What had these men done to deserve dying this way? And at the hands of Brittany Foy? I'd asked Lafitte and De Luca that very question, but they had no answers. We decided to give Rodney Clemens a call. He was the personal assistant for both of the Blakes. I had only seen him in passing, but he seemed like the type who would know every move his clients made.

I got Fingers to find a cell phone number for the man and punched it in. I put the phone on speaker so Lafitte and De Luca could listen in on the call.

"Mr. Clemens? Hello. My name is Detective David Porter HPD."

"I know why you're calling, but there's nothing I can tell you about what happened to them."

"Slow down, Mr. Clemens. You aren't in any trouble here. I believe the person who killed your former bosses is also the person responsible for a string of murders I'm trying to solve. I need to catch her, and if I can find out why she killed the Blakes, it will help me complete her profile."

"Neither of the Blakes had any enemies. I mean, no one who would want to kill them, anyway. No more than your typical politician."

"Well, considering they're both dead, Mr. Clemens, I'm going to have to disagree with you on that. How long have you been working for them?"

"Over ten years, sir. John had only one assistant prior to me, and he only lasted a few months. I'm the only assistant Carl ever had."

"Which tells me you know everything there is to know about these two, both good and bad. Correct?"

"I'm not sure what bad you're alluding to, but I knew every move they made every day I worked for them, yes."

"Either of them having an affair?"

There was a long silence.

"Carl Blake may have been. I can't be certain."

I didn't prod any further. I really wanted to know about their character, what these men were like behind closed doors. There was my answer. I already knew big brother was a strip club fiend.

"Listen, Mr. Clemens. I have reason to believe a woman— the same woman—killed the Blake brothers. I also have reason to believe she might have been a dancer at Heartbreakers, which was also the last place anyone saw him alive."

"What would make you think either of the Blakes was there?"

"Don't you want me to find this girl and bring her to justice? Don't play games with me here. I've already confirmed that John Blake was at the club that night, which I'm sure you knew. If I had to guess, you dropped him off. Don't see a guy like that driving or using Uber."

"Okay, he was there. He had a regular. I've been back a few times looking for her to ask her a few questions myself, but she hasn't been back since that night."

"Don't you find that rather strange? Have you gone to the authorities with that?"

"No. And this is off the record or I quit talking."

"Fine. I'm just trying to catch this girl. It feels like I'm working by myself here."

"You swear this is off the record?"

"Scout's honor."

He had my attention. What in the hell was he about to tell me?

"Carl had a bachelor party, a pretty wild one, before he got married. John was drunk; hell, all of them were drunk. My job is to control everything, and I failed miserably that night. They'd hired a few strippers and . . ."

"And what, goddamn it?"

"And John took a girl up to a room. About twenty minutes later, he came and got Carl. I saw the girl about an hour later when she came downstairs. I could tell she'd been yanked around pretty badly. All the guys, including Carl and John, were passed out, of course. I tried to help her out and asked if she was okay, but she was so frightened that she wouldn't let me get close to her. I offered her some money, but she wouldn't take it. Her clothes were a mess. I could tell she was pretty shaken up. I just couldn't let myself believe that they'd done that to her. Neither of them ever talked about it again, and I sure as hell didn't bring it up."

"After hearing this, I'm almost one hundred percent sure the girl I'm hunting is the same girl that killed your bosses. She kills rapists, Mr. Clemens. Only rapists. I might not have figured it out without your help, so thank you. And like I promised, this remains confidential. There anything else you might've left out?"

"Well, yeah, come to think of it. About six months after that night, John and Carl both started getting death threats in the mail."

"What did the police do about it? Did they do an investigation?"

"I didn't go to the police. In fact, neither of the Blakes ever knew; I never told them. I sorted through their mail every day. It was part of my job."

"Did you not think it was worth sharing with them that someone was threatening their lives?"

"I just figured it was the girl making idle threats. I mean, she was only a tiny thing. I didn't really believe she'd go through with it. People get mad and say they're gonna do shit all the time, and it's nothing more than lip service. And when the letters stopped, it only made me believe that even more."

"Can you tell me what the letters said?"

"They weren't long letters, just one- or two-liners. Threats like 'you fucked me so I'll fuck you,' or 'you're going to die soon, rapist scum.'"

"Sounds like my girl. You've done a great thing here. I'll call you if I think of any more questions."

I had everything I needed, and De Luca was right—both of the Blake brothers had raped Brittany Foy; their murders weren't some random crime.

Chapter 40

"We need to get ahead of them and set a trap," I said.

"What do we know about the cities they're killing in?" De Luca said.

"They travel all day and kill at night. So far, the crime scenes are about a day's drive apart," Lafitte said.

"That's good. Let's pull out a map and see where that'd put them tonight if they keep up the same schedule," I said.

According to our calculations, their travel would put them somewhere near Gulfport, Mississippi.

"Let's go through the remainder of the files I was able to get from that vault. We need to see if there's more info that might be helpful to us."

De Luca and Lafitte each took a handful of papers and started reading. Just as I had suspected, many of them were medical records, appliance manuals, and the like. And then I found a gem.

"Guys, you aren't going to believe what I have in my hands,"

I said.

"What now? Another sister?" De Luca asked.

"No," I said. "Maybe worse."

Somehow, they'd wiped this from any initial searches we'd made on the family. Even Fingers hadn't found it. The girls had a brother—Michael Crease. He was two years older than Stacy. The way things had been going, I had to assume Michael was just as sinister as the rest of the family. Hell, even their grandmother was a part of the madness. Reminded me of Jax Teller and his parents from *Sons of Anarchy*, one of the few television shows that actually peaked my interest.

"Could this guy be watching us, too?" Lafitte said.

"Maybe. Or maybe he's dead. Says here he's a diabetic. Where or what he is only God knows at this point. Hell, maybe he's a Sunday school teacher and youth pastor at a church somewhere."

"Wouldn't that be something? Hell, that family needs some church," Lafitte said.

"We all need some church," I said.

The honest truth was, if Michael Crease was a bad guy, his opinion of me wasn't too good. If he was watching, I'd need more than church. More like divine intervention. The last thing any of us needed was another goddamn enemy, but it appeared we could have one nonetheless.

"One last thing I found here. Looks like Stacy was pregnant once before. If my math is correct, it was after the incident, around the same time she left Tech. Some records here from Planned Parenthood. Looks like she had an abortion."

"God! With half the damn football team joining in, there's

no telling who fathered that kid," De Luca said.

"Yeah, if she hadn't had an abortion, the kid would be about eighteen or nineteen. I'm not pro-abortion, but if a woman is raped, she should have the right to do what Stacy did," I said.

"Don't get me started," De Luca said.

"No, let's not. David, have we made it through everything?" Lafitte said.

I stood up and stretched my legs. "I believe so. Let's get out of here."

We packed up, loaded the truck, and headed out on I-10 east, destination Gulfport, Mississippi.

Chapter 41

Brittany's dance ended, she stopped and stared at the brothers. Both men lay sprawled on the couch, covered in lust and saturated with Stacy's drug concoction. Both were fading further and further away.

"I didn't drink any more tonight than I usually do," Bubba said, struggling to keep his eyes open. "I don't know what's come over me. I feel so weak."

"Aww, honey. You weak in the knees over me?" Stacy said.

"Yeah, yeah, that's it exactly." Bubba grinned, barely getting the words out.

Claude was in even worse condition. He was lying there, speechless, with a stupid grin on his face and his limp penis in his hand.

"So, what now?" Brittany whispered to Stacy.

"Now we have some fun. Put your clothes back on. You didn't actually need to have sex with him, ya know."

Brittany knew, but she'd wanted to . . . so she did.

"You'd better hope the piece of shit doesn't have AIDS or something."

Brittany rolled her eyes. "He doesn't have AIDS, Stacy."

Stacy decided their routine had become too predictable; time to mix it up a bit. First, they'd remove all of the guys' teeth. Neither of them had tattoos or any other distinguishing marks they had to worry about, so they'd only need to burn off their fingertips. "Are you sure they can't feel any of this?" Brittany asked.

"I'm sure. And fuck them if they can."

"We didn't even tell them what we were going to do to them."

"You think they bothered telling the girls they raped what they were going to do to them? Just hurry up and keep working. We still have to load up both of the bodies and dump them."

Brittany didn't understand how this was supposed to buy them some time.

"Why are we doing this again?"

"Well, there are several things about this scene that will be different than our other work: two guys at the same time; bodies not found at home. Add to it all this extra work we're doing. Hell, it'll take 'em a day or two just to identify them when they're finally found. It means more travel time for us."

"You are so smart, Stacy."

The drug mix Stacy had made this time was much stronger. She needed to make certain they'd both be knocked out cold for a long time.

"We still have to kill them, don't we?" Brittany said.

"The drugs I gave them will take care of that. These boys won't see another sunrise."

"Wait, you put it in their drinks?"

"Yes, why?"

"I finished off Claude's drink! Am I going to die?" Brittany said in a panic.

"Why the fuck would you do that?"

"Gotcha!"

"You bitch," Stacy said, smiling.

After they'd finished, Stacy turned off all the lights and went outside to make sure no one was out and about. The coast was clear. Stacy knew this would be the hard part. Neither of these guys was small; and together the girls probably weighed a little over two hundred pounds. They started with Bubba. It took nearly ten minutes to drag his body from the house and get it loaded in the trunk.

"That was hard," Brittany said.

"Yeah, moving dead weight isn't easy. I'm kind of used to it from hauling your ass around!"

"Ha! I pull my own weight around here," Brittany said.

"I was just joking. I owed you that one."

They went back to get Claude's body. Bubba was the larger of the two, and moving him had already worn them both out. It made dragging Claude to the car even more difficult.

After they finished loading the bodies, they put the bloody teeth in a Ziploc bag to take with them. Now they needed a good place to dump the bodies. Stacy wanted to find someplace remote but public enough that they'd be found in a day or so. She just wanted to space the bread crumbs out a little farther this time.

They drove around for thirty minutes and finally agreed on a location. They pulled off the road and dumped the bodies out.

Stacy took out her pistol, screwed on the silencer, and fired four rounds. Cause of death? Apparent gunshot wound to the head. It would definitely buy them more time to move across the country.

Chapter 42

We traveled down I-10 toward Gulfport. I wanted to brainstorm ideas for setting up and catching these two maniacs. I was tired of just heading to the next murder scene and following Thelma and Louise down the highway.

We'd been driving an hour or so when my cell phone rang.

"Hi, Dad, it's me!"

"Hey there! It's good to hear your voice. Everything okay?"

"Yes, everything's okay. Can't a girl just call her dad to say hello?"

"Yes, I suppose a girl can. You happy to have your sister back home, or is she driving you crazy already?"

"She's okay for now. I'm sure she'll be back to her old annoying self soon. I'm sorry about all the mean things I said to you before about Stacy and what happened back in college. I'm just sad and I really miss Rodney."

"It's okay, Hil. We all say things that are out of line from time to time. We just have to learn, try to grow from our mistakes. Getting over Rodney is going to take some time."

"Yes, Father I know. Don't get all soft and make me regret calling you."

We shared a laugh. We needed to do more of that. I knew it wouldn't be long before she'd be on to the next phase of her life. She'd hinted about joining the ranks of law enforcement, which scared the hell out of me. Actually it terrified me. Hilary was bright and intelligent when she applied herself, but it wasn't her that made me nervous. It was the psychopaths that doing this job required you to deal with day in and day out.

"I'll give you a call in a few days. We need to do a lunch date when I return. I'm going to catch this girl, Hilary. Stop worrying. I can hear it in your voice."

"I know you will, Dad. That's the scary part. What happens when you do? I love you. I just don't want anything to happen to you."

"Nothing's going to happen to me. I love you, Hilary."

Hilary was right to be worried. Wounded and cornered animals always posed a much greater threat. Chickens aren't that big, but trap one in a corner, and you'll find out exactly what I mean. And sooner or later, I'd have Stacy and her sister trapped in a corner, too.

"You guys want to stop and get something to eat? I really could use a big juicy ribeye right about now. We could also use the time to hatch a plan for wrangling up Stacy and Brittany. What do you say?"

I knew Paul's answer already. That man had never turned down a meal in his life. De Luca nodded. We'd covered as much ground as we needed to.

"One of you find us the nearest steakhouse."

Lafitte pulled out his phone. "Longhorn Steakhouse, 15270 Crossroads Parkway, 39503. We're about twenty five minutes away, David."

"Longhorn it is."

Chapter 43

We pulled into Longhorn Steakhouse, and the parking lot was jam-packed. This restaurant had some of the highest ratings in the entire state, and from the size of the crowd, I believed it. We headed inside, trying our best not to look like out-of-towners.

We were told the wait would be about fifteen minutes and I was handed a buzzer. We stood outside and recapped everything we knew this far. Right at about fifteen minutes the buzzer went off.

We went inside and a waitress took us to a table. We'd asked to be as secluded as possible so we could at least hear ourselves talk. We were seated at a table in the back of the restaurant.

"What'll you have, sugar?" the waitress asked me.

"Water for me," I said.

"We'll both take water as well," De Luca said.

I looked away, trying to hide my amusement.

"Something funny over there, David?" Lafitte said.

"Nope. Nothing at all."

"I'm not ordering for him, David. We'd already discussed our drink preferences in the truck, wiseguy," De Luca said.

"Hey, you don't have to explain yourself to me," I said, smiling.

The waitress came back with our waters, and we all ordered monster twenty-ounce steaks that none of us would finish.

"So here's what I'm thinking. We get an undercover from back home and create a fake profile in or around where we think she'll be next, based on travel time."

"So you're talking about flying this guy out here and letting him hit the road with us?" Lafitte said.

"Yes, that's exactly what I mean. If we get cooperation from the local PD, we can use a rent house. Hell, that's the easy part. Getting her to bite on our guy with so many options is going to be the tough part," I said.

"Doesn't have to be. We know which sites she's been using. We have Fingers get rid of a few dozen accounts. Then we have him create our fake account and load it up with rape charges," De Luca said.

"Should we have Fingers remove all of the other profiles with rape charges except our fake one?" Lafitte said.

"Don't you think that would be a bit obvious??" De Luca said.

"Maybe. Check that. Probably. You can throw a dart in this room and hit a sex offender," I said.

I called Wilcrest and told him about our plan. I asked him to send us the profile pics of some Houston undercovers so the team and I could decide on who we wanted. De Luca called Fingers and filled him in as well.

"Wilcrest said we only have about ten undercovers whose looks could fool Stacy. Needed to be a little rough around the edges, but not too bad," I said.

The waitress brought out our steaks, and man did they look amazing! The grill marks were perfect, and the aroma was to die for. We dug in, and the conversation lagged as we savored every bite.

We washed it all down with a beer. Not exactly a bodybuilder's diet, but sometimes you just gotta live a little, I told myself.

My phone's email notification went off, and I looked down to check it. Captain Wilcrest had put together the profile pictures of the undercover officers we had available for our trap. De Luca and Lafitte glanced through them first, and both seemed to agree on an officer. I looked through them as well but didn't offer my opinion. I had a way of taking over investigations sometimes; I knew that. This time, though, I just nodded and agreed with their choice.

"How quickly can he be here in Gulfport?" De Luca asked.

"Captain said tonight. Flight isn't all that long. I'll call him now and get it arranged. I'll send the picture to Fingers, too, so he can get started," I said.

Chapter 44

We checked into our rooms in Gulfport, same setup as before. We unloaded our gear and got settled in. I unlocked the door between our room and De Luca's and waited for her to do the same. When the door finally opened, De Luca stood in front of me in a pair of tiny sports shorts and a bra-like thing.

"It's called a sports bra, David," De Luca said, shaking her head.

"I didn't say anything," I laughed.

I counted down from five in my head, and Lafitte joined us right on schedule.

"Can I help you, sir?" De Luca said over her shoulder as Lafitte followed me into her room.

"Just joining the team is all," Lafitte said, his grin so wide you could almost count every tooth in his mouth.

I set my laptop on the desk, logged in, and pulled up our fake profile.

"Should we activate it now?" De Luca said.

"I think we should wait. I mean, what if she wants to meet at a bar this time instead of this cat's house? He'll be here in a few hours, right?" Lafitte said.

We decided to wait. I told them both to get some rest, and I waited up to head out to the airport to pick up our undercover guy, Franklin Shuppe.

I spent the time rereading the case files. I did that often to make sure I hadn't overlooked anything. There was almost always at least one little thing that got overlooked or didn't make sense the first go-round. This time, however, I found nothing new.

I pulled into the short-term parking lot at Gulfport-Biloxi International Airport and turned off my truck. I woke up twenty minutes later to find five text messages from Shuppe.

I gave him a call.

"Franklin, it's Porter. Sorry I dozed off on you. Been a little sleep deprived the last few days."

"It's okay, detective. I've only been waiting ten minutes. My bags took longer than I expected, hoss."

Hoss?

"I'm parked in T3. You anywhere close to that?"

"Actually, I am. Be there in two shakes, partner."

This guy was as country as they come. Hoss? Partner? Did Wilcrest get this guy from the undercover program or an FFA group? As he strode toward me, I gave him the once-over. He was unshaven and stood about six five if I was guessing. His jeans and plaid shirt made me feel like I was watching an old rerun of *Dukes of Hazzard*. He wore a baseball cap turned backward with a fishhook on the bill. I could also tell he was a gym rat, which made me like him even more.

"How long you been on the force?" I asked as we pulled out of the parking lot.

"Three years, sir. Hope to be a legend like you someday, if all goes well."

I really liked this guy. And helping me apprehend Stacy and Brittany would look good in his file.

"The girls I'm after—"

"I know, sir; I read all the files on the flight over. I'm ready."

"I believe that, Franklin. Don't for one minute think those pretty faces won't hesitate to end your life, because they will. You had to kill anyone on duty? You even fired your weapon in the line of duty?"

"No, sir, neither. But I won't hesitate. I've killed about a hundred deer and twice as many hogs. Does that count?"

I laughed. "Not exactly, but it's a start."

I'd gotten Franklin a room on the other side of ours. I left him to get settled and called it a night.

Chapter 45

I woke up covered in a cold sweat. My heart was pounding so hard that I could feel the blood racing through my veins. I sat up and looked around the room. The clock read 3:30 a.m. I looked over at Lafitte who was out like a rock. I wasn't a big dreamer; in fact, I couldn't even remember the last dream I'd had. This one was a nightmare. I hadn't even had time to really process the idea that Stacy was indeed pregnant—and it was mine. How was I going to manage raising a kid who was conceived under those circumstances? What would I tell him or her about its mother and what she truly was? How could Miranda be loving to this child? I was wrong; nightmare didn't do it justice. Catastrophe summed it up better.

I got up and chugged a bottle of water. I wiped the sweat off my face and changed shirts. I still had a few hours of sleep time left, and I dearly needed it. I climbed back into bed and hoped the outcome would be different this time.

I woke up earlier than Lafitte and unlocked the door between our room and De Luca's. I spent some time searching the net to see if our girls had struck again, but it appeared they hadn't.

Maybe they were changing their pattern, or maybe they hadn't come this direction at all. We were kind of flying blind on hunches.

Franklin sent me a text message letting me know he was up. I sent him to the front desk to round up breakfast for the group.

Five minutes later, De Luca joined me in our room. I guess she'd heard me stirring around. She pointed to Lafitte and shook her head. "You just gonna let him sleep all day?"

"It's only six thirty and I'm not asleep, if you must know," Lafitte said.

"Never a dull moment with you two," I said.

"So what do you think about our guy?" De Luca said.

"I think he's perfect for the job, and he seems like a nice kid, too."

We heard a knock at the door.

"Got my hands full. Couldn't grab any coffee, partner," Franklin said as I held the door for him.

Franklin sat down the breakfast and went through some introductions with Lafitte and De Luca.

"It's okay. Lafitte and I will go down and grab some. Come on, princess. Let's go," De Luca said.

Lafitte groaned but he got up and followed her. I wouldn't have expected anything less from him.

———————————

"You always bust up guys you like this way?" Lafitte said as they headed for the lobby.

"Who said I like you?"

"Still playing hard to get, huh?"

"Just grab the door so we can get the coffee, Casanova."

"On a serious note, how do you think David is holding up? You know he wants to be home with Miranda and the girls right now."

"Well, you know him better than I do. I'm sure he'd rather be home with his family. But even more than that, he knows they'll never be safe unless he catches these two," De Luca said.

"Then let's make sure we get the job done."

Chapter 46

Paul and De Luca returned with the coffees and the four of us ate breakfast. I told them I'd looked online for news about the girls, but was unable to find anything.

"They sure have been quiet," Lafitte said.

"Yeah, I know. A few days now and not a peep. Maybe they went to Mexico," I said. I was joking, but who knows with those two?

I'd made a call to the Gulfport PD, letting them know we were in town and asking them to keep me in the loop if another murder turned up. As I downed the last drop of my coffee, my phone rang.

"Detective Porter? Captain Alstead, Gulfport PD. A pig farmer came across a couple bodies this morning. It don't fit the MO of the girls you're tracking, but we could use a little help getting started."

"Send me the address. We'll drive over and take a look."

It wasn't the call I was hoping for, but we really didn't have much going on. We were waiting until midafternoon to launch Franklin's fake profile.

I explained the situation to the others, and the four of us piled in my truck and followed my GPS to the crime scene. I wondered how often a town like this even had a murder case. The more I thought about it, the more curious I became.

"Lafitte, Google the murder and crime rate of Gulfport," I said.

"Okay. Give me a minute."

"What are you thinking, Porter?" De Luca asked.

I shook my head. "I'm not really sure. We've been here almost two days. The town seems really slow paced."

"You aren't going to believe this," Paul said. "You ready? Point zero one."

My hunch was right—Gulfport was not the murder capital of the world. In fact, the citizens of Gulfport just didn't commit crimes, for the most part. It was too early to draw any conclusions here, but I already had a sneaking suspicion about these two newly discovered bodies.

We climbed out of my truck and headed toward the taped-off area where a group of local officers awaited.

"Detective Porter? Captain Alstead."

I stuck out my hand, introduced myself, and asked him what they had so far.

"Well, two John Does. ME says they've probably been here two days or so."

"Why John Does? No IDs?" De Luca said.

"Both men were found naked here in this field. The farmer's dog brought back a piece of a hand, and the farmer came over to check it out."

"You guys already questioned the farmer, I presume?" I asked.

"I've lived here my whole life, detective. I've known Clive as long as I can remember. He and his wife, Ellie, wouldn't hurt a fly. We won't be able to match dental records or check fingerprints, either. All gone—every tooth pulled, every print burned off."

"You guys thinking what I'm thinking?" I said.

"Yes," De Luca and Lafitte said together.

"We have to find out who these guys are. I'd bet my life the two girls we're chasing did this. They pulled their teeth and burned off their fingertips to slow us down. Same with leaving the bodies here. They've gotten a two-day jump on us now, and we still have work to do here. It'll take hours just to ID them," I said.

Of course this was all a hunch, but my gut said it was a correct one. Folks here just weren't killing people, much less pulling out teeth so the bodies couldn't be easily identified.

"Did you scan the bodies for any kind of military chip?"

"No, sir, but we can once we get them down to the coroner," Captain Alstead said.

"Let's get them moved ASAP, captain. Give me a call when they start the autopsies."

"Autopsies? These boys were shot in the head. Hell, even a blind woman could see that."

"With all due respect, sir, gunshot wound to the head may not be the cause of death. Could be another ploy to slow us down and throw us off the trail. Please order the autopsies."

The four of us climbed back into my pickup. I didn't need the autopsy results or the names of these men to know who'd done it. But where the hell were they now?

"David, if they're still traveling on I-10, we just have to up our hours-traveled and expand our search area some. This doesn't take our fake profile trap out of play," Lafitte said.

"You and De Luca start looking a hundred miles out, based on this two-day gap they've created. And contact Fingers. Get him working on killing those other profiles and highlighting ours. Franklin and I will go to the coroner's office and wait on the autopsy reports."

"Hey, Franklin, do you have a name you'd like us to use for your profile?" De Luca asked.

"Well, Franklin's kinda stuffy, and I am a hillbilly at heart. Should've been named Buck or Bo or something. Hey, that's it—Bo Brown. I go by BB."

"Perfect," De Luca said. "Nice to meet ya, Bo."

I dropped the pair off at the motel so they could get busy figuring out where the girls might be. Franklin and I headed for the coroner's office.

"You really think it's them, sir?" Franklin said as we made our way through town.

"Yes, I believe it's them. All the signs point to it."

We arrived at the coroner's office and Alstead took us back.

"So here's what we got. I put a rush on these autopsies. Had to call in a favor. We don't have all those fancy gadgets like you big cities. Really don't have a reason to, I reckon. So we'll start with cause of death. You were right; they didn't die of a gunshot wound to the head. They both poisoned. Their blood alcohol content was five times the legal limit," Alstead said.

"That's good. What else do you know?" I said.

"Well, I think we've identified 'em both, too. Bubba and Claude Jenkins. Brothers. Claude must have spent some time in the military; he had a chip implant. Had some of my officers' check out his social media activity. Then we compared pics of the other vic until we found a match."

"You didn't recognize them? You said you knew everyone here."

"These boys are not from Gulfport. Town nearby called Long Beach is where they're from. But it's them for sure."

"Thank you, Captain Alstead. If I need anything else can I call you?"

"Sure thing, and thanks for your help today. I think we can take it from here."

Chapter 47

When we left the coroner's office, I called De Luca to fill her in.

"We're about ten minutes out. Call Fingers and have him start profiling the Jenkins brothers. I want to know everything there is to know about them, starting with the obvious: are they convicted rapists? Were you and Lafitte able to zero in on a new search zone and get Franklin's profile going?"

"Yes, yes, and yes, sir. We can go over the details when you get here."

I drove way too fast, ignoring all the long yellow lights and a couple red ones. It looked like we'd finally gotten another break, and I wanted to jump all over it. When we reached the motel, I slammed the truck in park and we ran inside. Paul was rattling out the details before the door closed behind us.

"So, both were convicted rapists with multiple charges.

Claude was actually kicked out of the military due to a rape case. We have the Franklin profile going, and we have a new search zone. De Luca and I think we should travel to Jacksonville. It's the end of the road for I-10 unless we head north or south," Lafitte said.

"Let's take this operation mobile and work from the road. We all have hotspots, and Fingers can help us out with anything else we need. We need to make up some time. Good job on the intel, very good job."

"David, let's have Fingers pull up the Jenkins's bank records for the last two or three days. Maybe they hit a bar or club with Stacy and Brittany, and we can get some video footage," De Luca said.

I nodded. "I think that's a great idea!"

We packed up everything again and headed toward Jacksonville. I felt good about what we'd learned, and even better about the trap we'd set up. Maybe we could force them into taking the bait.

Chapter 48

"Does Marci know we're coming to see her?" Brittany said.

"Who? Her name is Kim, remember. Marci no longer exists."

"Oh yeah."

"No, she doesn't know we're coming, and it's too risky to call her. We're going to spend the night in Lake City. You up for another job tonight?"

Just the thought of it made Brittany tingle from head to toe. She loved the feeling of power that killing these scumbags gave her. She no longer felt like a pathetic, powerless, victim; instead, she was a mighty, fearless advocate for women's rights.

Brittany slammed her fist on the dash. "You know, one day we're going to give this movement the national attention it deserves. Maybe then we'll have fewer and fewer rapes until we've ended it for good."

"It won't ever end, Brittany. There are countries where

men's dicks get cut off as a punishment and those misogynistic assholes still find ways to rape women. I love what we're doing. I wish I could bring the bastards who raped me back to life so I could kill them again and again," Stacy said.

The look in Stacy's eyes scared Brittany a little.

They made it to Lake City and found a motel room for the night. They logged on to their favorite hookup website and started their search within a twenty-mile radius. Much to their dismay, there were no hits on sex offenders.

"A city this big and not one damn sex offender? That seems odd. Those creeps are literally everywhere," Stacy said.

"Well, maybe they have two hundred of them, but none are on the hookup site. First time for everything, right?"

They expanded the search to fifty miles. Even then they only got one hit. Stacy expanded the search zone to one hundred miles. They had ten hits total.

"I think we should just take the closest one. It's already an hour away," Brittany said.

"Well, let's check him out," Stacy said.

Stacy cross-checked the name with her sex offender database. Looked to be a perfect match. And to make it all the sweeter, his fantasy involved a pair of sisters.

"Why do you think men are so stupid, Stacy?"

"It's simple: they have a penis. It's not a very scientific answer but, hey, if the shoe fits. Let's send Mr. Bo a message and see if he's free tonight."

Hi Bo! My name is Stacy and guess what if you are free tonight I may have another girl with me . . . my sister.

Stacy waited for a few minutes but didn't get the quick

response she was hoping for.

"I think I'm gonna try someone else. Maybe Mr. Bo went somewhere and left his computer on. It showed he was online. Oh well."

As Stacy checked out other potential matches, she received a message.

Hey Miss Stacy it's me Bo. Sorry I was hitting the weights and I accidentally left my computer open.

"Brittany, get over here! We got a live one!"

I was starting to think you looked at my profile and didn't like what you saw.

Oh no I'm very interested. I'd like to see a picture of that sister of yours too. I think I can make you both happy. And BTW I go by BB.

Gimme a second and I'll upload a picture of her. What does BB stand for anyways? Big Boy? Big Bo? Haha

Stacy found a sexy photo of Brittany on her desktop and sent it.

Wow she's smokin too! So what's the plan for tonight? Its four pm now. Wanna meet around nine? My place? Big Boy is right... how'd you guess?

Sure BB we're gonna have some fun tonight baby. Make sure you rest those muscles before then.

I'll be ready.

Chapter 49

Stacy and Brittany felt good about losing Porter, at least for now. Leaving Bubba and Claude the way they had surely slowed him down. It was nearly four p.m. now, and Jacksonville was only an hour away. They decided to pay Marci a visit a day earlier than they'd anticipated.

Stacy pulled up her address on her GPS. She'd never been to Marci's house before but knew she had to be pretty close.

"There it is, Brittany," Stacy said, pointing at a one story brick house on the corner.

Stacy parked in a shopping center across the street, and they made their way over on foot. They'd had brief phone conversations with Marci but hadn't seen her in years, so they were both extremely nervous.

Stacy knocked on the door, and they waited what seemed like an eternity. Marci opened the door a crack and peeked out in amazement.

"Get in here," she said to them.

"It's so good to see you, Marci," Stacy said as the three of them hugged each other.

"I've been reading about you two. Think you might be moving a little too fast? I can't believe you came here; you shouldn't have! The last thing I want this asshole Porter to do is nail us all. The work you're doing for the movement is amazing, though, I must say."

"We were careful. We parked far away, and we haven't been tailed. Come on! Who do you think you're talking to here? And where's your better half? I was hoping to see him, too," Stacy said.

"Well, I have neighbors, too. I'm sure at least one of them just saw two young women enter my home and close the door behind them. I never have guests here—ever. You know how fuckin' nosy people are, Stacy. It is good to see you, though. Both of you. And he's at work. He'll be sad he missed you, I'm sure."

"We actually have a meeting tonight."

Marci gave Stacy a look of disapproval.

"Don't worry; it's the last one for a while. Then we're going to disappear," Brittany said.

"How are you finding these guys anyway?"

"We just go to a hookup site and then do a cross-reference on criminal backgrounds," Stacy said.

"You've played this same ruse a few times now. How are you double-checking to make sure they aren't sending a fuckin' cop in on you?"

Stacy and Brittany hadn't thought about that.

"You're right," Stacy said. "It's a public website, though. What are the chances we'd be targeting their guy?"

"Little sister, they have IT guys who can manipulate data. It's not that hard to tweak some profiles and force you into one or two choices. You should see some of the things I can do with the programs I run here. Or better yet, they could hack a website and make every choice you click on correspond with them. I could do that in five minutes. Security isn't number one on the agenda for a hookup site."

Marci was a self-taught hacker who'd turned into a big deal in the hacker world.

Stacy thought about it for a minute. The number of sex offenders *had* dropped dramatically in her last search.

"We just wanted to drop in and say hi, but now you've got me worried. How long would it take you to check out the guy we're meeting tonight?"

"Shit, that's easy. Less than ten minutes. Do you have a picture of this guy?"

Marci loaded Bo's picture into facial recognition software used by the FBI. The program was scanning the picture, looking for a match.

"This will only take a minute. We'll have his Social Security number, DOB, and every other piece of information available."

The screen flashed and a name popped up; it wasn't Bo. The name on the screen was Franklin Shuppe.

"Well maybe he just goes by Bo, or maybe Bo is his middle name," Brittany said.

Marci put Franklin's Social in another FBI database program to find out more about him.

"Who are you, Mr. Shuppe?" Marci said.

The next image on the screen stunned them all into silence.

Franklin Shuppe was an undercover cop for HPD.

"Holy fuck!" Brittany said.

"Holy fuck is right! You were about to walk into a booby trap. Did you notice anything out of the ordinary when you performed your searches?"

"Sort of. There were a lot fewer perverts to choose from. We even talked about it. That fucking Porter," Stacy said.

"He has a great police mind, Stacy. You know that already. This is what cops do, and, for the most part, they're really, really good at it. Don't take it personal."

"So what do we do now? If we back out, they'll know we're onto them," Brittany said.

"Well, we sure as hell can't meet him at his place like he suggested," Stacy said.

"Yeah, his place will be wired to the max and surrounded by a SWAT team," Marci said.

"We need a plan. I still want to meet this guy and put two in his skull. Teach Porter a lesson," Stacy said.

"I can help you, but are you sure you want to go through with this? Killing a cop raises the ante," Marci said.

"Yes."

The three of them spent the next hour devising their plan for getting Franklin away from the trap that was set for them and into a trap of their own.

"I have an idea, but I'll need a sample of his voice. Can you send him a message and get him to call you? I only need about ten seconds. A few sentences would be good. Basically, I'll use a program similar to the ones they use in Hollywood movies. We'll need it for the cops and anyone else who might be listening in."

Stacy logged in to her laptop and sent Bo a message and the number to one of her burner phones.

"You think he's going to call?" Brittany said as they waited.

"Yes. Remember, they think they're setting us up. He'll call," Stacy said.

She was right.

"Hello?" Stacy said, answering her phone on the second ring. Marci was recording on her phone.

"Hey there, beautiful! It's me. Bo."

"Oh, hey, sorry to bother you. I'm sure you're probably busy, and I actually have an appointment here in a bit. I just had to hear your voice. I keep looking at your pictures over and over again."

"No problem. I'm actually about to meet with a client myself. I may be tied up for a few hours, so I wanted to call you now."

"What a gentleman. Well, I'll let you get to it. We still on for tonight?"

"Hell, yeah! See you soon, sexy."

Stacy ended the call and looked at Marci.

"Good job. That's all I need. Actually, that's more than enough," Marci said with a smile.

Chapter 50

I needed to see the bank records on Bubba and Claude. I wanted to know exactly where they'd been the last few days. Before long, I had an email from Fingers.

"Where was the last charge made, David?" Lafitte asked.

"Looks like a bar in Gulfport, and I'm betting they weren't alone. We need to call the manager and see if they have surveillance video they can send us."

"We can narrow it down by asking for the times between his first and last charge, give or take ten minutes," De Luca said.

"It'd finally give us a look at Miss Brittany and confirm our suspicion that these two are indeed behind those murders."

I called the bar. This wasn't a gentlemen's club, so I hoped for a lot less resistance with this request for video footage.

"This is Detective David Porter with the Houston Police Department. I need to speak with a manager, please."

"I'll do you one better. This here is Ron Willis. I own the

place. What can I do you for, detective?"

"I'm investigating the murders of Bubba and Claude Jenkins and need a little help. For starters, I need surveillance video from two nights ago. I have bank statements that show both men used their debit cards at your bar. Actually, it's the last place either of them was seen alive."

"I was here that night. Hell, I'll help in any way I can. I should be able to get those files pulled quickly and emailed over to you. There any questions I can answer for you? I liked Bubba and Claude. I felt terrible when I heard the news. They were both good guys—real good guys. They'd had their troubles in the past; don't get me wrong. But they'd turned it around and were doing right."

"I'd bet you guys get pretty busy. Probably a few hundred people in a place that size. Did you happen to notice any new faces that night?"

"Actually, I spend a lot of time serving drinks at the bar during busy nights. And yes, we were busy. Bubba and Claude were regulars, though, so when I noticed them with those two girls, of course I was curious. Hell, to be honest, everyone was. Bubba and Claude weren't exactly what I'd call lookers, and those girls were both *A* material, if you get my drift."

I was afraid of that. Bubba and Claude could have picked up two different women killers that night, but it wasn't likely at all.

"Yes, sir, I believe I get your drift. Can you describe them for me?"

"Well . . . you'll see on the video, but they were both blonde, about five three-ish, pretty large . . . you know . . .

up top, short skirts. Real pretty little things. People was asking me where the hell they came from. I have three cameras here in the bar and one at the door. All four of them left together, I know that for sure. You think those girls had something to do with this? Bubba and Claude were grown men, detective. I don't know if those girls could've brought them big boys down."

"Alcohol and drugs have a way of leveling the playing field, Mr. Willis. I've reviewed their autopsy reports, so I know they'd both drunk to excess."

"I sure am sorry to hear that. If those two girls are behind this, I hope you catch 'em."

"Thanks for your time. I'll be in touch."

Chapter 51

Franklin's meeting with Stacy and Brittany was a go. I'd cleared the op with the brass back home, and the Lake City PD was on board as well. They were lending us a few of their SWAT-trained officers, as they didn't have a full-fledged SWAT program. Stacy and Brittany wouldn't be expecting any company, so a few would be more than enough

"Franklin, you did well on the phone. You okay? You seem a little nervous," I said.

"No, I'm good. I just get really excited when I get an assignment."

"We'll have the place surrounded, and we'll be in a van parked at the end of the street. Lake City PD is working now on securing a location. We'll go over and check it out here in a bit. I don't want any surprises tonight. I know you looked at those crime scenes, but I want you to go back and look at the photos again. These girls are the real deal, and they're getting better and becoming more violent. We'll need a code phrase for you to use when they're in a position for us to breach the room. Got anything in mind?" I said.

"I don't know; let me think for a second. How about this: *are you girls into bondage?* When you hear me say that, it means all systems go."

"I think that'll work, David," Lafitte said.

"I agree. You have a concealed weapon? What are you carrying?"

"Glock G30 Subcompact, .45mm. Holds ten plus one, sir."

"Each of the guys they've killed so far has been four to five times over the legal limit. Apparently they take it slow and warm up to each other, so don't rush it. We're having a special cup brought in for you to use. Do not drink anything from any cup they give you, no matter how persistent they are. Otherwise, you're going to find yourself at the bottom of the Mississippi."

"My wife wouldn't like that. We're expecting our firstborn here in a few months. Definitely not drinking anything they have to offer."

"Listen up, everyone. The chief does not want this on the local news tonight. Everybody needs to be on their game. We can't fuck this up," I said.

I'd gotten the call from Lake City PD that the location was picked out and being wired. I gathered the group and we drove over.

"So, we'll have a unit parked there," I said, pointing to a spot down the street from the house, "and we'll be here in the van, Franklin. If something goes wrong and you need to abort at any time, *Schlitz Malt Liquor* is the phrase."

"David, that's the best you could come up with?" Lafitte said, poking fun.

"It's fitting," De Luca said.

I smiled. "And what in the hell does that mean?"

"I think it was a black joke, sir," Franklin said.

I shook my head and didn't bother to tell Mr. Clueless that I was fully aware of what it meant.

We climbed out of the van. A few curious neighbors milled about, which I didn't like. But I guess on such short notice this was the best they could do. I would have preferred somewhere a little more remote in case shit got hairy.

We walked inside and scanned for entranceways and exits. I wanted to be overly familiar with every way in and out of the place. I needed to be sure Franklin was comfortable as well.

I put a hand on Franklin's shoulder. "You good, Franklin?"

"Piece of cake. I'll try to get cozy with them on that couch. You guys can bust in the front door, and I'll act equally surprised to see you."

De Luca put a wire on Franklin. Then she checked out the coms to make sure everything was working as expected.

"Officer Porter, I'm Tony Davis with Lake City PD. My team and I will be ready to go on a moment's notice. I'm honored to be working here with your crew for tonight."

I thanked him for his service and turned my attention back to Franklin. He was way too amped up.

"You sure you're okay, kid? If not, I'll pull the plug on this thing."

"I'm good; I swear. And I just got a text from Stacy. They're in route. About an hour out."

We gave Franklin a few final instructions and headed for our van.

"I need a minute. I'll be right back," I said as the others piled inside.

"Everything okay, David?" Lafitte said.

"I'm good. Be right back."

I needed to do something I hadn't done in a long while— pray. I walked over to a nearby bench, sat down, and told God everything I'd been holding in since Miranda's disappearance: my pain, anger, sadness, frustration. Everything. I thanked Him for bringing Miranda and Karen back home to me. More than anything, I prayed for protection over Franklin and this mission. I knew we were sending him into the lion's den.

After I finished, I felt such relief, like a huge burden had been lifted off my chest. I headed back to the van, upbeat and ready to go.

"You good now, Davie?" De Luca said.

I think I detected a note of sarcasm in her voice, but I let it slide.

"Yes, I'm fine. Time to catch the bad guys."

We'd staged a plainclothesman on the street to do a walk-by every five minutes. We had the blinds positioned in such a way that he'd be able to get a quick glance in. Franklin had been instructed to stay on the couch to make sure we had eyes on him at all times.

"Okay, Franklin, say something so we can hear you, buddy." Franklin cleared his throat and put on serious face. "Rock me, momma, like a wagon wheel. Rock me, baby, any way you feel. How's that?"

I couldn't stop laughing. "Absolutely terrible! Was that singing?"

We all sat quietly and waited.

"Got a car moving in. Two women. Looks like our girls," our street cop said over the radio.

I pressed the button on my walkie-talkie. "Okay, guys. No mistakes here. Let's look alive. Franklin, you're on, kid."

The car came to a halt and, sure as shit, out climbed Stacy. They'd been so clean and precise on the other murders that we had nothing more than circumstantial evidence. Even her kidnapping of Miranda and De Luca wouldn't keep her behind bars forever. I needed to catch this pair in the act and put them both away for life.

Stacy was carrying an oversize bag on her shoulder. I was willing to bet it contained everything I'd need to pin the other murders on her, most importantly the 9mm pistol I was eager to turn over to forensics. I was sure she had her concoction of drugs in there, too—the same ones she'd used on Sam Wilson, Jon Rogers, and, most recently, Bubba and Claude Jenkins. I watched her glance around, being extra cautious.

Only Stacy got out. Unfortunately, I didn't have another unit I could put on Brittany to tail her. I banged my fist on the van wall. "Where the hell is she going?"

"I don't know," De Luca said.

I turned my attention back to Stacy and Franklin.

I waived at De Luca. "Turn up the volume some."

And then all hell broke loose.

Chapter 52

Franklin let Stacy inside and reached out to give her a hug. "Hey, there. God, you look amazing. Your pictures don't do you justice."

Stacy returned the hug. "Your muscles . . . they're so big!"

Franklin was nervous, but he was trying not to show it. "Aren't you missing someone?"

Stacy pointed to her abdomen. "Oh, Brittany? She started her . . . you know . . . girl stuff."

Franklin laughed. "Ahh! Yeah, that wouldn't be much fun."

Stacy opened her bag and took out a bottle of whiskey. "I brought this for us to drink. You a whiskey guy?"

Franklin walked over to the kitchen. "Don't insult me like that. I'm not going to invite you over here and then expect you to bring your own drink. I have a fully stocked bar here."

Stacy followed Bo into the kitchen. "I'm kinda picky about what I drink. A girl can't be too careful, ya know."

"Don't trust me?"

Stacy put her hand over her mouth and giggled. "Well, we did just meet, silly. Do you like to dance?"

"I've been known to cut a rug. Wait, do people still say that?"

Stacy laughed as she followed Franklin back into the living room.

"Too bad we don't have any music," he said, pulling her onto the couch.

They snuggled for a few minutes. Stacy squeezed Bo's muscles, trying her best to make him feel sexy. Then she pulled her phone from her pocket and started flipping through it.

Bo laughed. "So, I'm not good enough company? You'd rather text right now?"

"I'm sorry, baby. It was my sister. She wanted to make sure I was here and okay."

"Well, that's nice of her."

"She's a sweet girl. She'll do anything for me. She'd probably even kill someone if I needed her to. I pretty much raised her on my own, so I'm like a mother to her."

Stacy opened the music folder on her phone and turned on some slow jazz.

She stood up and reached out her hand for Bo. He could see the plainclothesman walking past the window as he reached up and took her hand.

Stacy wrapped her arms around him and held him tight as they swayed to the music. As the sultry saxophone blared, Brittany tiptoed into the room behind Bo, a baseball bat in her hand. Stacy pulled away just as Brittany began her swing. She caught Bo squarely on the side of his face. He fell in a heap on the floor without uttering a sound.

Stacy ran over to her bag, got the voice gadget Marci had given her, and spoke into the microphone. She reached into Bo's shirt and pointed out the wire he was wearing to Brittany.

"I haven't slow danced like this in a long while. It's nice," Stacy said into the machine, hoping it really transmitted her words in Bo's voice.

"I'm glad you're having a good time," Stacy said.

Brittany was scribbling on a piece of paper. She handed the message to Stacy.

Plainclothes cop out front

Walks by every 5 minutes

Last saw him about a minute ago

Stacy checked Bo's pulse; he was gone.

Stacy pulled a can of spray paint from her purse and left a message on the wall:

I told you cops not to fuck with me. I always win!

Stacy grabbed her bag and followed Brittany out the back door and into a car Brittany had stolen while Stacy was with Bo.

"We don't have much of a head start, so let's go!" Brittany said.

Chapter 53

I was up pacing back and forth in the van. "They're too quiet! What are they doing in there?"

I picked up a radio. "Do a walk-by. I know it's only been three minutes, but it's way too quiet."

"Maybe they're just getting friendly," De Luca said.

"I don't think so. I don't even hear the music playing anymore. Come on! Hurry it up!"

"I'm coming up on the window now. I don't see them, sir," the officer said.

I slammed my clipboard on the floor. "What do you mean you don't fucking see them? They're both in there! Walk back by and look again."

I got a sick feeling in my stomach. *Why would Franklin go off-script?*

"Still no sight, sir."

"Ring the goddamn doorbell!"

I watched as the officer followed my instructions. Nothing.

"What do you want me to do here, sir? No one is answering."

I yanked my headphones off, burst out of the van, and sprinted across the street. A car screeched to a stop in front of me, but I kept running. I'd drawn my weapon; I knew this was bad. I could hear De Luca and Lafitte scampering behind me. The officers who had been parked down the street came running, too. By the time I reached the porch, the plainclothesman had kicked down the door. I rushed inside and stopped dead in my tracks. *My God! This couldn't be!*

Franklin lay lifeless on the floor, a pool of blood around his head. I looked up and saw the message on the wall. We'd been made. But how? And when?

The sick feeling in the pit of my stomach morphed into rage. The officers were clearing the house, but I knew they were gone.

Lafitte confirmed it two minutes later.

I reached down to check Franklin, though I already knew what I would find. I was right again; he was gone, too. This wasn't fair. Franklin was way too young for this. He had his whole life and career ahead of him. And his poor wife! My God, this was terrible! I could feel my blood pressure rising.

I waived my Glock in the air as I reread the message on the wall. "She doesn't get away with this. Not this time."

Anger coursed through my veins. I ran out the front door and back into the street. I flagged down the first car that approached me, my gun raised in one hand and my badge in the other. "Out! Now! Police! I need this vehicle."

The man and woman gawked at me; I could tell they were

afraid. They scurried from the car, and I jumped in. I rammed the car into drive just as De Luca and Lafitte slammed their doors.

I felt my skin burning, and I saw red as I sped down the street.

"Call Captain Alstead. Tell him what's happened. Have him set up a fifty-mile perimeter around the city," I said.

They only had about a five minute head start. Much of the city was surrounded by woods. I knew they'd traveled out of the neighborhood on the road behind the house, the same one we were using. The fastest way to the freeway was the direction I was taking. I knew Stacy and Brittany would be traveling the speed limit so they wouldn't attract attention. I was already doing ninety.

The darkness of night was making it increasingly difficult to see into the cars as we sped by. Lafitte and De Luca shined their powerful Maglites into every car we passed. About a half mile ahead, I noticed a car weaving in and out of traffic. Lafitte spotted it, too. "David, look! That our girls?"

"I'm betting it is."

I punched down on the accelerator even harder. I was doing a little over a hundred now, and I had no plans of slowing down. Not after what these monsters did to Franklin.

As I closed the gap to ten car lengths, Stacy's car swerved all the way to the right lane and exited the freeway. I had no time to think; I yanked the wheel hard to the right, cutting off a handful of cars. I heard screeching tires, but De Luca reassured me that there were no collisions in our wake.

It appeared I was chasing a black, late-model Dodge Charger. Luckily for me, we'd jumped into a Taurus SHO, so keeping up wouldn't be a problem.

De Luca called in the plates when we finally got close enough to make them out. The windows were tinted, so we couldn't tell who was driving.

We were two car lengths away when Brittany hung herself out the window and fired her weapon. The first few shots went right through the windshield. I swerved left and right to keep her accuracy down. De Luca jumped in the passenger seat, hung her head and weapon out of the window, and fired back.

Stacy made a hard right at the next street we came to, running a red light at the intersection. I followed close behind. I couldn't tell if she was driving me into a trap or just being reckless. Lafitte joined in the firefight. The sound of gunfire was deafening.

"Aim for the back two tires!" I yelled over the commotion.

De Luca and Lafitte leaned out of their windows and fired. A barrage of bullets whizzed by my head; my ears ached from the gunfire.

Finally, De Luca lowered her gun and leaned back into the car. "I got a hit on the right rear tire. I can see it wobbling."

"C'mon, Paul! Take out the other tire!" I said.

Sparks flew from the car ahead of us as the back tire began to give way.

Stacy made a quick right. I slammed on the brakes, and the car behind us nicked our bumper as it swerved to avoid us. I made a hard right and looked at the stretch of road ahead of me. No sign of the Charger.

"Goddamn it! Where the hell is she?" I couldn't let her get away.

I sped down the road. I looked down each side street hoping to catch a glimpse of the Charger.

"There!" De Luca said, pointing down an alley.

I pulled to the curb and slammed the car out of gear. We jumped out, our guns drawn as we sprinted to the Charger.

I pointed my gun and light in the driver's window. "Freeze! Police! Put your hands up!"

But there was no one.

A man on the street pointed east when we made eye contact.

"You looking for the two blondes that nearly ran me over?" the old man asked.

"Yes! Did both of them go that way?"

"No, they split up. I seen 'em do it."

"Thank you, sir. De Luca, you and Lafitte go that way," I said, pointing them in the direction the bystander had indicated. "Watch each other's back!"

I took off in an all-out sprint. Everyone stared as I ran by them. Finally, I caught a glimpse of Brittany. She turned into a store then I saw the door fly back open. She let out a flurry of gunfire. Some of the shots were close, I could hear them smashing into things behind me.

I wanted to fire back, but there were people everywhere. I couldn't just start firing into the crowd. I'd have to wait.

I reached the store and eased the door open. I slipped inside, my gun leading the way. A few customers ducked behind the aisles. I held up my badge to the cashier, and he pointed me toward the back of the store.

"Is there a way out back there?" I asked.

"Yes. It leads to an alleyway."

I ran towards the front door. I crept around the building hoping to sneak up on Brittany. She'd be waiting for me to follow her through the back door. I got to the corner of the building and stopped. I took out my flashlight and turned it on, hiding the beam in my hand. I spotted her about fifty yards away. Her weapon was already raised and pointed right at me.

I tried to duck back behind the wall of the store, but it was too late. Brittany had already let several rounds fly, and one of them found a home in my left shoulder. I fell hard; the pain was intense. I reached my hand under my shirt. Warm blood oozed from the wound and ran down my body. It was almost the same place I'd been shot by Prodinov's men in Russia.

I wasn't going to let it stop me from catching her. I scrambled to my feet and grabbed my flashlight. I cleared the corner with my weapon raised and aimed my flashlight in the direction she was running. Brittany was about a hundred yards away from me. I could barely make her out in the darkness. I couldn't lose her.

I ran again. It felt like I was running even faster than before. Maybe it was the adrenaline. I couldn't be sure. I saw her turn into an abandon apartment building. I figured I was about twenty seconds behind when I finally got to the run down building.

Another cluster of shots slammed into the concrete by my feet. I scurried left and right then darted into the building. The shots came from two or three flights up. I slowly walked into the stairwell. The building was almost pitch-black. The only thing I could hear were Brittany's footsteps as she ran up the staircase. I fired several rounds in her direction, hoping to slow her down.

I heard a door open above me. She'd left the stairwell or wanted me to believe she had. I finally got to the door Brittany had taken. I shined my flashlight down there was blood on the floor. I shined it on the door handle more blood.

I didn't know where I'd hit her or how badly she was hurt, but at least one of my bullets had hit its mark.

I heard a noise coming from my right, and I headed that direction.

I took one more step and felt my feet slip from under me.

Suddenly I heard three fast steps behind me. Instinct took over. I rolled onto my back to find Brittany standing over me, her arms raised over her head. She was holding something, but I didn't have time to figure out what it was, nor did I care. I fired three shots, hitting Brittany dead-center. She fell to the floor and lay motionless.

I called 911 and gave them my name and our approximate location. I only had the name of the apartment building.

I crawled over to Brittany. Her pulse was weak, but it was still there.

I lay on the floor for what felt like forever. I was trying to move as little as possible the pain in my shoulder was intensifying as my adrenaline began to subside.

"Freeze don't move," I heard a voice say.

They shined a flashlight my way and I held up my badge. "I'm a police officer. Detective David Porter, I called this in. You've got a wounded officer here. Your perp is laying here on the floor. She's got several bullet wounds but she still has a slight pulse."

The medical crew came over and helped me to my feet. They brought over a chair and sat me down on it. I'd forgotten how bad it felt to be shot. Excruciating didn't do it justice.

They loaded Brittany on a stretcher and handcuffed her to it. She was in pretty bad shape. They listed her condition as critical.

I jumped into an ambulance to have my shoulder looked at. I reached for my phone to call Paul and De Luca. I prayed their luck was as good as mine had been.

Chapter 54

Immediately I could hear the disappointment in Paul's voice.

"I'm sorry, David. We gave it everything we had. It just wasn't meant to be this time. I've never wanted to catch someone so bad. We have a team checking out a blood trail. We fired a few shots at her, and it looks like one of us may have wounded her. "

I winced as the first responder tightened a bandage on my arm.

"Paul, I know you tried your best. I would never question that. I'm sure you guys left it all on the table. We'll get her. She just made a mistake here, didn't she? She'll make another before it's over, trust me. Maybe that blood will prove useful later. We can get a sample and get it in our database."

"De Luca got banged up a little. She'll be okay, though. Went down hard. Tripped over a homeless guy and took a tumble. It was so freakin' dark out there, man."

The EMT was finished with my arm. I stood up to get the blood flowing in my legs again. "So where's De Luca now?"

"The medical crew down here is cleaning her up. She scraped up her knees pretty good."

"Okay. Take care of her. I've got another call coming in. Gotta run."

I switched over to the new call. It was Captain Wilcrest.

"Well, that didn't take long," I said, skipping the standard niceties.

"Bad news never does. What the hell went wrong?"

"You want the short version or the long version?"

"Five minute version. I can get the rest of the details later. First things first: I heard about Franklin. He just got married, you know? His wife is going to be devastated."

"I know. I feel like shit about that. They definitely knew Franklin was a cop before the meeting."

"He was undercover. How the hell would they know that?"

"The bad guys have hackers, too, Cap. When Stacy and Brittany drove up, only Stacy got out. We were thinking Brittany may have gone to grab something from the store. Or maybe they were going to let Stacy do this one alone, for whatever reason. We were listening in. Everything seemed normal. Franklin was playing right along."

"What made you guys realize something was off?"

"We had a boot doing a walk-by every five minutes. He'd switch shirts and toss on a hat so it wouldn't be obvious on a quick glance. The conversation slowed to a snail's pace, and we assumed they were . . . you know, making out or whatever. But it just didn't feel right. The conversation was too sparse. I actually sent our window peeper on a walk-by two minutes early. He confirmed Franklin couldn't be seen, and we all rushed in. It was too little too late. Franklin was already gone. The girls were long gone, too."

"Mary mother of Jesus! The three of you okay?"

"Just some bumps and bruises. Nothing that we can't handle."

"I'm sorry about Stacy, David. I know how bad you wanted her."

"We're still going to catch her. I won't rest until we do. I suppose you got a call from Alstead?"

"Yes. He said you guys ran a circus through his town. You'll have to go down and tell this story again."

"Yeah, I know. The whole operation was understaffed. The city is small with an even smaller force. So, I understood when they couldn't lend us the support we asked for on such short notice. But that's one of the reasons the girls got out of that house."

"Any leads on where she might be headed next?"

"No clue. We're going to sift through everything tonight. We may end up coming home with our tails tucked between our asses."

"The entire mission wasn't a failure. You did manage to catch Brittany."

"I'd rather her still be out there than to have an officer dead. I'll let you know which way we're heading tomorrow."

Chapter 55

I hitched a ride to the hospital with a local cop. The doctor who looked at my shoulder noted the bullet had passed straight through. He stitched me up and told me to take two Advil, keep the area clean and dry, and that was it.

As I was walking out of the exam room, I saw Alstead heading my way.

He got really close to me, right up in my personal space, like he had something to say that he didn't want anyone else to hear.

"Porter, first off, sorry about your guy. Secondly, you guys caused a lot of damage here. You left a mess in the streets—a couple wrecked cars, shot-up stores. We ain't used to all that big city shit here. You picking up what I'm laying down here, buddy?"

Alstead was about five foot seven and one seventy, if that. He definitely had little man syndrome. And if that wasn't clear before, it sure as hell was now.

"I got it, Alstead. Just trying to do my job here. We're all on the same team. You think I wanted to get my guy killed? I been chasing those girls clear across the southern United States. You think I wanted one of them to get away? Especially the one that did."

"I don't know what the hell to believe. Heard she used to live with you, and you might even have gotten her pregnant. Same girl we talking about, no?"

I stood tall and crossed my arms. My eyes locked on his. "That a question?"

Alstead got my drift and took a step back. "No, it's an observation is all."

"I'll be down to give an official statement soon." I turned my back to him and walked away.

"Hey, Porter. Thought you might wanna know Brittany Foy didn't make it. They pronounced her dead about ten minutes ago."

I just kept walking.

Chapter 56

I went down to give my statement to Alstead and his boys. I'd been thinking about what our next step should be. The conclusion was the same every time: we needed to head back to Houston to regroup. It made no sense to wait anywhere else but home.

Maybe Stacy would go into hiding or lay low for a few months . . . or years. Hell, for all I knew, she might take up piano, never engage in crime again, and die an old woman. The latter seemed unlikely, of course, but we really had no direction.

Lafitte and De Luca shared a hug and said a long good-bye. Even ended it with a forehead kiss from Paul. He was headed back to New Orleans to decide whether or not he was joining me and my new team back in Houston. What I'd just witnessed told me his mind was pretty well made up.

De Luca and I were taking a flight back to Houston. I'd hired a company to get my truck back home. I never even considered driving back. I wanted to get home to my wife and kids as quickly as I could. Man, did that sound good!

I walked over to Paul and gave him a big hug. "Until we meet again, old friend."

"Indeed. I'm going to be thinking about making that move to Houston as well. I'll let you know something soon," Paul said, smiling at De Luca.

We boarded the plane and got settled in our seats. Paul was taking a separate flight back to New Orleans. I couldn't wait to lay my head back and shut my eyes for a few hours. De Luca gazed out the window at Paul, who watched from the tarmac as we got underway.

"He really likes you," I said.

"Don't try and lay it on thick for your friend. And I know he likes me; who wouldn't?"

I laughed. "I can think of a few people."

"Ha fucking ha."

"I'm going to try and get some sleep. See you on the other side."

Chapter 57

I felt the airspeed begin to slow and my eyes instinctively popped open. I couldn't wait to get off this bird and see my girls. Miranda told me they would all be waiting for me in baggage claim. I hurried off the plane, darting in and out of people as I went. Finally I arrived at the baggage claim area, Karen spotted me first.

"Daddy!"

"Hey, Karen! Daddy is so happy to see you. Did you miss me?"

"You know I missed you. You can't ever leave me again, okay?"

I smiled. "I'll do my best."

I finally made it to Miranda and Hilary. We stood there and hugged for a long time.

De Luca came over and exchanged pleasantries with my family as well.

"David, I'm going home. I'm exhausted. Will you be in the

office tomorrow?"

"First thing in the morning."

We loaded up in Miranda's SUV and headed home.

Miranda looked over at me, her eyes clouded with worry. "You look worn out, honey."

I reached over to hold her hand. "It's been a trying few days, and it's not over yet. I do believe I can finally get some decent sleep in my own bed. I have one stop I need to make on our way home."

I gave Miranda the address to Franklin's house. I needed to stop in and speak to his wife. I felt sick to my stomach about what happened. I was the officer in charge; it was my mission. I wanted—no, I *needed* to look her in the eye and apologize from the bottom of my heart. I knew it wouldn't bring Franklin back, but it was the least I could do. I owed her that much.

We pulled up to the house. Everything in me wanted to back out of that driveway. This was by far the hardest part of my job. It was my job to protect the innocent and keep them safe.

Miranda placed her hand on my shoulder. "You okay? You don't look so good."

"No, not really. This part of the job is no fun. I'll need a few minutes here."

I climbed out of the SUV and made the long walk to the front door. Before I could ring the doorbell, the door swung open.

"Detective Porter?"

A young woman no older than twenty-four or twenty-five stood before me. She was tall and thin with long, blonde hair. Her deep blue eyes looked heavy and swollen. "Mrs. Shuppe, I presume?"

"Yes. I recognize you from TV. Can I help you with something?"

"I won't take up much of your time. I wanted to come by and offer my condolences for your loss. I was the officer in charge the day—"

"It's okay, detective. Don't get me wrong, we're going to miss Franklin, but he loved his job. His goal was to be a detective like you someday. He often talked about the cases you were working on. He couldn't wait to chase bad guys and solve cases while wearing that detective badge."

"I'm so sorry I failed him and you. And before you say it's not my fault, it is. It's my job to see every possible outcome and scenario. Quite simply, I didn't do my job well enough this time. For that I am sorry."

"Thank you for your humbleness, detective. Franklin and I both knew how dangerous his job was, especially being undercover. I'm so proud to have been his wife and to have shared some of it with him. No need for you to apologize. If you know who did this, and I assume you do, the best thing you can do for Franklin is to catch them."

I gave Mrs. Shuppe a hug and my business card. The department had counseling services available that I also made sure she was aware of. What she said to me about catching them hit me like a gut punch.

I turned and started walkingaway then I stopped. One more thing I needed to do. I headed back for the front door. Mrs. Shuppe was still standing there.

"Is there something else I can help you with, Detective?"

I unclipped my badge from my side and handed it to her. "Please take this. It's for Franklin."

She offered me another hug. The tears were flowing now. I even shed a few myself.

"Take care of yourself and that kid," I said, pointing to her stomach.

We rode the rest of the way home in silence. I wasn't really in the talking mood after seeing Mrs. Shuppe. She was right; the best way for me to honor Franklin's memory was to catch the maniacs who murdered him. One down and one to go.

Chapter 58

Once the girls were in their rooms for the night, Miranda and I lay cuddled in our bed.

I pulled my arm out from under her. "Give me a minute. I've got to look at something."

Miranda had a confused look on her face. "Okay, but you better hurry back, mister."

The cop in me had to check out the house and look around outside one last time. I had an uneasy feeling in my stomach. I unset the alarm and walked outside. The company I'd hired to get my truck to Houston had delivered. Only my truck and Miranda's SUV sat in our driveway.

The night was quite still. The neighbors appeared to be tucked in tight for the night, their houses dark. The moon was full and sat high in the sky, providing almost enough light to read a book by. I headed back inside and set the alarm, laughing at myself for my paranoia.

I walked around the kitchen and checked the guest bathroom. Nothing. It was starting to feel like the only ghost I was chasing was an imaginary one in my head. I laughed at myself again.

I headed upstairs and, just for grins, I opened the girls' bedroom doors for one last peek. Karen was tucked in tight and dead to the world. Hilary had headphones on and didn't even realize I'd opened her door.

I went back to my room, took off my house shoes, and climbed into bed.

"David, is everything okay?"

"Everything is more than okay. Our family is whole again."

A single tear rolled down my face. I couldn't explain how rewarding it was to capture a fugitive. It gave me a high I couldn't find anywhere else. Weeks and sometimes months of investigation all leading to one glorious moment.

But not even that came close to comparing how I felt right now. Nothing meant more to me than having my family together again.

"Dav—"

I placed a finger over Miranda's lips. I pulled her close to me and guided her lips to mine. We kissed for what seemed like hours. And then I made love to my wife. It was the first time in over a year, so I was extra careful. In some ways, it reminded me of our first time together so many years ago. After a few minutes of hesitation on both our parts, the passion intensified. Before long, we reached a level that had only been matched a few times in our relationship. It was amazing.

After our lovemaking session ended, Miranda lay in my

arms. I still couldn't close my eyes, so I just laid there and listened until her breathing steadied and her body stilled. Finally, my eyes began to get heavy and I was out.

Chapter 59

The clock had yet to strike seven a.m. when our bedroom door flew open. Karen zoomed across the room and leapt into our bed, just like old times.

"Well, look who's already up and at it," Miranda said with a smile.

"Good morning, Mommy!"

If I were honest with myself, deep down I didn't know if my family would ever be whole again. I'd told myself this time would be different. I knew what it was like to have my family torn apart. The last year reminded me that each day was a gift that needed to be cherished as such.

"Come and give your old man a kiss."

I grabbed Karen and tickled her for a second and got her even more wound up than she already was. I gave them both a final kiss, and then I headed down to make us all some breakfast.

We all loved bacon—who didn't? Soon the entire

downstairs smelled like bacon and fresh coffee. I popped some bread in the toaster and poured Karen a glass of orange juice.

Miranda came down first, and Karen trailed her a few seconds later. I don't think any of us expected to see Hilary this side of noon and she didn't disappoint.

As the three of us ate, I sent De Luca a text letting her know I'd be heading to the station within the hour.

We small talked a little, I simply couldn't get over how happy even a simple breakfast with my girls made me. After I finished I kissed them both on the forehead.

I headed up the stairs to get ready for work. I stopped midway and winked at Miranda. She blushed and shooed me away. God, I'd missed that woman.

We said our good-byes, and I headed for the station. It was great being able to spend a little time with my family, but I knew what was waiting for me. I still had a fugitive on the run; I still had work to do.

As I walked through the station toward my office, several officers stopped to congratulate me on my new role as captain of the MCDH. Before I had my laptop powered on, Wilcrest was at my door.

"Glad to have you back, son. Chief Hill wants to meet with us in thirty. They tell you this isn't your office anymore? You and your new team have an office space cleared out for you in the north wing."

"Morning, Cap. Hell, I haven't even assembled a team yet. I did make an offer to a couple candidates."

"I won't tell you how to run your team, but I'll offer you this piece of advice: build your team with people you like and trust. Find people who are outstanding in their jobs, even if you don't know them well enough to trust them completely. And lastly, make sure you have someone who is amazing but who you probably wouldn't be friends with outside of work."

I had an idea where he was going, but I guess my face didn't convey that.

"What I'm saying is, the more diverse your team is, the more they'll keep you on your toes in regard to managing them. It will teach you to trust people who are different than yourself and give you the opportunity to grow as both a leader and a man. I'll see you in thirty, Chief's office."

As I sat down to check my email, I thought about what Wilcrest told me. That old-timer was a lot wiser than everyone gave him credit for. I was just grateful I hadn't fallen into the trap that so many others had over the years. When I was a young boy, my grandmother taught me that you could learn something from everyone if you just shut your piehole long enough to listen. *God gave you two ears and one mouth for a reason, son. He wants you to listen twice as much as you speak.* I tried to remember her lesson, especially being a detective; listening to what people had to say was ninety percent of my job.

"Hey, I see you made it," De Luca said, standing in my doorway.

"Yes, ma'am. Early bird gets the worm. I got a date with the chief here in about five minutes."

"Everything okay?"

"I'm sure he just wants a debrief and maybe to talk a little more about his plans for MCDH."

"That what we're calling it?"

"Got a nice ring to it, no?"

"Yeah, I think so. Just busting your chops. Someone's gotta keep you from getting the big head around here."

I got up and headed for Chief Hill's office. *Let's get this over with,* I thought.

I knocked on his office door and waited.

When I opened the door, I found Captain Wilcrest had already arrived.

"Good afternoon, gentlemen," I said.

Chief Hill gestured to a chair. "Have a seat, Porter."

He wasted no time getting started.

"I was disappointed to hear about Franklin. I think I've heard most of the details. I know you'll learn from this. I know how badly you want to catch Stacy—we all do. I can't say I blame you, but remember this: you have a duty to yourself, to this department, and to the families of the officers here to make sure no one gets put carelessly in harm's way."

What the hell was he saying here? Was he officially blaming me for Franklin's death? Was I about to be put on leave?

"With that said . . . personally, I don't believe you were reckless with Franklin. But I'll be honest with you; there are others who disagree, but my opinion is the only one that counts. We've set up an office area for your team. I'm excited to see what you'll be able to accomplish."

I breathed a slight sigh of relief. "Thank you, sir," I said.

Chief Hill clasped his hands together on the desk. "Have you made any hiring decisions?"

"Officially, I've made two offers. I also have a third I plan on making later today."

"Care to tell me who they are?"

"I'm trying to make sure my team is diverse as well as highly skilled. I made an offer to Detective De Luca. I feel like she's seen a lot, and she brings a well-cultured background. She's also got a unique perspective on perps, and she goes with her gut when she believes it to be correct. Those are probably some of the same reasons she was hired on the force here, I would suspect. I also made an offer to a detective out of New Orleans—Paul Lafitte."

I could tell the news of Lafitte caught the chief off guard. "Isn't Lafitte an old buddy of yours?"

"Yes, sir, we served in the military together. We did a couple tours in the desert. I've trusted that man with my life in some of the toughest situations, and I'd do it again in a heartbeat."

"I don't want you to feel like I'm questioning your choices. It's your team, your officers. I'd just like to be kept in the loop. Who is the third person you're making an offer to?"

I hesitated before answering. I knew my third offer would be sure to field a few questions and raise some eyebrows. I didn't care I felt like it would make my team stronger and that mattered more to me than anything else.

"I plan on offering Brett Smith a position leading my data analysis team."

"Brett *Fingers* Smith?" Wilcrest asked.

The room fell silent.

"I know he's had a checkered past, but I've been able to use and trust him for quite some time now. He's the best at what he does. He's provided me with valuable intel that others, quite frankly, wouldn't have found. No one outside this room knows that I'm even thinking about this. I plan on having a meeting with him at his house before I make him the offer."

"Porter, you realize this means we'll be giving a former criminal access to classified information in some cases?" Chief Hill said.

I smiled. "No offense, sir but Fingers has *always* had access to those files and any other files he's wanted to have access to."

It was out of character for Chief Hill to have anything but a scowl on his face, but even he grinned at that one.

"Touché, Porter. Duly noted. You do understand not everyone will be a fan of this."

"Sir, not everyone was a fan of me being promoted to detective or being your choice to lead the Major Crimes Division. I'm following in your footsteps, doing things that not everyone agrees with."

Again Chief Hill smiled. "I like you, Porter. Always have. You're a no-bullshit guy, and I like that."

"I always try to let people know exactly where they stand, sir. There anything else you'd like to discuss? I'm anxious to get back to work. I still have a perp out there to get my hands on. I doubt she's sitting around sculpting pottery."

"No, that'll be all, Porter. Good luck."

I stood up and shook hands with both of them. Then I headed to find De Luca. I wanted to run the Fingers hire by her to make sure I wasn't completely off my rocker before I made him the offer.

I'd sent her a text asking her to meet me in my office.

"What's up, Porter?"

I gestured for De Luca to close the door.

 "Have a seat. I need to run something by you."

She pulled up a chair, a puzzled expression on her face.

"I'm thinking about bringing Fingers on board and making him a part of our team. Tell me I'm not crazy."

"Hmm. Will my opinion have any bearing on your decision?"

"Yes. I value your opinion. I mean, if it's a crazy idea and I'm nuts for thinking it, just say so."

"Well, obviously you think he would add value to the team, and he's the best person for the job. Will everyone agree with it? No. But if you start making choices for this team based on everyone else's opinions, then you're not the guy I thought you were."

"Do you think we'll be exposing the department in any way? I mean, his past isn't exactly spotless. Am I making a mistake here?"

"Well, Porter, neither is your past, if you're basing your criteria solely on that."

"Slightly different scenario but I get it."

"Not really. Guys, especially black men, have been convicted of rape and other crimes with much less evidence and circumstance."

"You always give it to me straight, don't you?"

De Luca got to her feet. "Only way I know how to give it. If he's your guy, stop talking to me and go get him."

What De Luca said made a lot of sense. She was right; my mind was about ninety-eight percent made up before I'd even called her in. There was no doubt now.

Chapter 60

I left the station and headed for Fingers' house. I stopped at Starbucks to get myself a fresh cup of coffee. I got Fingers a tall mocha frappucino. Computer nerds like those, or so I'd heard.

Fingers' house looked more like a hideout than a home. It was tucked behind a thickly forested plot of land. He had an electronic gate with a video camera. I guess he saw my vehicle approaching, because the gate swung open right as my truck neared.

I parked and headed toward a door concealed in the side of the garage.

"Come on in, Porter."

Fingers was tall and slim. He probably didn't weigh more than one hundred fifty pounds, and that was being generous. He wore black-rimmed glasses that I imagined all technology buffs wore.

I handed Fingers the Starbucks drink. "A lot different than

your last digs, Fingers."

"Yeah, a lot more secluded. You found my last hideout, remember?"

I laughed. "And I suppose you didn't think I could find this one if I wanted to?"

"Pleading the fifth. So what's up? What brings you here? A simple phone call wouldn't have worked?"

Fingers had established quite the lab. As I looked around the room, there were at least twenty monitors. Wall-mounted TV screens also filled the room. I counted ten security cameras, and those were just the ones I could see. I didn't want to guess what all this equipment cost or how long it'd taken to set up the network.

"Well, I'll get right to it. HPD recently started a new Major Crimes Division that I'll be heading up. I've been promoted to captain and tasked with building the team, including the hiring. I need a data analyst, and I want you to be that guy."

Fingers face went blank. "Let me get this straight, Porter. You want *me* to join the good guys and actually work for a paycheck that, like, gets taxed and everything? You do remember arresting me seven years ago, right?"

"I remember all too well. You broke the law; we arrested you. That's how it's set up to work. But I'm here because I believe you turned over a new leaf. I'm putting together the best Major Crimes Division in the world, and I need the best of the best on my team. That means you. I've already looked past your background and taken into account all the cases you've helped me solve since then. So what do you say?"

"I say you have a boss, and he'll never be okay with this.

Besides, I don't think I'd fit in down at the station."

"Like I said, I'm making the hiring choices. I've already cleared this with my superiors. Also, I don't need you at the station; I need you right here in your office, doing what you do best. This is where I've always needed you. Why should that change? Just going to put you on the payroll and make it official. I'm giving you a second chance. A clean fresh start."

"Don't act like you're doing me a favor here because you like me. You need me to make yourself look good."

I wasn't sure where Fingers was coming from. I hadn't expected this type of response. Then I realized that, besides a quick call and a bunch of data requests, I didn't really know Fingers the man—what he was about, his story, or what made him click.

"Listen, I'm not trying to pull the wool over your eyes here. This would be a win-win for both of us, and yes, it would make me look good. Honestly, it would make both of us look good. I've mentioned this to only a few people down at the station, and I already have doubters. You have a chance to prove them wrong."

Fingers stared down at the floor and rocked back and forth in his chair.

"Let me tell you a story, something that isn't in my file. My parents were both special ops. They were both assigned to teams that were run undercover and off the record. They were promised a huge sum of money for obtaining certain information for the government. Someone ratted them out and they got ambushed and killed. I never got the money my parents were promised. No one even acknowledged that either of them worked for the government. They just moved on to the next two suckers. I was twelve when they were killed."

Fingers eyes welled up. I could tell the pain of his loss was still raw. I surmised from his account that he had negative feelings toward authority and the police. I couldn't say that I blamed him. No wonder he had reservations about me and my motives.

"Fingers, for what it's worth, I'm sorry about what happened to your parents. Sounds like they got the shitty end of the stick. That's not going to happen here. Like I said, I believe we both have something we can offer the other. You have the chance to turn the tables around and make your mark here. Rewrite the history book on Brett Smith."

Fingers and I talked for more than an hour. In the end, we came to terms. Fingers was officially a member of the MCDH, effective immediately.

One of the terms of our agreement meant him meeting with me and Chief Hill. This would give both sides a chance to meet face to face, man-to-man.

Chapter 61

Stacy arrived in New York City ready to get back to work. She'd spent a few days mourning the death of her sister and deciding who she would target next in her sister's memory. Porter needed to be taught another lesson. A painful lesson. Franklin, she decided, was only her first cop. There would be more, many more. They wouldn't get off easy like Franklin did, either.

She'd purchased a dozen nine-inch Bowie knives from a string of stores along her drive from Lake City. The killings in honor of her sister would be gruesome, bloody, and extremely painful. She would make her victims suffer a slow, agonizing death. She'd also picked up some new goodies that she couldn't wait to put to use.

She wouldn't need her car here. She'd never ridden a subway but couldn't wait to try it out. She needed to learn how to get around. There was little time to waste. She couldn't wait to shop for new clothes to fit in with the locals. Every corner of every street was filled with hundreds of people. Everyone was moving a million miles an hour. Not a blade of grass in sight. The high-rises here were breathtaking.

It was nearly one thirty p.m. Stacy walked by a storefront window and caught a reflection of herself. She absolutely loved the red hair and was a bit envious that she hadn't been born that way.

After she'd finished stuffing herself with pizza, she hurried back to the apartment she'd rented. The Metro Apartments were less than one minute from a subway station, and she wanted to be able to get home and out of sight as quickly as possible.

She'd sent a text to Marci a day earlier asking for a hit list of sorts. She wanted the names of the five officers who'd had the most run-ins—be it before or after becoming an officer. She was looking for the worst cops NYPD had to offer.

Marci finally sent a list of names: Mark Romero, Luke Rasmus, Bryan Sills, Justin Dudley, Jermaine Carter.

Now it was time to do her research and pick her next victim. It didn't take long to discover that all of them had one glaring thing in common: each had been placed on administrative leave at least once. Three of them more than once. And one three times.

The more she dug, the more she knew Mark Romero was her man. He'd been placed on leave without pay three times and investigated for everything from excessive use of force to tampering with a witness. One of the accusations against him was that he forced prostitutes to perform sexual favors in lieu of going to jail. To Stacy that was the same thing as rape. He forced women to have sex with him against their will.

So why haven't they nailed this guy, she wondered?

A few more website checks and Google searches provided her with even more reasons not to like Mark Romero. Turns out the guy had married the chief's daughter. It explained how a prick like him managed to keep himself from getting fired or prosecuted.

A quick residence search told Stacy he lived in Columbus Square on Columbus Ave. She looked up the apartment complex online. The pictures blew her away. The place was luxury to the max. No way a piece of shit cop could afford a place like that. Why'd this asshole have the golden ticket? Father-in-law must be protecting him. Stacy wanted to make an example out of him.

Chapter 62

Stacy loved stakeouts. She'd become so enthralled with getting every possible detail; she was like a lion hunting its prey, carefully stalking for days or even weeks and then attacking in one fell swoop.

"Come on, Stacy," she said as she watched from her hideout across the street from the luxury apartment high-rise. "Open your eyes and find this guy." No sooner had the words left her mouth when he finally appeared.

Mark was tall, late forties, bald, and clean-shaven. His eyes were ocean blue. He had an e-cig in one hand and his Starbucks in the other. Stacy followed at a discreet distance. She followed him into the parking garage and watched as he got into his red Corvette which she'd already placed a tracking device on.

"Not in uniform? Where you headed, Mr. Romero?" she muttered.

She already had a cab waiting in the garage. Twenty-five

minutes later, her question had been answered and several other assumptions were starting to become clearer.

What the hell was this guy doing in the middle of the Bronx? She followed him as he stopped at four different buildings in the projects and spent way too much time in each one. He damn sure wasn't doing an investigation. And as she watched him argue back and forth with what appeared to be a gangbanger at the fourth stop, it became crystal clear: Romero was shaking down bad guys. Another reason to get rid of the piece of shit. The man he was talking to now was even taller than Romero. He wore a do-rag, was tatted down and, if she was seeing correctly, had a pistol tucked into the side of his pants. No surprise there. He talked with his hands and was clearly in charge of the other men who stood behind him. Romero stood emotionless and puffed on his e-cig, blowing his smoke right into the man's face.

"These guys don't look happy, Mr. Romero," she said.

Maybe these guys were sick and tired of getting shaken down. They didn't know it, but they wouldn't have to worry about it much longer.

Finally, the man shoved a package in Romero's chest and not too friendly-like, either.

Romero smiled and headed back to his car. Stacy nudged the cabdriver to follow.

"You some kind of cop, lady?" the taxi driver asked.

"Just drive, hombre."

Romero didn't stray far from his last stop before his brake lights flashed again.

Stacy gasped. Romero pulled right next to the curb on a street full of prostitutes.

"Goddamn you, asshole!" she said.

"You his wife or something, lady?" the taxi driver said.

"No. I told you to just drive. If that bastard was my husband, he'd be dead . . . and not figuratively. I mean dead. Gunshot to the head. No more questions. Got it?"

The taxi driver nodded.

Stacy watched Romero motion girls over to his car. Not a single one of them had gone over before he called them. They knew he wasn't a paying customer. He was a disgusting pig abusing his power. Finally after a few minutes of negotiations, one of the girls got into the car and off they went.

Stacy had an idea. She told the taxi drive to take her to Smoke Heaven, a smoke shop she'd pulled up on her phone. It was about ten minutes from the spot where she'd seen Romero pick up the girl. Once they arrived, Stacy told the taxi driver to wait for her and went inside. She asked for a manager and went to the back of the store. Fifteen minutes later, she came out with a small bag in her hand.

"Okay, let's go. Take me back to the place we were before."

They arrived back at the corner where Romero had picked up his girl She looked around for the girl Romero picked up. No sign of her; that was good. It meant Romero had yet to return.

She grabbed her bag and told her taxi she no longer needed his services. Paid him out and off he went.

Stacy walked over and found herself a spot on the wall.

About a minute later, a man came hurrying toward her from across the street.

"What the hell is this?" The man looked like a seventies

pimp. He wore a cheap suit that screamed, I-bought-this-out-of-the-back-of-a-van.

He leaned against the wall next to Stacy. "Hey, girl, you lost?"

Stacy rolled her eyes. "This must be your shithole street I'm on, no?"

He leaned even closer and got right in Stacy's face. "If it's such a shithole, what are you doing here? Get the fuck outta here before I make you disappear, bitch. Unless, that is, you want to work for Uncle D?"

Stacy returned the favor and leaned in close before she responded. "Listen. Uncle D, is it?" She'd taken her gun from her waistband and pressed it up against him where no one else could see it. "I won't be here long, and I'm not looking for trouble. But you have about two seconds to slowly back away from me and walk back across the street. I'm not trying to move in on your territory here. I've got some unfinished business with an old friend. You're a business man, so I'm sure you can appreciate that."

He stepped away and gave Stacy a hard stare. "If I ever see you around here again, it won't be pretty."

The next hour was uneventful. Several cars pulled up near her, all looking for the same action, and she quickly dismissed each one. Suddenly, she noticed the red Corvette heading in her direction. Romero stopped fifty yards away from Stacy, and the girl he'd picked up earlier got out. As he pulled away from the curb, Stacy pretended not to see him and stepped out in front of his car.

Romero slammed on his brakes and glared at Stacy. She pushed her sunglasses down and peered at him over the top of them. She turned around and strutted back to the curb, her minidress leaving little to the imagination on either end.

Stacy hurried down the sidewalk and was several yards away from the car by the time Romero called out to her.

"Hey, you! Red!"

Stacy stopped and waited for the car to pull close to the curb. "Hey Red? That usually work for you? I'm a lady, not a fucking dog."

"I'm sorry, Miss. I'm Mark. Do you want some company? I sure wouldn't mind some."

Stacy sauntered over to his car. "Whatcha got in mind, big boy?"

Romero offered to take her to his private party spot. She climbed in and they were off.

Chapter 63

Stacy nibbled on her finger. "So where are we going, handsome?"

Romero smiled. "Somewhere real special. Only be me and you, baby. No interruptions."

Romero's cell phone rang.

He put a finger to his lips. "Don't say anything. I gotta take this."

Stacy nodded.

"Hey, baby. How's the shopping going?"

Baby? Stacy thought. *This guy's taking his wife's call with a girl he'd just picked up in the car.*

"Yeah, I just left the station. I'm going to the gym. I'll be home in a couple hours."

There was a pause. "I love you, too," Romero said before disconnecting from the call.

He smiled at Stacy. "Sorry about that, sweetie. We're almost there."

Stacy couldn't wait to dig into this guy. She'd get two birds with one stone with this kill—a cop and a rapist pig.

They pulled up to a tiny non-descript house that was isolated. The closest house was too far away to even hear someone scream. This guy's poor wife probably had no clue that her asshole of a husband had another house where he took his whores. How long had he been doing this? How many girls had he taken advantage of?

"Come on, baby. I don't have much time."

Stacy followed Romero into the house. He didn't know it, but he was about to be all out of time—permanently.

Before she'd even closed the door behind her, Romero had already started unbuttoning his shirt.

"Gotta take a leak. Wait here," Romero said. He gave Stacy a deep, wet kiss.

He set his keys, e-cig, cuffs, and gun on the table and headed for the restroom.

After Romero was completely out of sight, Stacy grabbed his e-cig and quickly changed out the canister with the drugs she'd acquired from the smoke shop. *Damn! This shit is easier than I thought it would be. Buy a set of tits and you can literally have whatever the hell you want,* Stacy thought as she returned the e-cig to the table and made herself comfortable on the couch.

When Romero came back into the room, minus his shirt and pants, Stacy gave him a once-over and a seductive smile. "Moving kinda fast there, Mark, aren't we?"

He picked up his e-cig and took a few drags. "I told you I don't have much time. So let's just get this over with."

He walked up to Stacy and wagged his finger at her. "And

don't think I'm paying you anything either, fucking skank."

Stacy stared at him with a puzzled look on her face. "What? You think I'm gonna fuck you for free? You're cute but not that damn cute. It's two hundred for a fuck and one for a blow. What's it gonna be, hon?"

Mark laughed and took another long drag on his e-cig. "I think you're going to do whatever the fuck I want you to do, bitch. There's something I guess I forgot to mention." He pointed at the gun on the table.

Mark paused, blinking hard. Stacy could tell he was becoming disoriented.

"I don't pay whores for sex. I'm fucking NYPD. Where do you think the gun came from? My badge is in the right-front pocket of my pants, if you don't believe me."

Stacy tried to act surprised. She hoped he'd take a few more drags. The smoke shop manager told her that if she wanted to get fucked up fast, this was the shit to do it.

"So you just pick up whores and fuck them because you're a cop? It's either fuck you or what, go to jail?"

Mark took another drag. "That's exactly what it is. But I know you don't want to go to jail, so that just leaves fucking, right?"

Mark tried to remain on his feet but lost his balance and fell. He dropped his e-cig and put both hands on his forehead.

"What the fuck did you do to me, you bitch? You fuck with my E-cig?"

"Ahhh, the stupid little whore girl has outsmarted the big-time NYPD cop. You like to rape prostitutes. Making a girl fuck you because you want some ass is pretty low, Mark.

You're a piece of shit."

He managed to stand up but not for long. His breathing labored and he couldn't move.

Stacy went over to her bag and took out everything she needed. She took out a set of rubber gloves and put them on. She rolled him to his side and cuffed his hands behind his back. He put up a little resistance but not nearly enough. The drugs had delivered as promised. She used her heavy-duty zip ties to bind his legs together.

"Listen up, Marky Mark. I'm going to carve you up real good. Been in the business a long time, so I'm pretty good at it. Should we record this for your wife?" she said as she selected a Bowie knife from her stash.

Mark tried to respond but couldn't get anything out of his mouth.

"How many girls have you raped? Thirty? Forty? One hundred? How about I slice you once for each girl you've raped?"

Stacy rolled him onto his back and started on his thighs. She drew back and thrust the knife deep into Mark's leg. Blood shot out like cannon fire, spraying all over the carpet.

"Lift, lower, stab," she whispered over and over again. *God, this feels amazing!* The more she stabbed the more of a rhythm she developed. It invigorated her.

Mark's body trembled. He yelled, but no one was close enough to hear. She lost count, but from the looks of it, she'd stabbed his legs at least fifty times.

She was exhausted.

Stacy walked over to her bag and took out a vial.

"Mark? Open your eyes, baby. Do you know what this is?"

She held the bottle close to his face and smiled as he tried to focus on it.

"No? It's called hydrochloric acid. You familiar with it? Probably not but let's do a science experiment, shall we?"

Stacy opened the vial. Mark's eyes rolled back in his head as his body quivered. Then she poured, beginning with his legs. His skin sizzled and popped, melting away as the acid ate at his flesh.

Stacy thought about hitting him with her knife a few more times but was having way too much fun with the acid for now. She held the vile over his eyes and slowly dripped the acid into each of them. Mark roared in pain.

"Shut up! Shut the fuck up!" Stacy yelled.

Mark was still sobbing, so Stacy decided to stop him on her own. She poured the acid around Mark's lips and watched as pieces of his face oozed away.

"Goddamn! You look like shit. You look like that character from *Batman*. What's his name? Come on. Help me out here, Mark. Two-Face! That's it. You look like a real-life fucking Two-Face. Good for you, Mark."

Mark lay motionless and silent.

"Fuck! I'm sorry, Mark. I didn't know that shit was so strong. I really wanted you to suffer longer. Maybe I should have diluted it or something, huh?"

Stacy checked his pulse. It was weak, but she wasn't done with him. She grabbed her knife and came back to finish him off.

Lift, lower, stab. Lift, lower, stab. Again and again and again. She delivered blow after blow to his chest until she could no longer lift her arm. Exhausted, Stacy dropped the knife and slumped over onto Mark's lifeless body.

She took off her rubber gloves and jumped in the shower. She took out a sundress from her bag and slid it on. She had panties in the bag but decided not to bother with them. She caught a glimpse of herself in the bathroom mirror. She wasn't showing yet, but she knew it wouldn't be long. Stacy thought about leaving a calling card for Porter, but she wanted to kill a few more of the cops on her list first. There was probably GPS on Romero's phone, but by the time they found him she'd be long gone, and nothing here could tie her to the scene.

Stacy peeked outside to make sure no one saw her leaving. She walked about a mile to a convenience store, found an Uber driver, and scheduled a pick up.

Chapter 64

I had two members of my team already in place. I hoped Lafitte would be joining us soon. The Rapist Killers Club was our first official assignment. Fingers, De Luca, and I spent time scouring websites looking for breadcrumbs, any clues Stacy and Brittany might have left on their murderous trek across I-10.

The chase had gone cold. We were analyzing more murders than I ever had at any one time. And not just in Houston—nationwide. We scoured every murder that even vaguely looked like something Stacy might have been responsible for. So far we'd come up empty. Maybe she took a sabbatical to mourn the loss of her sister. Perps often did that. It would explain why she'd suddenly become so quiet. I knew she wouldn't remain in hiding forever, but when she resumed her killing, where would she be? If she left no DNA at the scene, pinning her to something would be next to impossible. *What if she stopped leaving her calling cards for me?* David thought.

The more people she killed, the more blood she felt was directly on my hands. In her sick, twisted mind, the murders were my fault instead of hers. She wouldn't stop killing until she was dead or in jail.

We made sure her picture was everywhere. We got it out nationally and hoped every beat cop and department in the country had their eye out for Stacy. Sadly, the pictures we had were outdated. Hell, her hair could be purple, and she could be sporting green contacts. Even those two simple changes would allow her to walk right past a cop without a second glance.

Two weeks passed with no new leads, and then everything changed.

My desk phone rang. It was a number I didn't recognize.

"Detective Porter, this is Michael Ozzo NYPD Homicide Division. Do you have a minute?"

I sat up straight. "Sure, detective. What can I do for you?"

Just then I heard the *ding* of my laptop's email notification. I listened to Ozzo as I logged in.

What he said next chilled me to the bone.

"We think we have your killer here in New York. Someone killed an officer here two nights ago. Stabbed him over one hundred times. Most gruesome, sickening thing I've ever seen, and I've been a cop for over thirty years. Poured some kind of acid all over him, too. Real horror movie shit."

As Ozzo talked, I scanned my email. It confirmed a hit on Stacy's blood. She was definitely their killer.

"You there, Porter?"

"Yes, sorry. Go ahead."

"One of our own gets killed, we pull out all the stops. I'm sure you can appreciate that. We worked and worked on Officer Romero's body and finally got what we were looking for. Found a trace of blood that didn't belong to our guy and ran it through all the databases. Sometimes, you know, these overkill stabbers cut themselves. Knife handle gets slick; they're going ape shit. It's bound to happen. She probably didn't even realize she was cut till she left and the adrenaline wore off. Anyways, got a hit on a Stacy Demornay, aka Lisa Crease, and a note to notify you if there was a positive hit. So who the hell is this girl?"

"Well, Ozzo, as you found out for yourself, she's an extremely dangerous woman. I'm going to tell you something you aren't going to want to hear right now. She's part of a gang of women who go around hunting down rapists. So if she killed your guy, either he was a rapist or she thought he was. Honestly, I haven't found them to be wrong yet."

"She some goddamn vigilante or something? Mark never raped anyone. That's bullshit, Porter. Give the dead guy a little respect."

"All I'm saying is that's who she targets. She's a rape victim. So was her sister. The two of them and another woman started a Rapist Killers Club to go after rapists. They're seeking justice for all rape victims out there. My Major Crimes Division here in Houston has been tracking them, but we've been a step behind for much of the investigation. If she's unaware that she left a trace of her own blood at the scene, it might be the big break we needed. Was there a note left at the scene for me?"

"A note?"

"Yes. She normally taunts me with a note or a calling card after each killing."

"No note."

"Romero a good cop? He have any troubles?"

There was silence on the other end. I knew if Stacy had killed this man, he must have been a discipline problem. And undoubtedly a rapist.

"Some of the boys thought he might be banging prostitutes in exchange for not arresting them. Plus, he'd been put on leave a few times for some other shit."

"Wait, what? He was—"

"Yeah, you heard me right. That was the rumor."

"That's it, Ozzo. Stacy must have found out what he was up to. I bet that's how she got him alone. He probably picked her up and tried to have sex with her. She trapped him when he thought he was trapping her. He was forcing prostitutes to have sex against their will to avoid charges. It's rape any way you slice it."

"I'm not telling anyone about that right now, Porter. Everyone here is hurting. The department's on high alert, ready to burst."

"I understand. Listen, my team and I will be in New York tonight. Keep all of this, even the blood match, to yourself. This may be our big break. If Stacy doesn't know I'm coming, she won't be running from me. In the meantime, see if you can find out where Romero typically picked up girls. I want to interview some of the girls when I get there."

Ozzo laughed. "Interview whores? What do you expect to get from a bunch of prostitutes?"

"Please just get the information for me. I gotta run. I'll see you tonight, Ozzo. And thank you."

Chapter 65

I called a quick meeting with De Luca and Fingers to fill them in on what I'd learned from Ozzo.

"So when do we leave for New York?" De Luca said.

"You and I will leave tonight. I've already made travel arrangements. Fingers, we may need you; if so, I'll shoot you a text or call. I'm not leaving New York without Stacy, one way or the other."

I left the office and went home to gather my things. I knew Miranda and the girls wouldn't like this one bit. We'd just gotten back together and settled into a somewhat normal routine, and I was already running off again. Hunting down bad guys. Being away from my girls was the only part of my job I didn't like. That and getting shot at, I suppose.

I parked my truck in the driveway and headed for the house. I wasn't looking forward to telling them I was leaving.

Miranda was waiting for me at the door. I guess my face

gave me away.

"What's wrong?" she said before I could open my mouth.

"I've got to leave. Tonight. We got a huge lead on Stacy's whereabouts. I think I know where she is. DNA evidence isn't usually wrong."

She put her hands on my shoulders. "Where? The girls are going to be devastated, David."

I shook my head. "I know they are, but I have to end this."

I heard footsteps bolting down the stairs. "Daddy!" Karen cried as she leapt into my arms.

"Hey, princess. How was your day? Did you do anything fun? "

"Me and mommy always have fun, silly."

"I bet you do. Where's Hilary?" I kissed the top of Karen's head and set her on the ground.

"She's out with friends," Miranda said. "When do you have to leave? It's almost Thanksgiving David; you can't miss Thanksgiving."

Karen crossed her arms and pouted. "Where are you going? Why are you leaving again?"

"You know Daddy chases bad people. It's my job, and I do it to protect all the good people, like you and Mommy."

I scooped Karen up and tossed her on the couch. I tickled her, smiling as her sweet giggles warmed my heart. Nothing made me feel better on the inside than seeing joy in my little girl.

Finally, she pushed away from me. "Don't think I forgot that you're leaving me, mister. I'm still mad about that."

I laughed. "I know you didn't forget. I'll make it up to you. I promise."

She held up her hand. "Pinky promise?"

"Yes, pinky promise."

I kept a bag ready for emergency trips, and this no doubt qualified. I tossed in a couple extra shirts and headed back downstairs. I hugged Karen and told Miranda how much I loved her.

"I promise I won't miss Thanksgiving," I said as I headed out the door.

I met up with De Luca at our terminal a half hour before our flight was set to leave.

"You all set?" De Luca said as she walked up to me.

"Yup. We got about a, what, four hour flight? That should give me time to make it through both of these."

I held up two books on forensic psychology.

"Is there anything else out there for you to learn on the subject?"

"The more I learn in life, the more I realize I don't know. Funny how that works."

"Meh. I got something much lighter."

She held up her copy of *Fifty Shades of Grey*.

I laughed. "I don't know if Paul is into that whole submissive thing."

"Very funny, Porter. So if you know that much, I suppose you've read it?"

I didn't reply. It was more fun to keep her guessing.

The flight to New York was uneventful. We waited for our bags and then headed outside to catch a cab.

"So what's the plan, Porter?" De Luca asked while we waited.

"We need to meet with Ozzo. First thing we need to do is

find out what Stacy looks like now. Then I want to head over to the spot where Romero had been picking up girls."

"I agree. Someone had to see something."

We waited another ten minutes for the first available cab.

"Where to?" the cabbie said after we got loaded in.

"43rd Precinct, the Bronx," I said.

He peered at me in the rearview mirror.

"Don't worry, we aren't going to blow the place up. We're police officers," I said, flashing my badge.

I sent Ozzo a text letting him know we'd touched down and were on our way to see him.

I stared out of the window. Even though I'd made many trips to New York, the city never ceased to amaze me. Here it was, almost midnight, but you wouldn't know it by the level of activity. Every street corner, nook, and cranny was bustling with movement.

We pulled up to the station and climbed out of the taxi. I paid our fare and grabbed our bags from the trunk.

Ozzo, or at least I presumed it was him, was outside waiting on us, a cigarette in hand. He didn't look like what I expected. He stood about five eight and was as big around as he was tall. If I had to guess, he was in his early forties, and he was balding.

"Detective Porter?" Ozzo said, reaching out for a handshake as we walked up.

I set our bags down and extended my hand. "Yes. Pleasure to meet you. This is Officer De Luca. Again, we're sorry for your loss. We recently lost an officer at the hands of this same perp, so believe me, we want her just a badly as you do."

"Well, everyone here is chomping at the bit to get their hands on her."

"We need to go to the corner where Romero was picking up girls."

Ozzo glared at me. "Still not easy to hear."

"I'm sorry, but we both know it's probably true. One of those girls had to have seen something."

Chapter 66

We climbed into an unmarked car and headed to Romero's old spot. We parked at the end of the street and sat watching for a few minutes.

"Damn! You guys could come down here and clean up," De Luca said.

"We both know there'd be a whole new crew here tomorrow doing the same thing. Supply and demand. There's a lot of both here," Ozzo said.

I'd convinced De Luca to be bait for the pimp working this corner. She stepped out of the car and walked toward a vacant spot against the wall. Less than five minutes later, our guy crossed the street and headed toward De Luca. The instant he hit the sidewalk, she was on him. Ozzo stepped on the gas. Before the pimp could even react, we were less than five feet away.

"What the fuck is this?" he said, staring down the barrel of my Glock.

"Listen to me closely, and everybody goes home in one piece. You got it, bud?"

The man pointed to Ozzo. "Fuck you! I know that fat piece of shit. He five-oh. You five-oh too, brotha?"

I understood his overtones, the way he referred to me as *brotha*. As if I was somehow less black than him or had sold out.

"I'm a detective, yes. Listen, we just want to talk. You can take my word for it. I just need some information."

He stared at me. I could tell he was trying to get a bead on whether he could actually trust me or not.

"So if you just wanna talk, why you got your gun in my face?"

We'd created a scene and had attracted way more attention than I wanted right now.

I slowly put my gun in my holster. "You're right. Can we talk now?"

He was quiet for a moment, weighing his options, no doubt.

"Whatcha wanna know, pig?"

"You know that cop who used to come by here picking up girls?"

"Man, I don't know what the fuck you talking 'bout. Don't no five-oh be comin' 'round here."

"Help us out here. We both know I can run you and your girls in and make this night longer for us all. None of us want that," I said.

"How do I know you not gon' take me in anyways if I talk?"

"Well, quite frankly, you don't. You're going to have to trust me here. What's your name?"

"My name don't fucking matter. I don't wanna get involved

with this shit."

"His name is Dwight Miller. He goes by Uncle D," Ozzo said. De Luca stepped forward.

"Listen, Uncle D. We know Officer Romero was coming here, shaking you and your girls down. And I'm sure you've heard he's dead now. We need to know the last time you saw him down here and which of your girls he might have picked up that night."

He turned to De Luca. "Yeah, that bitch was coming down here and messin' wit' my bidness. Taking my girls off whenever he wanted. Not like I coulda ran to the cops on his ass. Can't say I'm gon' miss him any."

As Ozzo took a step in the pimp's direction, I put my hand on his chest to stop him. We might actually get something out of this guy, and the last thing I wanted to do was piss him off.

He turned to Ozzo. "What you gettin' mad for, fat boy? Why you care 'bout a piece of shit crooked-ass cop for? He give all y'all a bad name. And if his wife wasn't the chief's daughter, they woulda fired his ass. Errebody know that."

"Be that as it may, he was a cop and someone killed him. We need to find out who and bring them to justice," I said. "We aren't investigating because he was a cop; we're investigating because someone was brutally murdered."

The man looked at me intently. I could tell that what I was saying was sinking in a little. I could also sense when his guard dropped. He was still a pimp surrounded by three cops, but he relaxed a bit.

"I don't know no names. Girl came around here that nobody seen before. So I ran up on her like I did your girl here. She got straight gangsta, though. Pulled her strap on me. Then she said I'd never see her again, so I backed off. Told her not to come back."

"This girl . . . what did she look like?" Ozzo said.

"Lil' bit taller than her," he said, jerking his head in De Luca's direction. "Big fake tits, tight little body, red hair. I asked around, but ain't nobody know who she was. Romero came by and dropped off my girl that he'd picked up. That redhead bitch walked right out in front of him. Shit, I thought he was gonna hit her. Slammed on the brakes and shit. Then I see her lean in his window. Next thing I know, they drivin' off. Ain't seen neither one of 'em since. Shit, I ain't thinkin' no girl took him out."

"Sounds like our girl," I said. I reached out to shake his hand. "Thank you for what you did here, Dwight. We'll get out of your hair now."

We stood there for a moment, but he finally grasped my hand. I'm sure he'd had his share of run-ins with cops, so I couldn't blame him for hesitating. Not that pimping girls helped his cause any. But I also knew it hadn't always been sunshine and roses between cops and the black community. And five minutes of CNN would have you believing it hadn't gotten a whole hell of a lot better.

We watched him walk back across the street before we loaded back up in Ozzo's car.

"Can you take us to the murder scene?" I said.

"We've combed that place from head to toe. You're not going to find anything we hadn't already found," Ozzo said. "You think you're going to come to New York and suddenly find this girl in our town?"

"I've got something else in mind. I'm not actually going into the house. I'm not coming here to step on toes, Ozzo. But yes, I am here in New York, and I plan on finding Stacy."

He turned the car around and headed toward the house. My idea was a long shot, but it might work now that we had a description.

"Okay, so there are at least four things we know now that we didn't an hour ago. Number one, Stacy hustled her way into Romero's car by pretending to be a prostitute. And we know she's going as a redhead now," I said.

"So, she probably didn't have a car. That means she either used Uber or took a taxi from the murder scene," De Luca said.

I pointed to her in excitement. "Bingo!"

As we pulled to a stop in front of the house where the murder took place, I downloaded Uber onto my phone and scheduled a pickup.

"Uber drivers usually work the same areas at the same times of day. Most of them have other jobs, too, so their schedules are pretty regular. We can eliminate Suburbans, Escalades, and other SUVs. She wouldn't have needed anything that big for just herself," I said.

Ten minutes later, a Nissan Altima—Ryan, Uber said— pulled to the curb behind us. I climbed out of the car and walked over to greet him.

"Hi. I'm Detective Porter. You're not in any trouble, but I need to know if you made a pickup here two nights ago. Would have been a busty redhead, slim, maybe even dressed like a hooker, if you catch my drift."

"No, sir, I didn't make a run over here, but my friend Hasan picked up a girl who sounds a lot like the girl you're describing. We like to compete on who picks up the hottest chicks, and he had all of us beat that night."

My face lit up. "Can I have Hasan's phone number? It's really important that we speak to him tonight."

"Yes, sir. Heck, I can do you one better. Hasan snapped a picture when she got out of his car."

I waited while he thumbed through his gallery. Then he handed me his phone. Her hair was shorter and red, but it was Stacy without a doubt.

I handed him back his phone. He gave me Hasan's number and then drove away.

"So he pick up your girl?" Ozzo said when I returned to the car.

"No, but he told me who did."

I punched in Hasan's number and held up a finger to Ozzo as I heard the call connect. I turned the speaker on so Ozzo and De Luca could hear.

"Hasan? Detective Porter here. I'm investigating a murder, and I believe you might have some information that can assist me with the case."

"Oh? Well . . . I don't think so. I'm just a mechanic and a part-time Uber driver. I think you may have the wrong man."

"I know what you do. That's why I want to talk to you. We just spoke with one of your fellow Uber drivers. He told me that a few nights ago you picked up a redhead, a really hot one. You sent him a picture of her. You remember that, Hasan?"

"No, I do not. Sorry, I must go."

"Hasan, wait! Please don't hang up. I believe that girl is in over her head and needs some help. And she's very dangerous. I really need you to tell us where you dropped her off. Your friend already told us she was your client. Just tell me where you took her, and I'll be on my way."

"That's all you want to know?"

"Yes, Hasan; that's it."

"Metro Apartments on 41st Street. Can I go now?"

"Yes, Hasan. Thank you."

I disconnected from Hasan. "Let's go pick up your cop killer."

"Goddamn you, Porter. You've been here a fuckin' hour, and you already know where she is?"

I winked at De Luca. "I didn't do anything special, Ozzo. I just knew where to start, and I got a little lucky. Let's head for the Metro Apartments on 41st Street."

"Should I call SWAT?"

"Hell no! Call no one. Right now she has no idea we've tracked her to New York. She won't be expecting us. I sure as hell don't want to startle her."

"Okay, but you better know what you're doing here. This girl gets away . . ."

I laughed. "Haven't I proven myself enough already? And besides, if it weren't for us, you still wouldn't know where she was. We do this my way."

"Well, shit, you got me there. Fine. We do it your way. I'm letting you know, though—I'm not a fan of this no-backup-cowboy-shit, Mr. Texas."

As we pulled up in front of the Metro Apartment complex, my heart was racing.

"Let's go," I said.

We walked in and headed for the front desk.

"David, I think I'll head around the back just in case she has a quick escape plan."

I nodded. "Be careful out there, De Luca."

"Detective David Porter," I said, flashing my badge at the gentleman at the desk. "Do you have a resident by the name of Stacy Demornay?"

"Why, I don't believe so, sir. Do you have a description?"

I gave him one. "Ohhh, I know just the girl you're looking for. She moved in here a few days ago. Real looker, that one."

"I need to know what room she's in."

"Room 504. Would you like me to ring her?"

"No, we'll go up and see her. Thanks."

We rushed for the elevators and waited forever for one to open. I sent De Luca a text letting her know where we were headed.

When the elevator opened on the fifth floor, we sprinted to room 504. Both Ozzo and I had our guns drawn. He motioned for me to kick the door in and did a silent countdown.

I kicked the door with all my might and followed my gun into the apartment. We hurriedly cleared the front room. It was after two a.m., so I assumed she'd be in the bedroom. We heard what sounded like a window slamming open in one of the back rooms and ran that direction.

We reached the bedroom to find the curtains flapping next to the open window on the far wall. We scanned the room but saw no one. As Ozzo sprinted to the open window, I heard a cluster of gunshots from behind me. Ozzo went down hard. I whirled around to find Stacy standing in the doorway.

We stared at each other, guns drawn, neither of us saying a word. I'm not sure which one of us was more surprised.

"Goddamn, you're good, David. Real fucking good. I didn't think you'd find me here. So what now?"

"Now you put the gun down and go to jail for the rest of your life."

Stacy laughed. "Do you really see me going to jail, David?"

She pressed the gun to her temple.

"Don't do it, Stacy."

"Why the fuck not? What do you care about me? You never cared about me. Did you care about me when you told the football team they could all come and get a free piece of ass?"

"Stacy, I feel terrible about that, but I didn't know what they were going to do. That wasn't part of the plan. But right now I need you to put the gun down before you do something—"

And like that, it was over. Stacy pulled the trigger and fell to the floor in a heap. Brain matter spattered the walls, and a pool of deep-red blood spread on the floor around her. I didn't have any real feelings for Stacy. Not after everything she'd done to my family. Not after all the innocent people she'd murdered. But as I stared at her lifeless body, part of me felt sorry for her in a way. If I hadn't gone to the party, maybe none of this would have happened. Stacy had gotten a pretty raw deal for much of her life, and it turned her into a bitter, hateful, woman. And then there was the child that had just died along with her. Was it mine? I guess I'd never know for sure, but I was relieved. What a nightmare that would have been for me and my family. Regardless, an innocent little life had been needlessly taken.

"David, what happened?" De Luca said as she ran into the room.

"She shot herself. Didn't want to go to jail, I suppose."

De Luca placed a hand on my shoulder. "You okay? You don't look so good."

"Yeah, I'm fine. Ozzo took a shot to the shoulder. Can you call it in? I'm gonna step outside for a bit."

I took out my phone and sent Wilcrest and Miranda the same text.

We found her, cornered her. She took her own life. It's over.

The medical crew ran past me with a stretcher. I didn't wait for them to carry Ozzo out. I figured I'd touch base with him later. De Luca and I went down to the precinct to give our statements. It was daybreak by the time we finished, and both of us were ready to get the hell out of New York.

"Tell Ozzo to give me a call when he's feeling better. I owe him one," I said to the officer at the front desk as we headed out.

I booked two seats on the next available flight. Hell, we'd fly standby if we had to. Neither of us could get to Houston fast enough. I called Miranda to let her know I was coming home.

De Luca wasted no time passing out when we got on the plane. I was exhausted, but I was much too wired to sleep. I spent a few minutes rehashing the last two years of my life. If I had to pick one word to describe it all, it would be *whirlwind*. On second thought, *nightmare* worked just as well. But now it was over. The girls and I could get back to our lives. I could focus on setting up procedures for our new team. I'm sure the respite wouldn't last long; I'd be back on a case before you could blink. But I was going to enjoy the mental rest as long as I could.

Chapter 67

I didn't know if the spark that had been lit between Lafitte and De Luca would turn into anything, but deep down I hoped it would. Maybe she could settle Lafitte down, something I didn't believe would ever happen. Maybe it was true that everyone has a soulmate. I'd certainly found mine. Lafitte and De Luca were meeting us for a double date at Main Event. We'd talked about giving Top Golf a go, but I figured the wait would be too long without a reservation.

"Miranda, you look stunning," I said as I walked into our bedroom. She smiled over her shoulder at me. "You know we have the house all to ourselves tonight, right?"

Miranda yawned. "Yeah, but I'm already a little tired. It's been a long week," she said.

"A little tired or *really* tired?"

We both laughed. I pulled her close to me and laid a soft kiss on her lips.

As we headed out, I sent Paul a text to make sure they were

also en route. Unless there was a wreck, the traffic in League City, Texas, was generally light. Tonight was no different.

We turned into the parking lot, and I spotted our friends just heading inside. By the time we found a parking spot, Paul was already putting on his bowling shoes on in lane nine.

We joined our friends and exchanged warm, friendly greetings. But then it was time to get down to business. Lafitte and I were fiercely competitive at everything. I was looking forward to beating him tonight.

"Ready for an ass-whoopin', my friend?" I said as I laced up my shoes.

"Have you ever beaten me at anything, David?" Lafitte said.

"Are these two always like this?" De Luca asked. Miranda rolled her eyes and nodded.

"If memory serves, the last time we bowled I beat you one ninety to one seventy-five," I said.

"We'll see."

We ordered a round of drinks as the game got underway. This was nice. No police work tonight. Just a little fun with my wife and old friends. After my talk with Lafitte about moving to Houston went so well, I figured us spending time together would cement his decision.

As I picked up my bowling ball, my phone vibrated in my pocket. Then it started to ring. I took a look.

"That one of the girls, dear?" Miranda asked.

"No. I don't recognize the number. It's international. I have no idea who it could be."

"No police work tonight. You promised," Miranda said half joking.

"I'm only going to answer because I don't know who it is. I suppose it could be important."

"Porter," I said as I put the phone to my ear.

"Detective Porter, dis is Clifton Dixon. I am a homicide detective in Negril, Jamaica. Do you have a moment? I have something I need to read to you. We need your help solving a murder."

The man's accent was heavy, and I could barely understand his broken English. Why was a cop from Jamaica calling for my help?

"Sure, go ahead," I said.

"Thank you. I will read to you a note found at de scene of a double homicide last night at one of our resorts."

"I'm listening."

"Thank you. I read de letter to you now.

Detective Porter, catching us won't be as easy. My wife and

I have been watching you. We know everything about you.

To us you're nothing more than a cocky ex-jock and a

fucking rapist pig. You've caused my family a lot of pain over

the years, and most recently you murdered my Aunt

Brittany. Until I kill you, I'll be watching your every move. I'll

be close enough to tickle the hairs on Miranda's pretty little

neck. A young couple needlessly lost their lives tonight and many more will die before it's over. When will we stop? Not

until everyone realizes that you're an inept fraud who had

everyone fooled. After we have humiliated you, ruined your

career, and destroyed everything you love, maybe we'll find

a new hobby.

See you soon, Dad.
With all the hate in the world,
Caleb
PS – you'll be joining my mother soon in the pits of hell."

I was stunned silent. The bowling ball I was holding slipped from my grasp, missing my foot by only a few inches. Miranda, Lafitte, and De Luca all came over to where I was standing. I wasn't looking at them, but I could hear them talking to me, their voices buzzing around me from every direction.

"Detective? Hello? Are you still there, sir?"

The phone was still at my ear, but when I opened my mouth to reply, no words came out. I felt light-headed. The room swirled around me. I lost my balance and fell hard to the floor.

Lafitte helped me sit up. I frantically reached for my phone.

"I will be in Jamaica tomorrow afternoon. And yes, I know who your killer is."

"If we're going to have any success in catching dis maniac we will need your help, Detective Porter."

"I know. I have your cell phone here in my call log. I will call you first thing tomorrow, Mr. Dixon, to give you my travel plans. I'll want you to meet my team and me when we land."

I hung up and realized I still hadn't moved. I was seated on the floor, my legs crossed under me, the bowling ball I'd dropped still at my feet.

"David, honey, are you okay? What's wrong?" Miranda asked. I could see panic all over her face.

"Yes. I mean . . . no. I don't really know," I said, befuddled.

"David, who was that? You're scaring us, man," Lafitte said.

"A detective from Jamaica. It looks like the three of us will be heading to the island tomorrow. The files we found . . . the abortion . . . I guess Stacy didn't go through with it after all. A man and his wife killed a couple last night in Jamaica. They left a note for me, and they warned there would be more."

"How do you know Stacy didn't get that abortion, David? What does that have to do with the killings in Jamaica?" Lafitte asked.

I heard the question, and even though my mind processed the answer, I said nothing. The words were stuck in my throat. I just sat there, staring off into no-man's-land. Finally, after what felt like an eternity, I answered.

"Because the killer is my son."

As if the complexities of stalking a cold-blooded murderer weren't already daunting enough, hunting a murderous son who wants you dead took things to a level I wasn't sure I could handle. In an instant my worst nightmare had become a mind-numbing reality. There was no forensic psychology book out there to help me with this one. I was literally writing the book myself—and I was scared shitless.

Part 3 of the Trilogy!
See how it all ends...
Coming Winter 2016

Turn the page for a sneak peek!

Prologue

Houston, Texas 1 a.m.

Watching video surveillance of a man who would be dead in thirty minutes but had no idea he was about to die was eerie. Caleb sat in their motel room anxiously waiting for *go* time. His stomach growled so loud he could hear it. It was close to lunch time, and he hadn't eaten anything all day. He couldn't eat, not right now. Action, danger, excitement—all made him way too jittery to eat, so he didn't. He stared at the monitor in front of him. It was one of three that surrounded him. Marci, sitting ten feet from him, was surrounded by three monitors as well. Every detail of their plan had been perfectly set in motion. Now it was time to watch the actors play out the scene.

Caleb got up and stood behind Marci. He stared at her for a second. He'd learned almost everything he knew from Marci, and he loved her dearly. He bent down and gave her a long, deep kiss, sneaking a quick feel in the process.

Marci smiled and pushed Caleb away. "Hey! Stay focused, you sexy man."

The fact that Marci was twenty years his senior didn't matter to Caleb. He didn't know if he liked older women in

321

general or just this older woman in particular.

Caleb ruffled Marci's hair and smiled.

"Okay. It's noon straight up. Let's do this," he said.

He put on his headset and dialed a number using a burner phone. He gave Marci the thumbs-up.

"Hello? Officer Patton speaking."

"Officer Patton, good afternoon. My name is . . . well, it doesn't matter what my name is. I need you to listen very closely to every detail I'm about to tell you. One mistake could be fatal. Okay?"

"Who the fuck is this? John, is that you playing games again?"

Caleb stood up and paced the room. "Sorry, Tom, this is not John. This is your guilt game, and I am your host. I plan on being with you from now until the very end."

"John, shut the fuck up. I know this is you."

"No, Tom, *you* need to shut up and listen. Right now you're in your squad car heading toward . . . Damn! I almost spoiled it. Let's start with the basics. Your car's controls have been overridden. Well, some of them anyways. Like the locks, for example. You can no longer unlock the doors. Go ahead and give it a shot."

Patton hit the *unlock* button but nothing happened. Caleb could hear him pounding on the door. "What the hell is happening? Who the fuck are you?"

"Mr. Patton, you need to calm down. You must be mentally aware and invested in this game or you'll miss something. So let's go over the rules. You are not allowed to contact anyone. Anyone includes . . . well . . . everyone. Your cell phone has been programmed to communicate only with me. But contacting also means pulling over and trying to wave someone over to your car. Don't do that. You see the computer in front of you? It's transmitting directly to a monitor that yours truly is watching. Yup. That would be me."

"What the fuck do you want from me, you little piece of shit? Do you know who you're messing with?"

"Oh, snap! I almost forgot. The video is also being broadcast to your 72-inch flat-screen at home. Your wife, Julie—say hi, Julie—can see and hear you, too. And your three-year-old, Matthew. So I'd watch the potty mouth."

Patton's eyes widened. "Julie, I'm so sorry you've been drug into whatever this is. You're going to pay for this, pal."

"Patton, listen to me. She can hear you, but right now her mic is off, so you can't hear her. We'll get to that later. So here's what's going to happen. You've been a cop for what, twenty-one, twenty-two years? We've been reading and studying and learning all about you for over a week now. You've done some pretty naughty things, haven't you?"

Patton didn't respond.

"Okay. That didn't go so well, Mr. Patton. Let me explain something. If I ask a question, it becomes your job to answer. I did leave out one small detail. Your wife and son can't move. You see, they're what you might call *tied up* at the moment."

"You better not hurt them; I swear!"

"Ohhh, stop it, Tom. We aren't going to hurt them. Well, maybe we are. You'll be glad to know this is your game, and you actually get to decide if they get hurt or not. You see, I'm going to stop talking and give you the floor. I know where you're headed right now, but I'm not going to spoil the show. So here's what I need from you. You are going to tell your lovely wife all your dirty little secrets. All of them. Or the room they're in will fill with hydrogen cyanide gas and they'll both die. Right now it's 1:10. The canister in your home is set to go off at 1:30 . . . unless someone turns it off. Again, can you guess who that someone is, Tommy? Yup, me again."

Tom did a U-turn and headed for home. He was speeding and darting in and out of traffic. "So all I have to do is tell her the bad things I've done, and all of us live? That's the game? What kind of sick shit is this?"

"Patton, did you forget who else is listening in? Can you clean up your language a little? I mean, I did ask nicely. Yes, if you tell the truth, they'll live and you'll die at 1:30. Oh, I didn't mention that, did I? You see, someone has to atone for your sins, but you get to decide who. Isn't this fun? And Julie has already been warned that if she makes it out of this and we suspect even an ounce of evidence has been given to the cops, we'll be back to finish them off."

"They are going to catch you, and when I find out who you are—"

"Now, now, Tom. Let's not get ahead of ourselves. You're angry; I get it. And you're used to always being in control. But you're all out of options, bud. The GPS shows you aren't going for your noon nookie, Tom. Why did you turn around? You headed home now? Don't answer that. So here's what's going to happen. In ten seconds, Julie's mic will be turned on. I want you to tell her everything. Do you hear me, Tom? Everything! The truth shall set you free. Time's atickin'.There's C4, a remote detonator, and timer all wired to your car. And . . . go!"

Tears poured down Julie's face. Matthew was crying, too. He really didn't understand everything that was happening, but fear is contagious.

"Tom, can you hear me?"

"Julie! Yes, I can hear you. I love you, baby, and I'm so sorry. I'm going to take care of this. Don't you worry."

"Tom, who are these people? Please come get us, Tom. We're both so scared."

Caleb turned off Julie's mic.

"Julie, you were given your instructions back in the locker room, remember? If I see Tom's car anywhere close to Pearland, both of you lose—you first. So Tom can watch, of course."

Julie cried out, but Tom couldn't hear her.

"Okay, now that we're all playing nice again, both of you get one last chance. Oh, silly me. I forgot to turn the split screen on your monitors so you crazy kids can see one another. There."

Tom stared at the screen in horror. There in the middle of his living room sat his wife and son. He knew it was all his fault.

"They want me to talk. They want me to tell you how bad of a husband and father I've been. I mean, none of it's true, but I'll say what they want to hear. You believe me . . . right, honey?"

"Tom, listen to me. Look at your son. For whatever reason, these people have gone to a lot of trouble here. They have to think you've done something. Why would they do this if it isn't true?"

"Ding. Ding. Ding. Score one for Julie," Caleb said. "Tom, we've followed you for a week. We've read your police files, even the unofficial ones. The best pattern to have is what? Say it, Tom"

Tears poured down Tom's face. "No pattern."

"That's right. No pattern. But I'm guessing you've been doing this for so long, you felt invincible. Anyway, I'm talking too much. This isn't about me. You have ten minutes left, Tom. You should really use your time wisely."

Tom finally composed himself enough to speak. "Julie, I need you to listen to me."

Caleb leapt from his seat. "Stop the presses. Tom, right now you're traveling seventy-two miles per hour on Interstate 610. You're about to pass Reliant Stadium. Don't forget what I said. Do not get on 288 South. Anywhere near Pearland and boom. Don't fuck with me, Tom. I mean it."

"Okay! I got it. Please don't hurt them. Please! I'll tell them everything. Just promise me you won't hurt them."

"Tom, I always keep my word. If you talk, I won't lay a finger on them. I won't need to hurt them. You're about to do that for me."

"Matthew? Hey, little buddy. Look at Daddy. I love you, son. Julie, don't believe all the bad things they say about me. Know that I love you. Twenty-five years of my life I have loved you. Good-bye my love."

"Tom, no!" Julie screamed.

Tom slammed his computer shut. Caleb and Marci were still tracking him via GPS, and the audio feed was still live.

Tom removed his service weapon from his side holster and

fired one shot into his skull. His patrol car spun out of control and crashed into the freeway barricades. Then it exploded.

Julie screamed.

"God, that sounded terrible," Marci said.

"Julie, I'm sorry you guys had to listen to that. It's not how I planned it to happen. Protect and Serve—that is what they sign up to do. But some of these assholes find every way possible to abuse their power. It's really, really sad."

"No, *you* are the sad one. I hope you burn in hell for this," Julie said between sobs. "Not all cops are bad. You killed a good man. You're the real piece of shit, whoever you are."

"You're right, Julie. Most police officers do a fine job, a really fine job. And guess what? I'm not after them. I'm hunting men like Tom—men who lie, cheat, and steal."

"Well, who made you the goddamn judge? Why not let him have his day in court?"

"No, no, no. He had his day in court. It was today, in fact. The judge found him guilty on all counts, and he was sentenced to die."

"You sick bastard!"

Caleb cut the transmission.

"Julie, listen to me, dear. Your mic is off. After Tom is identified, officers will be at your house to inform you of your husband's death. Remember the rules of the game. Please don't make me turn on those canisters, because I can and I will. There will be a lot of officers there, a lot more people for me to kill. And if you change your mind in a week or so, I'll come and visit you and Matthew then, too. Hey, look at the bright side. You're still young, still got your looks.

If you remarry, please don't pick another asshole. Ta-ta."

Caleb killed that transmission as well.

"Our work is done. Let's get the hell out of here," Caleb said.

Marci held up a finger. "First we have to spin the wheel."

They'd created a wheel that contained the numbers one through fifty. Each number had a corresponding city, country, number of victims—one or two—and gender written on a sheet of paper. Using the wheel meant no pattern could ever be established.

Caleb spun the wheel, and they both watched in anticipation as it slowly landed on the number seven. Marci took out their handwritten list to find out the details of their next adventure.

"Let's see . . . seven. Honolulu, Hawaii. One female victim. That should be fun," Marci said.

"Jamaica, Houston now Hawaii. Never been to Hawaii – I'm excited."

"Makes two of us. Who's ready for a tropical vacation?"

ABOUT THE AUTHOR

Terry Keys is a novelist, songwriter and poet. He writes for Examiner.com and works as a project manager in the oil and gas industry. A native of Rosharon, Texas Keys spends his free time hunting, fishing and working out. He lives in Dickinson, Texas, with his wife and two children.

Please visit his website at www.terrykeysbooks.com

Twitter: @tkeys15

Facebook: terrykeysbooks

Email: terry@terrykeysbooks.com

Made in the USA
San Bernardino, CA
27 August 2016